clovermead

DAVID RANDALL

clovermead

IN THE SHADOW OF THE BEAR

MARGARET K. MCELDERRY BOOKS

NEW YORK LONDON TORONTO SYDNEY

Margaret K. McElderry Books
An imprint of Simon & Schuster Children's Publishing Division
1230 Avenue of the Americas, New York, New York 10020

Book design by Abelardo Martínez
The text for this book is set in Cochin.
Manufactured in the United States of America
2 4 6 8 10 9 7 5 3 1
Library of Congress Cataloging-in-Publication Data
Randall, David, 1972–
Clovermead / David Randall.— 1st ed.
p. cm. — (In the shadow of the bear)
Summary: Clovermead, twelve-year-old tomboy, learns that her father has been lying about the past and that the truth may be the key to ending the epic battle raging between the followers of Lord Ursus and those of Lady Moon.
ISBN 0-689-86639-9
[1. Fantasy.] I. Title.
PZ7.R15638Cl 2004
[Fic]—dc22
2003009934
FIRST EDITION

To my parents,

Francis and Laura,

who supported me, encouraged me, and inspired me

as I worked to make myself a writer

ACKNOWLEDGMENTS

I have been writing for fifteen years, and I owe a great many debts to the friends, family members, and teachers who gave me the heart to persevere in my attempts to get my stories published. I thank them all—and particularly my aunt Lois McConnell Randall, who has been both loving and professional in her improvement of my work. I am also especially grateful to Melvin Bukiet, Jennifer Lyons, and John Hodgman, whose recommendations of my writing provided me the opportunity to work with my agent, Simon Lipskar.

Many people read, commented on, and improved *Clovermead,* including my editors, Emma Dryden and Sarah Nielsen; my agent, Simon Lipskar; my parents, Francis and Laura Randall; my sister Ariane Randall; my uncle and aunt John and Lois Randall; and above all, my wife, Laura Congleton. Laura encouraged me to read *Clovermead* to her out loud, listened carefully, and fine-tuned the story line by line. This book would not be in print, or worth being in print, without her.

CONTENTS

Note

The currency of Queensmart includes pennies, shillings, and sovereigns. There are twelve pennies to a shilling, and twenty shillings to a sovereign. A penny is worth around $20, a shilling is worth $240, and a sovereign is worth $4,800. Pennies are sometimes sliced into halves or quarters, but most transactions below the penny level depend on barter or credit.

The Lands of Lady Moon

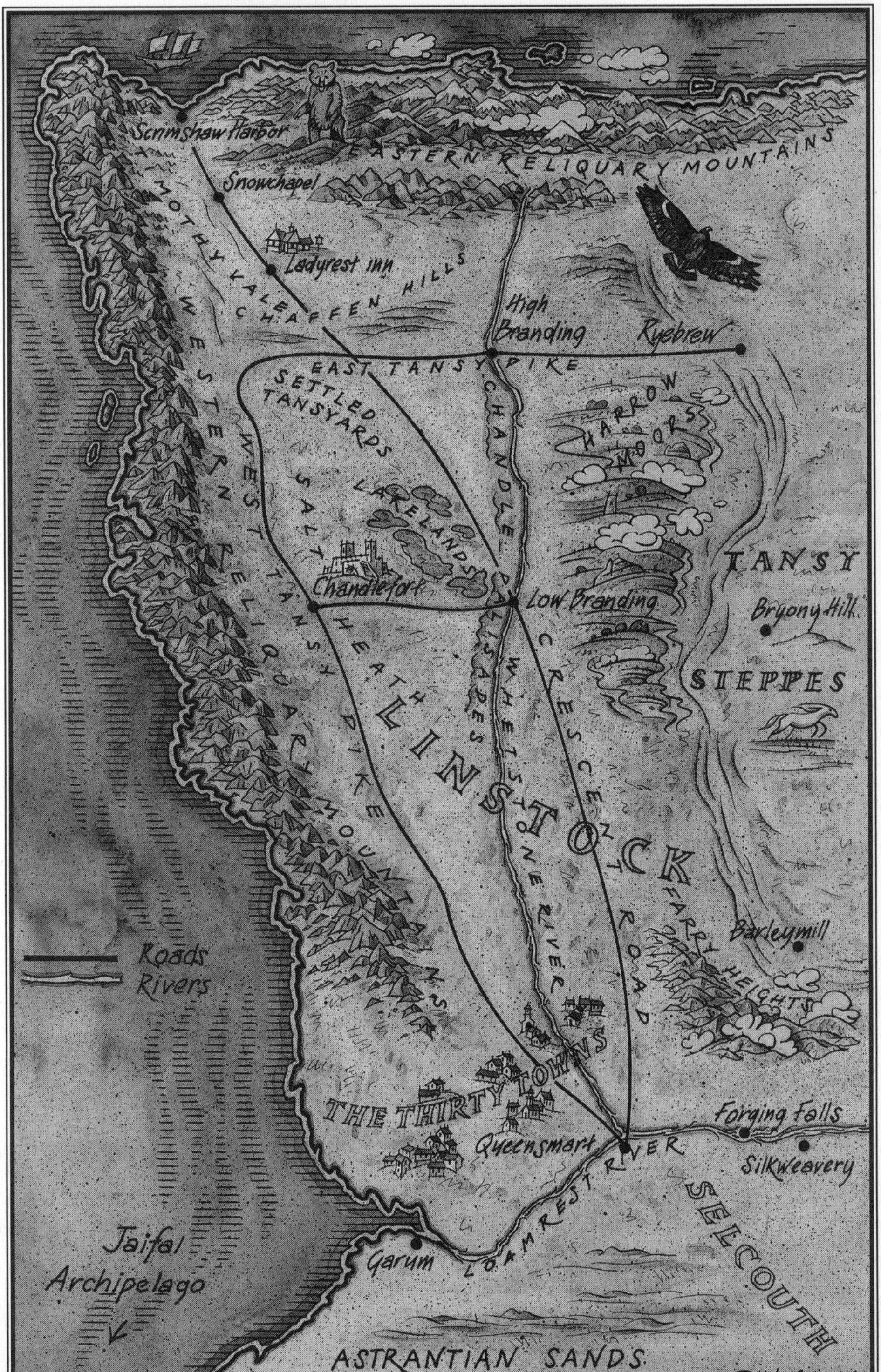

Chapter One

THE TANSYARD PILGRIM

CLOVERMEAD WICKWARD LEAPT ONTO THE BED, LUNGED with the sword, and battered a pillow. She laid about her with two-handed swings that sent the dust motes spinning and scratched the oak bed frame's dark polish. She crouched in front of the open window, growled a challenge out to the thick green slopes of Kestrel Hill as the cool and lazy autumn breeze caressed her cheeks, and smiled with unholy glee.

Clovermead's flailing limbs radiated an almost palpable energy as she sprang from pillow to bolster and back again. She was five feet tall—she had grown three inches in the last year, and her father said the way she ate, she was like to grow another three inches in the year to come. Her long golden hair, fine and soft as silk, billowed down to her shoulder blades in unruly tangles. Between her freckles her skin was white as crystal salt. Her eyes were bright blue. Over her wiry frame she wore an outsize woolen sweater and trousers—boys' wear in Timothy Vale, but Clovermead vehemently preferred comfort to feminine style. Her trousers were plain brown, but a bold Valeman pattern of interwoven yellow and blue crescents blazed forth on her new wool sweater. Goody Weft had made that sweater for Clovermead and given it to her on her twelfth birthday.

"Bold Lady Clovermead skewers the spider-priest of Great Jaifal," Clovermead announced to the room. The room was small and sparsely decorated, but, Clovermead noted with some pride, clean and comfortable. She had oiled the dresser and made the bed just last night. Clovermead leapt to the floor and rolled in a huddle under the bed. "The priest's servant-spiders skitter after her. She hides beneath the eight-legged altar—hah! There's a secret entrance to the rear." Clovermead slid out the other side of the bed. A large pile of dust followed after her. "Sweet Lady, I knew I forgot to do something—silly Clo, you'll have to sweep away this mess. Look! A secret passageway! It leads up—to daylight? No, that's a gem glittering in torchlight! Clovermead, it's the Spider Ruby itself! You've found it!" She snatched a candle from the dresser and held it aloft in triumph. "Time to escape. Where's that trapdoor I saw? I remember! It was behind the skeletons." She spun around to face the door.

It was open. A young man was watching her from the doorway of the room. A bemused smile flickered on his lips, and Clovermead's cheeks flared strawberry red. It was the owner of the sword.

The man was unmistakably a pilgrim—pilgrims often sported exotic fashions, but Clovermead had never seen anyone so bizarre. His jerkin and leggings were patchworks of horse skin, beaver fur, and leather ribbons. On his head he wore a fox-fur hat edged by the fox's face, paws, and tail. He had tied his long auburn hair into a thick braid like a horse's tail, and both his cheeks were tattooed from ear to nose with crisscross blue lines. Beneath his strange accouterments the pilgrim's eyes were dark brown. Baby fat still lined his square, sun-darkened face and his short, compact body.

Clovermead put the pilgrim's sword back on the bed and patted flat his rumpled coverlet. "I thought you had gone outdoors," she said.

"Evidently," said the pilgrim.

Clovermead flushed again. "I'm terribly sorry, sir. I know I was wrong to look through the keyhole, I shouldn't have unlocked your door, and I oughtn't to have picked up your sword—it's very sharp, isn't it? And heavy! I never realized how hard it is to lift one up—I'm sorry, I'm wandering. Father says I do that too much of the time, and Goody Weft says I do it all the time, but Goody Weft—"

"Clearly speaks the truth," said the pilgrim. His oddly guttural accent was half music and half braying. "You are a thief, yes? A snoop? How did you get into my room? Ladyrest Inn has a most excellent reputation."

"I'd never steal!" said Clovermead. "We Wickwards don't rob our guests—I wouldn't even steal a Spider Ruby, not really. Father's always told me never to touch anything that belongs to a guest, or to go into their rooms. . . ." Clovermead turned scarlet. "That came out all wrong. I did go into your room, but I'm not a thief. Don't blame my father, sir, he's always taught me never to lie and never to steal—"

"The innkeeper's daughter has penetrated my refuge, which I was assured was inviolable," the pilgrim said loudly. Clovermead worriedly eyed the stairway behind him to see if her father was within earshot. "She has made merry with my possessions. Her father's honor as host, so carefully built up and hoarded, so fragile, will be destroyed by his darling's daring pleasantry. When I report the truth to him, what will he say? What will he do? He will cry! Great innkeeperly globules of water will scour his face from eye to mouth. He will be distraught to learn to what depths his daughter has descended. Is it so, little magpie?"

"Not exactly, sir," said Clovermead gravely. "Father will be unhappy, but he's not the sort to cry. Goody Weft might switch me—she always says Father spoils me rotten and that she has to give me discipline for two. I suppose it won't help Ladyrest if people hear I unlocked a door, but I don't think it'll hurt us so badly. Where else in Timothy Vale are the pilgrims going to sleep? Anyway, sir, I wasn't stealing. I was investigating your effects. I was certain when you arrived this morning that you had a fascinating past. You have that air, you know."

"You cannot trust airs," said the pilgrim, his eyes twinkling. "It means only that my clothes are worn, and that I am no seamster. Little magpie, should I punish you? You do not seem penitent."

"I don't think Father would want you to do anything to me without his permission," said Clovermead more calmly than she felt inside. She could dive through the pilgrim's legs, scramble down the stairs, and gallop outdoors to the wide pastures and secret hideaways of the Vale—but she'd have to come home sometime, and then Goody Weft really would switch her. "You should come downstairs with me and tell him what I've done wrong. Oh dear, it's only a week since they caught me taking apple pie from the pantry, and I promised I wouldn't make trouble for a month. I'll give you a penny if you don't tell Father. It's all I have in the world. Except the robin's egg I'm trying to hatch, and my books, and my pony, Cripple Malmsey, but I don't think you'd want any of those, would you?"

"Sweet Lady, girl!" the pilgrim laughed. "Do you always chatter so much?"

"No," said Clovermead with dignified cogency.

"I do not think I believe that claim," said the pilgrim. He walked over to his bed, checked his sword for nicks, and slid it into his scabbard. "You do not know how to fight with swords?"

"No," Clovermead said again—but then she couldn't bear to stay silent any longer. "I've always wanted to learn! I've heard ever so many stories from pilgrims, about knights who kill dragons and about battles and strange temples and heroes with magic swords. And the nicest old man with red eyebrows stayed here one winter and taught me to read. He gave me the *Garum Heptameron* when he left. Have you read it? It's all about the adventures of the queens and knights of Queensmart and the Thirty Towns, and there are seven times seven stories in it, which is forty-nine. The next summer a silly lady with a face like a prune let me have *The Song of the Siege of the Silver Knight.* Sir, I couldn't stay away when I saw your sword—there aren't any like it in Timothy Vale. All we have is daggers and axes and bows for hunting deer. Sweetroot Miller and I played sword fighting with pieces of wood, but I scraped her arm and the blubberer threw down her stick and ran home. Now none of the girls will play with me. Not sword fighting, anyway. The little ones play with rag dolls, the big ones are mad about dancing with the boys, and now Sweetroot wants to dance too, and she's the only girl near Ladyrest my age. Dancing's all right, but oh, I did want to know what it feels like to hold a real blade! Is it a magic sword like the one the Silver Knight had?"

"Alas, no," said the pilgrim. "Sorcer-swords do not exist outside of books, I think. There are enough odd things in the world, O daughter of an innkeeper, but not enchanted chopping knives." The pilgrim looked slyly down at Clovermead. "You would like to learn to sword-fight?"

Clovermead's eyes shone. "More than anything!"

"Really so? Well, magpie, I have tired myself greatly crossing the Chaffen Hills, and more than anything I would like to rest and recuperate myself for a few days in your father's fine inn. Shall I make a bargain with your father? I will teach you a little fighting, and I will eat and sleep here at his expense while I give you lessons. You will plead my case to him, I will not tell where I found you this afternoon, and in the future locked doors will stay locked, yes? And you will be bruised hard enough while learning to blade-whack, which should be sufficient punishment for you. Is this fair?"

"It is," Clovermead said, and solemnly shook his hand. His fingers were supple and strong as oiled leather. "I'm Clovermead Wickward. What's your name, pilgrim? I think I heard you say it when you came in this morning, but I was rereading the *Heptameron* and I didn't pay any attention to you till I saw what you looked like. Pardon me, that sounds rude. It *is* rude, but it wasn't meant rudely, if you see what I mean."

"In my land we have a saying," said the pilgrim. "A man should not care if a bee buzzes in his ear or if a child babbles at his feet."

"I don't think I care for that saying," said Clovermead. "The tone is very superior, very lofty. It sounds very silly coming from a young man who can't be that much older than I am. Did people say that a lot to you when you were younger? It must have been very annoying to hear it from grown-ups on a regular basis."

The pilgrim grinned and the blue crosses on his cheeks crinkled. "It was infuriating. Miss Clovermead, I am Sorrel of the Cyan Cross Horde. I am from the Tansy Steppes, and therefore a Tansyard. I have lived through seventeen winters. Does that answer all your questions?"

"Of course not," said Clovermead. "I have dozens more! But I'll save them until I've gotten Father's permission to sword-fight with you." She dashed out of the room and downstairs. Sorrel blinked and chuckled as she disappeared from sight. Then he took a leisurely minute to check that all his possessions were where he had left them, locked the door, and headed downstairs.

The great dining hall took up more than half the space of Ladyrest's ground floor. Its floor and walls had been carved from sturdy lengths of oak. To the right of the kitchen door sat a huge stone hearth surrounded by four rocking chairs. A dozen long tables, each accompanied by a pair of low benches, occupied the rest of the room. Afternoon light glowed through four huge, square windowpanes that could have come from nowhere nearer than Glaziers' Street in Queensmart and imparted a dark-honey hue to the dining room's polished timbers. Every part of the hall was immaculately clean. A score of iron sconces around the room held torches, ready to be lit when night came.

As his daughter fervidly summarized Sorrel's proposal, Waxmelt Wickward cleared the dirty dishes that a patrician pilgrim had left on the table at the end of his late lunch. Goody Weft cheerfully sang a shearing song in the kitchen as she washed the dozen pots and pans she had used for lunch. Clouds of steam billowed out from the kitchen.

Waxmelt Wickward was a little man—inches shorter than Sorrel and not much taller than Clovermead. His thin gray hair had receded halfway up the temples of his round face, and he sported a mustache and a small, pointed beard, both neatly trimmed. His face was smooth except for the lines of delighted laughter that had deepened in him as he watched his daughter grow. Faint worry glimmered almost perpetually in his soft eyes. He was stout around the middle, though not quite fat.

He quietly piled the dishes in the crook of one arm, whisked them to the kitchen, and came back into the room drying his hands on his apron. "My daughter says you're the best swordsman north of Queensmart," he said dubiously to Sorrel.

Sorrel shrugged. "Men with swords have chased after me and I have not died. I was a boy not so long ago and I remember how to be gently trained. These are my qualifications, Mr. Wickward. I can add to that only my desire to eat more of your most delicious oatmeal and fried lamb chops, and my rapturous craving to sleep many nights on your soft mattress and pillows. My little money cannot satisfy my desires, so I must hope that you will take my services as payment. I will be most happy if you say yes. I assure you, this Ladyrest is a lovelier inn than any I have seen in all the lands of Linstock."

"Goody Weft cooked the oatmeal," said Waxmelt modestly, looking pleased in spite of himself. He coughed and tried to look stern. "I've heard that all Tansyards are horse thieves."

"It is the noblest sport," Sorrel acknowledged, humbly dipping his head. "But Clovermead is not a horse, and we do not steal from our hosts. You have heard that, too?"

"Ye-es," Waxmelt reluctantly agreed. "But I hear all sorts of stories about Tansyards. You're the first one I've met. Not many of you come out of your Steppes."

"Of course he's honest!" Clovermead burst in. "And he must be an excellent fighter! I've read the whole story in the *Heptameron.* The Tansyards were gallant warriors who struggled for their freedom, even after the legions of Queensmart had subjugated the Thirty Towns and Selcouth and the Astrantian Sands and made the Cindertallows of Chandlefort do homage to the Queen. The Tansyards refused to submit to the Empire, and against all odds they annihilated four Imperial legions and captured their banners. Then Queen Aurhelia swallowed a bitter pill to her pride and gave up trying to vanquish the Tansyards. Isn't it true?" she appealed to Sorrel.

"Most certainly, Miss Clovermead, but it was in my great-great-grandfather's time that we sent the legions fleeing back to Queensmart. Great-great-grandfather was an esteemed warrior, of whose glory the Horde sang many songs, but I have no such deeds yet to my name. Mr. Wickward, I can transform your daughter from an untrained girl to a rank novice. Will that be an acceptable trade for your hospitality?"

"It's a foolish idea, Mr. Wickward," Goody Weft bellowed from the kitchen. "Don't encourage that daughter of yours in her mischief. She'll lose an eye."

"You said I'd break my neck if I climbed onto the roof, and I didn't!" Clovermead yelled back.

"Ninny's luck!" Goody Weft retorted. "Mr. Wickward, it's a scandal how you indulge her. Tell her no for once!"

Clovermead gazed imploringly at her father. Waxmelt looked into her face, sighed, and glanced apprehensively at the kitchen door. "The answer is yes, Goody," he called out. He flinched as a pot crashed loudly to the floor. "This isn't just a treat, Clo," he continued softly. "You need to learn how to defend yourself. All the pilgrims say the fighting's terrible in Linstock—isn't that true, Mr. Sorrel?"

"It is a devastated land," said the Tansyard somberly. "The soldiers of Low Branding raid near Chandlefort, the soldiers of Chandlefort raid near Low Branding, and all of Linstock has become fire and blood. The farmers pray to Our Lady for the Empire to come back and keep the peace, but they know that the legions will never again march north from Queensmart. The Empire is dying, dead, and Chandlefort and Low Branding squabble over Linstock like vultures over its carcass. I hear there are more such wars in Selcouth and the Thirty Towns. You are lucky here in Timothy Vale, with the Chaffen Hills between you and the soldiers."

"I thank Our Lady night and day for their protection," Waxmelt said. "Mr. Sorrel, I think Clo should learn how to defend herself, in case our luck runs out and the soldiers ever do come this way. Clo, you understand you're not playing a game?"

"Yes, Father," Clovermead said. She was a little awed at how serious her father had become. Then she grinned. "You'd better not wait a single minute to start your lessons, Mr. Sorrel. You never can tell when a cruel and bloodstained soldier might decide to wander by."

Waxmelt laughed. "She won't give you any rest till you teach her something, Mr. Sorrel. You may as well start now. I'll come outside and watch." He took off his apron, folded it neatly, and hung it on the back of a chair.

Goody Weft came and looked through the doorway of the kitchen. She was a tall, rangy woman in a black dress whose plain, bony features lit up with a look of indignation as she eyed the apologetic Sorrel, the cringing Waxmelt, and the ecstatic Clovermead. "It's an absolute disgrace," she announced, then wheeled back into her domain. Loud, despairing commentary followed the three outdoors.

Sorrel looked around him. Ladyrest Inn, two stories tall and ten times larger than any other building in the

Vale, hulked on the crest of Kestrel Hill. Around the inn were a smokehouse, a barn, a yard piled high with firewood, a small apple orchard, a stable, and a midden where hairy, snuffling pigs rooted at the garbage. East of the inn were the mill, the bake-house, and the handful of steep-roofed log cabins that constituted the hamlet of Grindery, the largest settlement in Timothy Vale. West of Ladyrest were the rough granite flagstones of the Crescent Road, which ran from the Imperial city of Queensmart north through Linstock, the Chaffen Hills, and Timothy Vale, and at last over a winding pass threading the Reliquary Mountains to its terminus at Our Lady's shrine at Snowchapel.

Just north of Ladyrest the Road descended suddenly along the slope of Kestrel Hill to the ford through the cold, swift Goat River, then rose to meander in the middle distance past vast flocks of sheep, thick grass, and very little else. Besides the cabins of Grindery there were no more than sixscore shepherds' huts scattered through Timothy Vale. The Vale itself was an emerald string bean of verdant, hillocky pastures. On either side of the Vale the land rose precipitously toward firs, bare rocks, and finally the savage white tips of the Reliquaries. Except for a few hours around noon, one set of peaks or the other cast jagged shadows across the Vale's precarious aisle of habitation. Year-round, sharp winds plunged from the Reliquaries' heights to chill the Vale.

Sorrel shivered as he led Clovermead and Waxmelt over to where Ladyrest's firewood yard abutted on Kestrel Hill. His tatterdemalion jerkin was far too thin to protect him from the Vale's autumn breezes. Waxmelt blew on his hands and rubbed them briskly together, but Clovermead bounded unheedingly through the cold. Only her red cheeks registered the impact of the chill.

With Waxmelt's permission, Sorrel took the inn's axe and chopped each of two long oak branches roughly into the shape of a sword. He then took out his knife and whittled them till their hilts were easy to grasp and their blade edges thin but not sharp. He gave the lighter sword to Clovermead and walked with her and Waxmelt to the east side of the hill.

"Try to hit me," said Sorrel.

"Yaah!" screamed Clovermead. She rushed at him with all her might—and found herself flat on her back, her sword lying some feet away.

"Are you hurt, Clo?" Waxmelt asked, not very anxiously.

Clovermead picked herself up off the grass and patted her arms and legs. "No, Father. My fingers tingle and I'm out of breath, that's all."

"Out of breath and still talking—only you, Clo," said Waxmelt. He grinned, and Clovermead stuck out her tongue at him. "Mr. Sorrel will think you have no manners. Sir, I don't know fighting, but that looked nicely done. Would you like cabbage stuffed with lamb sausage for dinner?"

"I salivate ecstatically, Mr. Wickward," said Sorrel with a low bow and a lick of his lips. He looked curiously at Waxmelt. "I think your voice reveals that you are not from the Vale. You are from someplace south, yes? I think you are like me, not yet accustomed to this horrid cold?"

"I'm from Linstock," Waxmelt said flatly. "I came to the Vale twelve summers ago, when Clo was just a baby."

"That is so? From where in Linstock do you hail?"

"From where Clovermead's mother lies buried," Waxmelt said. He was scowling now. "There was fever that year, and she was weak after giving birth to Clo. I left her grave behind me and I've never looked back. I don't like to think about Linstock."

"I beg a thousand pardons," said Sorrel. "I sorrow for your sadness and I will ask you no more questions."

"It's nothing," said Waxmelt. "Don't bother yourself further." He nodded a farewell to Sorrel, ruffled Clovermead's hair, and headed back to Ladyrest.

Sorrel turned to more basic lessons once Waxmelt was gone. He had Clovermead hold the sword in her outstretched arm for three minutes, then had her hold tight to the hilt while he slashed furiously at the blade. He made her lunge, duck, jump, and leap backward while holding the sword as a shield in front of her face.

"Let's fight," Clovermead begged. "I can do these exercises later. I want to be in a battle!"

"As you wish, Miss Clovermead," said Sorrel. "We shall have a single combat! We will try to tap at each other's bodies with our blades. Please do not aim for my head, and please do not try to skewer me well and truly. If I hit you ten times, I will win, and if you hit me once, you will win. Yes? Then, we proceed!"

Clovermead immediately leapt at Sorrel and rained down furious blows on him. He parried them patiently and waited for her to exhaust herself. When she was panting, he shifted to the offense. He moved slowly and let Clovermead see exactly how his sword swept and thrust. The oak sword hit Clovermead ten different ways and left behind only light bruises.

Their bout ended as the sun set. Sorrel and Clovermead sat down on the side of Kestrel Hill, near a patch of pine forest that bulged down from the Eastern Reliquaries. Their oak swords lay by their sides in the tall grass. The two of them dripped with sweat.

"I haven't been so tired since Gaffer Miller's ram chased me into Goat River," said Clovermead. She took off her sweater. Her shirt beneath was stinking and damp. "Phew! Fighting's just as much fun as I imagined, but I hadn't realized there was so much hard work to it. It's easier to carry two buckets of well water or bathe a cat. Still, I think I see how it ought to be done. Tomorrow I'll be much better—don't you agree? I think I'm a natural warrior. I'll be as good as a Tansyard within a week!"

"Miss Clovermead, you are as skilled with the blade as any Tansyard with one afternoon of training," said Sorrel. "In five days you will be as good as any Tansyard with five days of training. No, I do not speak the truth entirely. You are a marvelous quick learner. Your parries improve most rapidly. But do not expect to perform miracles, nor to spit ten champions before sunrise."

"Hmph," said Clovermead. "Father always said I should have high expectations for myself, and high expectations are certainly a lot more fun than low expectations." She sat up, plucked a hayseed, and put it between her teeth. Her eyes widened. "Gracious Lady! What a huge bear. I've never seen one come so close."

Sorrel lifted his head. "Where do you see this bear, Miss Clovermead?" he asked.

Clovermead pointed to the near edge of the pine forest. There a white-furred bear squatted on her hind legs. She was enormous—sixteen feet high and six feet thick. Her hoar white claws were three inches long. She yawned and revealed teeth even longer than her claws and sharp as razors. She steadily inspected the two of them and sniffed gently at the wind.

"She has found me again," said Sorrel. His teeth began to chatter. He got to his feet. "Miss Clovermead, it is time for you to return to Ladyrest. You will please walk directly to the dining room. I must bid you farewell for a little while."

"I don't understand," said Clovermead. She spat out the hayseed and stumbled to her feet. "I know she's large, but she won't hurt you if you stay out of her way. She's just a bear."

"Times are changing," said Sorrel. Now his hands were shaking. His eyes darted from the bear to the Ladyrest stable. "Miss Clovermead, you should know that I am a coward. I am always fearful and I run very often. Now it is time for me to run from this creature. I will go to my sweet mare, Brown Barley, and I will gallop away from your fine inn, and if Our Lady smiles, I think I can make the bear lose my scent. Please make my excuses to your excellent father. Ask him my most weeping pardon that I must abandon his scrumptious lamb sausage and cabbage, and inform him that I will return when it is dark. And please do not tell your father about the bear. He will worry about your safety and require me to go away. He does not need to worry—she is only chasing me. Even if she discovers some days from now that I have returned here and she comes back, for now she will only watch." Sorrel fixed his eyes on Clovermead's with wistful urgency. "Please say nothing. In a week I will be gone."

"I wish I could go with you," sighed Clovermead. Her eyes blazed. "Danger in Timothy Vale! How wonderful. Of course I won't say anything, Mr. Sorrel. Father's a fuddy-duddy who raises a ruckus if I'm out of sight for an hour! He's just not reasonable. I wouldn't mind if the bear *did* come looking for you. I'd fight at your side against her."

"I will remember your kind offer," said Sorrel. He bowed to Clovermead with the utmost dignity. His eyes skittered back to the bear and his Adam's apple jerked. "But please, miss, now go."

"I won't tell Father," said Clovermead as she left. Then she ran as if a pack of wolves were yipping at her feet. Partly she ran for the pleasure of running and partly with a prickle of real fear to speed her on her way.

She slammed the dining-room door shut behind her and scampered to press her nose to the window. She watched Sorrel jog to the stable, and a minute later she saw him on Brown Barley, cantering north on the Road. The bear got to her feet and padded after him. She was an avalanche in fur.

"This is my first real adventure," Clovermead told herself solemnly. "I must treasure it. Funny, I always thought bears seemed nice. I wonder what that one's name was?"

Something roared in her mind and Clovermead suddenly knew the answer to her question. "Boulderbash?" Clovermead asked herself curiously. "Of course, Boulderbash. It suits her perfectly. How perfectly gargantuan she was!"

Chapter Two

The Vision in the Puddle

SORREL STOLE BACK INTO LADYREST AFTER MIDNIGHT. His clothes had been spattered with mud and Brown Barley panted with weariness. Clovermead met him at the stable. She put the mare in the stall next to Waxmelt's pony, Nubble, and helped Sorrel rub her down. Then she covered her with a quilted blanket and brought her honeyed oats. Brown Barley whinnied appreciatively and stamped her feet. Clovermead led Sorrel back to the inn and had him sit in the chair nearest the dining-room fire. She gave him a bowl of hot oatmeal.

"Father said to give you this first. There's cabbage and sausage waiting on the stove, and I can make you mint tea. Goody Weft and I plucked the mint leaves just last week and they're almost fresh. It's the best tea in Timothy Vale. Would you like some?"

"I cannot refuse so well-omened a brew," Sorrel said with a tired grin. Clovermead bounced into the kitchen and came back with a hot mug. Sorrel's teeth began to chatter as he held his face over the rising steam. "Now that I am warming, I realize what an icicle I had become. Eeyah. You have my profound gratitude, Miss Clovermead. Where is Mr. Wickward? I should also thank him for leaving me dinner."

"He's asleep—I told him I'd wait up for you." Clovermead peeked conspiratorially up the empty stairs and shuffled closer to Sorrel. "He's entirely in the dark about the strange event," she whispered into his ear. "So am I. Will you tell me about the bear, please? I think you owe it to me, and I don't care how long the story is. I don't mind staying up."

Sorrel thoughtfully sipped at his tea—then shook his head. "I think my guest-duty is to disappoint you, Miss Clovermead, and to be mouth-buttoned. You are safer knowing nothing. Alas, I give you poor recompense for your aid, and I am abashed, chagrined, ashamed, and contrite. In Tansyard we have seventy-three words to express these emotions, or maybe seventy-four, and I assure you from the bottom of my heart that I feel all of them."

"You rat," said Clovermead in amazement. "I even made you mint tea."

"I abominate myself," Sorrel said. He slapped himself on the left wrist. "Now, there is a dinner in the kitchen?"

And for all Clovermead's entreaties, he told her nothing more.

"I suppose he should not speak casually of great matters," Clovermead said to herself when she woke the next morning. "Still, it rankles to know that an adventure is finally happening in Timothy Vale, but not for me. It's like having your arm in a splint with an itch on your elbow. Ah, poor, deprived me. Clovermead, you must learn to fight well enough to whack that hoity-toity Tansyard once on the ribs before he leaves."

With that goal to inspire her, Clovermead kept rigorously to the fierce regimen of exercise Sorrel made her undergo. She ran up and down Kestrel Hill a dozen times, hung by her arms from an apple tree branch, and held her arms extended with a ten-pound piece of firewood in each hand. She lunged and parried for hours at a time, and after two days Sorrel taught Clovermead how to fight a formal duel. He also threw dirt in her face and kicked her legs out from under her in a desperate skirmish all over Kestrel Hill, and he stood at her side to show her how infantry fight together. The Tansyard mounted Brown Barley, charged Clovermead, and showed her how to sidestep a horse's hooves and slash at its belly.

Clovermead threw herself into the bouts with fierce devotion and slapdash style. Her lightning-quick assaults forced Sorrel into a desperate defense, but she was unable to sustain them. She would falter at last and Sorrel would press her back with a slow, methodical counterattack. Clovermead's parries would become slower, her sword would barely rise, and Sorrel would whack her stomach or her armpit with his blade.

"That signifies death," Sorrel said. "I think that this fighting is a game to you, Miss Clovermead—you want to razzle-dazzle, but you will not slow-and-steady. Slow and steady will keep you alive and make your opponent dead. Dead-making is the point of fighting—not to flash metal in air."

Clovermead laughed gaily. "I wager my razzle-dazzle will kill you a few times before the week's out, Mr. Sorrel."

It did. On the fourth day Clovermead's wooden blade rapped Sorrel's chest for the first time. On the fifth day she tapped him twice, and on the sixth she knocked him off his feet with a sudden whack to the ribs. Clovermead crowed with delight and danced jubilantly around the prone Tansyard.

Waxmelt and Goody Weft had been watching. Goody Weft barked with laughter at the Tansyard's sudden fall. "Teaching Clovermead how to fall down, is he? It's money well spent, Mr. Wickward, I see it now." She guffawed all the way back to Ladyrest. Sorrel blushed furiously as he picked himself up.

"Usually this does not happen so," he said to Waxmelt.

"I'm glad to see you've taught Clovermead well," said Waxmelt with a smile.

"I had not expected her to learn so quickly," Sorrel said, rubbing his ribs.

"I got him! I got him!" Clovermead caroled, stabbing her sword to the sky. "Ooh, I'm a dauntless warrior! And I'll get him again!"

"It must be very rewarding to have so enthusiastic a student," said Waxmelt.

Sorrel groaned. "Deep, deep down beneath the pain I feel great teacherly pride. Ouch."

Clovermead spent the next morning doing chin-ups from a branch of a poplar tree near the top of Kestrel Hill.

"They are very good exercise," said Sorrel. "Besides, I have been tossing and turning half the night. Bad dreams of bears afflict me, brrr! I will rest and you will bemuscle yourself, yes?"

"You don't feel well because you ate too much of Father's stew last night," said Clovermead as she chinned. "You are a lazy glutton who is pompous about being grown up, which you hardly are. You're a bad example to a tender maiden, and I disapprove of you. Who's in the right in this war between Low Branding and Chandlefort?"

"Like a butterfly, you flutter from topic to topic in your conversation," observed Sorrel. "It is hard to answer you. First I will say that I possess many faults, but I cannot be a bad example to a scamp like you. Second I will say that the answer to your last question is high politics and beyond the judgment of simple folks like us." He hesitated a moment. "It is often said in Linstock that the Mayor of Low Branding had much justice on his side when he began the war. It is also said that he has fought the war most savagely, most cruelly. There are few who think the freedom of Low Branding is worth the butcheries the Mayor has dealt out to achieve it."

"What butcheries?" asked Clovermead curiously. "The pilgrims don't talk much about the war when I'm around."

"They are kind to spare you that knowledge," said Sorrel shortly. "More chinning, less jawing." He settled down on the grass with a rock for his pillow.

"Still, I'd like to know." There was no response from Sorrel. Clovermead sighed and looked north, down Kestrel Hill to the Goat River ford and up to the north pastures of the Vale. Just across the river Gaffer Merrin and an assortment of his sons and dogs led their flock from the Vale Commons to the Merrin Paddock. The Gaffer's curly white beard made him look like a particularly large ram that had learned to wear clothes, stand on its hind feet, and wield a yew crook. His ruddy-blond sons were more like the Merrin dogs—hairy, dirty, cheerful, and forever on the run after a stray lamb. They halloed to one another, and the echoes floated over the grass stubble of the Commons, the rippling river, and the swell of Kestrel Hill to Clovermead's ears.

Clovermead let herself hang down. Her feet dangled half a foot off the ground. "Card Merrin over there wants to marry me," she said to Sorrel, nodding at the smallest figure. "He comes to Ladyrest and he stares at me. He's thirteen and I hate him. He gets all flustered and boring when he talks to me. He doesn't read and he doesn't hunt and he doesn't do anything exciting. He just likes wrestling with his older brothers and drinking beer when Gaffer Merrin lets him. If I had to marry him, I'd pinch him every day."

"Pinching and conjugal harmony go very badly together," said Sorrel. "That was not a saying of the Cyan Cross Horde, but it should have been. It is a wise saying and full of truth. Miss Clovermead, please return to your exercises. They are to your inestimable benefit."

"Phooey to my inestimable benefit," said Clovermead, chinning herself over the branch once more.

Now she saw a lone woman in a gray dress walking south on the Road, eating up the distance with a steady gait. She stopped while the Merrin flock eddied in front of her, and waved her thanks to the Merrin sons when they had pushed their bleating charges out of the way. They bowed respectfully.

"Someone important is walking this way," said Clovermead.

"Impossible. You must have a horse to be important. Any Tansyard will tell you that." Sorrel sat up and looked north. "A woman traveling by herself? That is most rare."

The woman crossed the Ford. She slogged through knee-high water—and slipped, falling headlong. Dripping, she got to her feet and disconsolately shook her sleeves.

Clovermead dropped to the ground. "Perhaps nefarious and cruel bandits have stolen her beast and murdered her companions. Not that I've ever heard of bandits between here and Snowchapel. If there are any, they would have to be nefarious indeed to rob a poor pilgrim. She must be awfully cold. I think we should do a kind deed."

"What did you have in mind?"

"Drying her off." Clovermead jogged up the hill to Ladyrest. Sorrel yawned, sprang to his feet, and loped after Clovermead. He caught up with her in the yard behind the kitchen. Clovermead plucked two fluffy towels from the laundry-line and tossed one to him. "Simple hospitality," she said, and galloped off toward the ford with the towel flapping loosely from her hand. Sorrel folded the second towel over his arm and followed after her.

They came to the woman at the bottom of Kestrel Hill. Clovermead skidded to a halt and thrust forth her towel. "Unknown lady, please use this to dry yourself, courtesy of Ladyrest Inn. Sorrel has one too. You have fought with Goat River, and Goat River has won. I know how you must feel. Once I dove into Bluehorn Lake to see if it was as cold as everyone said. It was. You're not a pilgrim, are you? I'd remember your face if you'd come north this summer."

"I am not responsible for Clovermead, madam," said Sorrel, stepping up behind her. He unfolded his towel, bowed, and proffered it as well. "This cloth has been provided by Ladyrest Inn and Tansyard Portaging Services."

The woman stared at them bemusedly, made the crescent sign, and bowed. "Thank you very much," she said. She took their towels and vigorously rubbed her sopping clothes.

Her thick gray dress clung to her from her shoulders to her feet. A white head scarf covered up her hair, her ears, and her neck. She wore a silver pendant of Our Lady at her throat and carried a drenched pack on her shoulders. She was a tall woman whose age-thickened face retained much of its youthful beauty. Raven black and cloud white wisps of hair danced at the edge of her scarf. She had a dreamy look to her that made Clovermead think that this was not the first time she had fallen into a river, or likely to be the last.

"There's no reason for you to remember my face," the woman said. She sat down on a granite boulder by the side of the Road and began to squeeze water from her dress. "I came on pilgrimage twelve years ago. I stayed the night at Ladyrest then, but I've been a nun at Snowchapel ever since."

Clovermead's eyes widened. "Heavens above! Though I suppose you know more about them than I do—professionally, I mean. I've never seen a nun before. I thought nuns never left the Chapel. What do you actually do there? What's your name? Are those a nun's robes you're wearing? Does everyone in the order wear that sort of pendant? Where are you going? Do you want to stop at the Ladyrest and have a meal or stay for the night?"

"Next she will ask you for lessons in nunnery," said Sorrel. "Miss Clovermead will devour you whole with questions and enthusiasm. You must fly for your life while you still can. For me it is too late; leave me to my doom."

The nun belly-laughed, low and loud. "I'm sure it's a very pleasant doom to have a pretty girl hanging on your every word. Sorrel is your name? I want to hear no more complaints from you! And you're Clovermead, miss? Let me see if I can answer your questions in order. The Sisters of the Holy Order of Our Lady's Sibyls spin wool, grow vegetables, host pilgrims, pray, and watch the Scrying Pool at Snowchapel for glimpses of the future. My name is Sister Rowan. These are my traveling robes, and very itchy linsey-woolsey they are too. The pendant belonged to my dear friend Sister Mendloom, who left the pendant to me when Our Lady took her home." Sister Rowan made the crescent sign again, slowly and sadly. "Poor Mendy, her arthritis hurt her terribly those last few years. Deary me, what were your last questions?"

"Where are you going?" Clovermead repeated. "Will you stop the night at Ladyrest?"

"Oh, yes! My dear, you should address your questions to me one at a time. I have an awful tendency to forget things. I'm traveling to the Royal Abbey in

Queensmart—Our Lady sent me a vision telling me to go. Actually, she sent me visions two nights in a row, but I didn't remember the first one when I woke up. The second time around she was furious! I woke with an awful headache. I don't know why Our Lady wants me to go to Queensmart, but there's no doubt I have to go. I don't think Abbess Medick really believes I've had a vision. I've always been terrible at scrying. I see roasts burning, but it always turns out to be me who forgets to watch the meat. Abbess Medick says it doesn't take prophecy to know I shouldn't be let loose in the kitchen. But she agreed to let me leave Snowchapel! 'So you can stop pestering me, Sister' were her words. But this definitely was a vision! Now, as for your last question . . ." Sister Rowan suddenly blushed. "What was your last question again?"

"Can you stay the night at Ladyrest?" Clovermead asked.

"I'm afraid not. Our Lady definitely told me to hurry. Dear me, I'm afraid I've disappointed you, miss. I'm disappointed too. I remember my night at Ladyrest very fondly, and I'd much rather be there than in Queensmart. Queensmart is my home, and I left it, which should tell you what I think of the place." Sister Rowan pressed her boots tentatively against the ground. They squished. She pulled them off her feet and water poured out. "I don't think Our Lady will mind if I sit and dry out a few minutes more. If I may ask, what gives you the right to speak for Ladyrest Inn?"

"I am Clovermead Wickward," said Clovermead portentously, "the innkeeper's daughter."

"Are you Mr. Wickward's baby? My dear, how you've grown!" Sister Rowan looked more closely at Clovermead, pinched her cheek, and laughed with delight. "You were just an infant in silk swaddlings when I saw you last. Your hair was as blond then as it is now. I remember running my fingers through it and marveling at how fine it was. Mr. Wickward had just become innkeeper. He hardly knew how to cook—the woman he hired yelled at him frightfully. He jumped a foot in the air every time a pilgrim knocked on the door, and he twitched if anyone looked your way. I told him I wasn't going to steal you, but he just glowered at me. Is he calmer nowadays?"

"Decidedly," said Clovermead. "He is so calm that a visitation of flower-priests from Hither Jaifal would not perturb him."

"I am Sorrel of the Cyan Cross Horde," Sorrel interjected, thrusting out his chest. "I am a Tansyard vagabond and pilgrim."

"Merely my tutor," said Clovermead. Sister Rowan gave Sorrel a sympathetic look. "Why don't you have a horse?"

A flash of annoyance crossed Sister Rowan's face. "Abbess Medick wouldn't give me one. She said Snowchapel couldn't spare a horse for 'gaddings about.' She was kind enough to give me the fare for the riverboat from High Branding to Queensmart, but I swear by Our Lady, she smirked when she said I'd have to walk to High Branding. She is a—never mind. It is part of Our Lady's plan, I suppose, to blister, chill, and drench me."

"I have always taken ease to be a sign of Our Lady's favor," said Sorrel. "I avoid discomfort as a sign of evil. Blessed are the lazy, as we say in the Cyan Cross Horde."

"I envy you your theology." Sister Rowan fingered her damp habit, made a moue of distaste, and reluctantly handed the towels back to Clovermead and Sorrel. She put her boots on again and got up with a sigh. Her boots squelched softly.

"Are you leaving already?" Clovermead asked plaintively.

"Duty is duty, as my mother vainly told me in my youth, so onward I must go. Walking will warm me, I suppose. Clovermead Wickward, I am delighted to see you have grown into a lovely young lady. Sorrel of the, um, Cyan Cross Horde, it is a pleasure to meet you. When I hear you profess your beliefs, I sincerely wish you were Abbess at Snowchapel."

"When I am Abbess, no nun will rise before noon," Sorrel devoutly murmured.

Sister Rowan laughed heartily. "I look forward to that day—I'm afraid we must part company now. I thank you both again for the use of the towels. The blessing of Lady Moon on both of you." Sister Rowan reached down to a nearby puddle, dipped her finger in the water, and anointed their foreheads with a muddy dribble. She muttered a few syllables of the Moontongue and glanced down at the murky water—

She screamed. The nun fell heavily on the rock and clutched at her cheek. Blood streamed down her face. Something had ripped her face from her nose to her ear.

"Ursus clawed me," Sister Rowan moaned. Her eyes

were wide with fear. "He saw me and he reached out. Lady preserve me." She shivered, and tears welled out of her eyes. They ran down her bloody cheek. Clovermead looked around wildly to see what had attacked the nun, but she saw nothing. She looked at Sister Rowan's slashed flesh, and her own cheek tingled.

"I saw more in the puddle." Sister Rowan's eyes sought out Sorrel's. Her pupils shone with silver fire. "The bear-priest is coming after you. He brings blood with him. You must ride to Snowchapel this instant. No more delays."

"You have seen truly?" asked Sorrel, his face stark with fear. "This is not the Scrying Pool."

"The Moon shines everywhere," said Sister Rowan. The silver fire faded from her and her voice was weak with pain. Clovermead gave her back the towel, and Sister Rowan staunched the wound on her cheek. "The Scrying Pool is crystal clear, but all waters reflect Our Lady's vision a little. I see that you carry a message, Tansyard. I see that the bear-priest wants to intercept it. I see Lord Ursus' teeth and claws. I see you must ride fast, Sorrel of the Cyan Cross Horde." She smiled faintly. "I never saw so much in the Scrying Pool. Our Lady's eyes must be in me."

"Night and stars," Sorrel swore. "Miss Clovermead, I fear our lessons are at an end. You have not done badly, but do not be rash if true-trouble finds you. And keep away from the razzle-dazzle! You are not yet a trained soldier."

"Are you going right now?" asked Clovermead. "It's not fair! I'm never going to know what this is all about. I'm horribly frustrated."

"When everything is settled, I will return and tell all to you," said Sorrel. He flashed her a grin. "Good-bye, Miss Clovermead. You have given me a delightful week. You have my profound thanks." And he was off and running toward the Ladyrest stable, his ragtag clothes flapping behind him.

"His condescension is insufferable," said Clovermead. "Stupid Tansyard. Sister Rowan, who is Lord Ursus?"

"Blood and killing," Sister Rowan said. Clovermead waited for an elaboration, but none came. Sister Rowan frowned and looked in the puddle again. "How do I avoid the bear-priests?" she muttered to herself. "Dear Lady, tell me which way to travel. His shadow is heavy on Linstock. I see him everywhere. Ha!" She grinned suddenly at Clovermead. "Abbess Medick is right—my visions never are very useful. Our Lady doesn't tell me which way to travel, but she's sent me a vision for you just now. My dear, something that belongs to you lies hidden in a nearby tree."

Clovermead's brow wrinkled. "I haven't lost anything."

"Sometimes the vision is unclear, but the water never lies. Did you misplace a doll when you were an infant?"

"Father says I broke them all."

Sorrel galloped out of the stable on Brown Barley and kicked her north on the Road. He waved farewell, then dwindled and disappeared out of sight.

Sister Rowan nodded approvingly. "Bravo, Sorrel. Too few people pay proper attention to visions. It makes you wonder why they come all the way to Snowchapel to find out their future and then refuse to believe what they've been told. Tell me, who would you expect to see heading south on the Road this time of year?"

"Hyssop Nunsman," Clovermead said instantly. "He always comes down to spend the winter in High Branding."

"Of course!" said Sister Rowan. "How could I forget? Hyssop's always good at sniffing out news for us. In fact, I believe he said he'd accompany me south if I waited a few days. Unfortunately, the vision said I couldn't wait even a minute. Well. Miss Clovermead, for your kindness I will reveal a Mystery to you. If there is great need, we nuns have ways of traveling discreetly." She uttered a few more words of Moontongue and her face began to melt.

"Oh, heavens!" said Clovermead. "Does that hurt? Your nose is getting as big as a Low Branding plum. You look like Hyssop! I'd recognize his squint and his greasy red hair and the wart on his nose anywhere. Your pack looks like his sack full of furs. You're not as big as Hyssop, but I don't suppose most people would notice. If I weren't paying attention, I'd swear you were him. How marvelous!"

"It is fun to sneak up on people unawares," Sister Rowan admitted. She stood up and gave the towel back to Clovermead. "Good-bye, good-bye! I'm sorry I bloodied the cloth. Look in the trees!"

"Good-bye," Clovermead called to the disappearing figure of Hyssop Nunsman. "Good luck! Lady bless you! Oh, it's good-byes all around, excitement's in the air, and here I am stuck in Timothy Vale the same as ever. How perfectly wretched. I suppose I'll have to challenge Gaffer Miller's ram to a duel if I want excitement." Her shoulders slumped and she let the towel fall to the ground.

The puddle lapped against the bloody corner of the cloth. A growl like distant thunder bit into Clovermead's bones as gore seeped into the water. She saw a claw flash in the puddle's muddy scarlet.

Clovermead gulped hastily, made the sign of the crescent, and steadied herself. She looked around, but saw nothing. After a second she whistled nonchalantly. "Frightened of nothing! Just like a child. Silly, silly Clovermead," she told herself disapprovingly. She paused. "But I don't think I'll tell Father about claws in puddles or Lord Ursus or anything like that. He'd worry about me and he'd send me to my room till I was a hundred and twelve and I'd never ever have a chance for another adventure. Did he see Sister Rowan through the window? I'll have to tell him some story about who she was and why Sorrel left so suddenly. But nothing about bears."

Then Clovermead smiled dreamily and flexed her fingers into claws. "Bears! Oh, I could do anything I liked if I were a big, strong bear. That would be fun. Rrargh! I wonder what it's like to bite people?"

Chapter Three

The Brooch of the Burning Bee

For ten days Clovermead searched under every elm, oak, pine, fir, beech, and nondescript bush near Ladyrest. As she ransacked the foliage for the lost whatever-it-was that belonged to her, the leaves in Timothy Vale began to turn color. The lower slopes of the Reliquaries became solid orange and yellow, while the sugar maples in the Commons flared a bloody, coruscating red. Already the night temperatures were close to freezing. Men and boys brought the sheep down from the high pastures, while their wives and daughters picked apples and harvested the barley and the wheat. Gaffers and Grannies with rheumatism and broken bones sniffed at the morning breezes and direly predicted a cold, snowy winter. Pilgrims anxious to pass south of the Chaffen Hills before the first snowfall hastened through the Vale. Waxmelt and Goody Weft kept busy serving their flurry of guests and scarcely noticed that Clovermead was spending long hours away from Ladyrest.

On the eleventh day Clovermead tramped west from Kestrel Hill and crept into Gorseberry Dell. She hopped onto the stone wall that marked the boundary of Gaffer Bolts' land and peeked in. Before her, unattended by man or dog, the Gaffer's sheep bleated in a low and fenced-off square of meadow. The flock had eaten the grass down to a green stubble, and now they huddled by the far fence and nipped what grass they could reach through the wooden slats. Beyond the meadow were marshy thickets crowded with thorns and blueberry bushes. In the center of the thickets rose a lone ash tree's skeletal crown.

"Trespassing is wrong," said Clovermead reflectively. "Not that Gaffer ever minded, except when I took carrots from his garden or when I dipped that lamb into the pot of blue dye. But he shouldn't care if I just steal a quick look at his tree. Sweet Lady, a whole flock of witnesses gazes upon my surreptitious misdeed! Fortunately the nearest court is in High Branding, and precedent does not allow sheep to testify in a court of law. Not that they could say anything but 'Bleat!' and 'Baa!' I dare Gaffer Bolts to prosecute me solely upon ovine testimony. I need fear nothing."

Clovermead jumped down from the wall, dashed past the startled sheep, and bounded into the thicket. Thorns tore at her clothes—one long spine cut through to her arm and drew blood. Clovermead cursed the offending barb with Tansyard oaths she had learned from Sorrel—*"Serla mordey, Mirra commeri,"* and best of all, *"Lempur madnerap ved heraka madnerap dim coralla tir madnerap!"* She didn't know what they meant, but they sounded wonderfully enraged and unladylike.

The ash stood huge and aloof within the thicket, neighbored only by dead leaves and wispy ferns. A ferocious blast of lightning had murdered the tree long since and left it leafless, barkless, and charred jet black. Shoulder-high to Clovermead, the lightning had gouged a jagged hollow. Years of rain had softened the wound with a green bandage of moss.

"I might have put something in that hollow," Clovermead said doubtfully. "I wouldn't have thought I'd forget coming here, but perhaps I was young and foolish. Goody Weft would say I still am young and foolish, but she'll say that when I'm one hundred and two. Are you there, lost whatever-you-are?" She sidled toward the ash's trunk and quickly thrust her hand into the cavity. Her fingers dug past leaves and crawling grubs and caught on metal. "I've found something!" Clovermead bugled. "Sister Rowan, you were right!" She shook off an inquisitive insect, pulled the object out, and raced back to the wall. She ruffled the fleece of puzzled sheep as she ran.

"I suppose I must have come here when I was knee high to a newborn lamb," said Clovermead as she hastily decamped to the safety of Ladyrest property. "Nevertheless, I don't remember that tree or that thicket at all." She rubbed at the metal thing. "This is disgustingly dirty. I don't mind a little grime—Goody Weft would say I don't mind a lot of grime—but there are limits to everything. I must remember in the future to bury treasure in tightly sealed metal caskets. Goodness, it's a brooch of some sort. I don't remember that I ever owned one. Does it sparkle when it's clean?"

Clovermead ran east to Billybeard Creek and squatted at the water's edge. The clear water loosened most of the grime from the brooch, and Clovermead's thumb scoured away further encrustations. She lifted the brooch into the pale sunlight and squinted.

"Very battered," Clovermead judged. "The color's dull—most likely it's pewter. But look at that design! The bee has a crown on her head, so she must be a queen bee. Those are flames around her. That isn't usually good for bees. Nor for queens, I suppose. One reads of fiery ladies, but I always imagined that meant something different. Still, the blaze doesn't seem to be hurting her. It must be an emblematic design of some sort. The bee wields a burning blade. Strange, I don't remember this brooch of the burning bee, either, but I suppose it must be mine. I can see how I forgot it. The coral earrings Daddy got me are much prettier. I wonder if he remembers the brooch?"

"Hello, Clo," said Waxmelt as Clovermead bounded into the Ladyrest dining room. "You just missed a pilgrim all the way from Forging Falls, in Selcouth. He sang a prayer before he ate, and he told all sorts of odd stories about a wise donkey. He had a wisp of a beard and twinkling eyes and fat cheeks. You'd have liked him. Do you want some tea? There's a pot still hot on the stove."

"Yes, please!" said Clovermead. She tossed the brooch from hand to hand while Waxmelt went into the kitchen. "Do you remember how Sister Rowan had a vision in a puddle and told me I would find something in a tree that belonged to me?" she called out.

"Sister Rowan was the nun you said fell into Goat River and banged her arm and got our clean towels all bloody?" Waxmelt poured steaming mint tea into two mugs. "You didn't tell me her name before. And I think this is the first time you've mentioned a vision. Is that why you haven't been underfoot lately? You must have been climbing every tree in the Vale."

"Just the ones around Ladyrest. Sister Rowan said it wasn't far off. Anyway, I found something." Waxmelt came back into the dining room with the mugs in his hands. "I dug into the hollow ash tree on Gaffer Bolts' land and I found this brooch—"

The mugs crashed to the floor and splintered with a crack like thunder. Fragments skittered in every direction and tea splashed on Waxmelt's boots.

Her father's face had turned pasty white. His hands shook. His eyes were large and round and filled with crawling fear.

"Put that away, Clovermead," Waxmelt whispered. He crept to the front door, closed it, and bolted the lock. Then he lowered the shutters over the windows and the room grew dim. Clovermead could scarcely see her father anymore. All that remained of him was a little man stinking of terror.

Clovermead got a leather cord from the kitchen, laced it through the brooch, and hung it around her neck, under her shirt. Her fingers were cold and clumsy, and it took her two minutes to make the knot tight. She tried to speak, but no words came out. Her father was as scared as a child.

"A vision in a puddle," Waxmelt said. He tried to laugh and almost choked. "Sweet Lady. Sweet Lady." He looked down at the broken mugs. "I have to sweep these up. The guests will hurt their feet." He walked rigidly to the kitchen, brought back a broom and a pan, and handed the pan to Clovermead. He swept in the broken pieces while she knelt.

Waxmelt gently took the pan from her when they were done, left through the door to the midden, and scattered the remnants of the mugs amidst the manure. Then he returned to the dining room and sat down by Clovermead. He could not look her in the face.

"Sister Rowan said this brooch belonged to me," said Clovermead. "Does it?"

Clovermead watched while her father's mouth opened and closed uncertainly. He had never before hesitated so much when Clovermead asked him a question, not even three years ago when Clovermead had asked him if human babies got born like calves or like ducklings. Clovermead watched his face twist, and it reminded her of how she looked when she was trying to tell a fib, to hide something naughty she'd done. But Waxmelt had always told her never to lie, that it was better to tell the truth and take the consequences. Waxmelt had never lied to her.

Until now. Until now. Clovermead watched her daddy's familiar face twist strangely, horribly, as he tried to think of what to say. Her heart ached as she saw him try to figure out what stories she would believe.

"You wore it as a baby," he said at last. "I pinned your swaddling clothes with it. So, yes, it is yours."

"Why was it in a tree?"

Waxmelt opened his mouth and shut it again. He cleared his throat. "I put it there for safekeeping."

"Why? Who are you keeping it safe from? What is it?"

"It's an old family heirloom," said Waxmelt with a painful, horrible smile. "It isn't worth much, but I didn't want it stolen. I didn't know the Valefolk when I first got here, so I thought I would hide it in a tree for a while. Then I was afraid soldiers might come north—"

"You're lying." Clovermead couldn't keep the words inside her. Then she stepped back from him, afraid, and waited for her father to be angry at her and yell at her for doubting his word. She hoped his face would smooth out, return to normal, and that he would tell her some simple, obvious truth. She longed for that lying face to go away.

Waxmelt hung his head. His eyes scuttled from hers. Lies, lies, her daddy wanted to tell her lies. Clovermead wanted to cry.

"Yes. I was lying to you." Waxmelt swallowed heavily. "I can't tell you about the brooch, Clo."

"Not even when I'm older?" Clovermead tried to make a joke of it, but she heard herself pleading.

"Not even then, Clo." She flinched at his words. His face was full of fear and lies, and he hadn't even noticed how shamefully his daughter had begged him for the truth. "Clo, the brooch has to stay hidden. Put it back in the ash tree—no." His arms, his legs, his whole body, twitched. "It's not safe there any longer. Your nun saw where it was. Keep it hidden on you instead. Beneath your shirt is fine. But you have to keep it out of sight."

"Why? Why would anyone care about a junky brooch? It's just pewter."

"I can't tell you why, Clo. You'd hate me if you found out. Dear Lady, I don't want you to hate me." Waxmelt let himself look at his daughter. Desperate, naked love filled his gaze. Clovermead had to turn away. He had lied to her and he was still lying to her and the lies clawed at her heart. It wasn't fair of Waxmelt to love her so much.

Waxmelt reached out a hand and stroked her shoulder. "Keep the brooch hidden and don't ask me questions. Please, Clo."

"Father, can't you tell me anything?" Her voice rose to an odious squeak.

"No," said her father. "Nothing at all."

Chapter Four

Lucifer Snuff

Clovermead scarcely spoke to her father for a week. Then, late on a bitterly cold night, they found themselves sitting side by side in front of the fire in the dining room. They let the roaring red heat wash over them. Waxmelt shivered now and again and rubbed his ears and nose. Clovermead spread her fingers toward the baking warmth.

A spark burst from the hearth onto the stones, burned brightly, and died.

"I've been thinking, Father," said Clovermead finally. "There's a lot about you I don't know. Where are you from?" She traced the outline of the brooch hidden beneath her shirt.

"Linstock." Waxmelt's voice was barely more than a whisper.

"Where exactly, Father? High Branding? The Lakelands? Low Branding? Chandlefort?" Waxmelt was silent. "Who are my grandparents? What did they do for a living? What did you do before you came to Timothy Vale?" The silence grew longer. "Who was my mother?" Clovermead's eyes started to glisten and she brushed the tears away, swearing furiously at herself for her weakness. *Lies and silence,* she groaned inwardly, and her stomach twisted. *I don't know my father at all.* She felt dark and hollow inside.

"Your mother was a beautiful woman." Waxmelt put his hand on Clovermead's hair and stroked it gently. "She had hair as yellow as yours. It looked like butter and sunlight."

Clovermead saw a reflection of beauty in Waxmelt's sad face, from a distant place and time. *He's telling the truth,* she told herself. *It's true: Mother was beautiful and I have her hair.* Clovermead bent into Waxmelt's hand and let it cup her chin. His grip was tender and familiar. He had held her so for as long as she could remember. Clovermead leaned on her father and let her anger melt a little. He had told her two truths.

"I wonder if she'd think I've raised you properly." Waxmelt laughed wistfully. "You ought to be a fine little lady, Clo. You should be in silk dresses. Your mother never meant you to wear trousers and fight with a wooden sword."

"What was her name?" Waxmelt was silent. A knot of rage filled Clovermead. She wanted to roar with fury, and she tore herself from her father's nestling support. "You tell me little scraps of truth and you keep everything else secret. When will you tell me the whole truth, Daddy?"

"Never," said Waxmelt.

That night Clovermead sobbed herself to sleep beneath her blankets. She dreamed that her father had plucked the stars from the sky and left her weeping in the dark. Her tears turned to howls, her howls to roaring, and she scraped at the lightless earth until it bled. The earth screamed, and Clovermead woke as the moon fell in the hour before dawn. She gasped a prayer to Our Lady for sweeter dreams. When she slept again, a beautiful woman with yellow hair rocked her in a cradle, caressed her, and sang her a lullaby.

Thunderstorms pelted the Vale for a week. Snow fell on the northern Reliquaries, faded, returned, and spread to all the peaks around Timothy Vale. Waxmelt caulked the cracks in Ladyrest's timbers and spent a day with Goodman Sawyer hauling a winter's worth of logs to the firewood yard. He filled the stable full of provender for Nubble Pony, Jessamyn Cow, and Ladyrest's assortment of chickens, goats, and pigs. Goody Weft collected her season's wages from Waxmelt, packed her belongings, and made ready to join her family in the North Vale for the winter.

"I'll stay another week," Goody Weft said. "No one in his right mind will come through here any later. Then I'll be off home. Lady bless me, I'll wager my nephews say less in a month than you do in a day, child! Ah, but they're good boys. And good listeners—I'll enjoy myself, telling them the tales of the year. They'll scratch their heads for a week when they hear about that Tansyard!" She chuckled as she went upstairs to the guest rooms to strip the beds and put the folded blankets in cedar chests.

Between the squalling downpours Clovermead practiced her swordplay. Now she fenced in grim earnest and sliced at lies and silence with smoldering anger. She parried and thrusted, ran and stretched, until she dripped with sweat and gasped with exhaustion in the biting cold.

One night she went with Sweetroot Miller to a dance at the Merrin house, but her feet were clumsy and she ached every time a Goody or a Gaffer asked after her father. Card Merrin asked Sweetroot to dance, and then to dance again. Sweetroot said yes both times, smiling, and Clovermead wondered if she should be jealous. She slipped away from the happy, dancing couples into the kitchen and spent the rest of the evening helping Goody Merrin prepare the food and clear the tables and wash the dishes. For once she enjoyed these chores: They kept her mind busy and blank.

A last clump of pilgrims fled south into Timothy Vale. Behind them storms disgorged snow and more snow. They blew on their fingers and huddled gratefully by the Ladyrest hearth.

"Did you see a Tansyard?" Clovermead asked a matron from Ryebrew. *Let her say yes,* Clovermead prayed. *Let her say Sorrel's finished his business and will come tomorrow. Then he can take me to some far land where fathers don't lie to their daughters.*

But Sorrel has secrets too, said a mocking voice inside her. *Ask him very nicely what they are and he'll purse his lips. You have to make people tell you the truth. You have to rip the truth out of them.*

"Do you mean the tatterdemalion?" the matron asked. Clovermead nodded. "We crossed paths with him a day south of Snowchapel. I never thought I'd see a pilgrim heading north so late in the season. I don't think he'll be back before spring, little girl. The storm behind us was a blizzard. The passes are shut for the winter."

That night Clovermead dreamed she was sprawled on her stomach deep in a cave. She was very warm and very sleepy. At the cave entrance Sorrel stood by his horse and stared out anxiously at the falling snow. Clovermead yawned and Sorrel whirled around to look at her. His eyes widened in fear. Then he leapt onto Brown Barley and galloped into the heart of the blizzard. Clovermead tried to call after him, but all that emerged from her throat were strangled growls.

The pilgrims left before dawn and missed a morning at Ladyrest so blue, crisp, and beautiful that Clovermead bolted from her half-eaten breakfast to squelch around the muddy firewood yard and gleefully exhale to see her breath turn to white mist. She galloped to the old maple tree by the Road, her wooden sword jouncing against her legs, plucked a last brown leaf from its lowest limb, and with her curious fingers traced its withered veins. The leaf had grown ragged and moldy with age.

Inside, Goody Weft was cleaning dishes in the kitchen. Waxmelt whisked the fallen leaves on Ladyrest's doorstep at Clovermead. Their soft pressure startled her as they fell on her feet. She squeaked with shock and sprang away. Her father grinned. "Mr. Sorrel should have taught you to watch for ambushes."

"Is it battle? Then, by my guerdon and my halidom and my gorget, have at you!" Clovermead snatched a clump of leaves from the ground and waggled them threateningly at Waxmelt. He raised his broom before him and swung it wildly at the foliage in her hand.

Clovermead sidestepped his mighty blows, dashed forward, giggling, and scattered the leaves on the newly clean doorstep. Quickly she whirled and drew her wooden sword against Waxmelt's vengeful broom. Sword and broom resoundingly thwacked each other, and great and loud was the combat that raged across Ladyrest's yard. "Ladyrest! Ladyrest!" cried Waxmelt, and his daughter clarioned her own battle cry, "For dirty doorsteps!" At last they tumbled into the pile of leaves by the stable door, dropped their weapons, and piled foliage on each other from head to foot.

"Oh, dear," Waxmelt gasped. He plucked a faded red leaf from his gray hair and wiped tears of laughter from his eyes. "Goody will have a fit when she sees the yard looking like this. Fuss and botheration, rapscallion, I'll have to clean it all over again. This is your fault."

"Who whisked leaves at whom?" Waxmelt smiled sheepishly and Clovermead giggled, until she remembered she was supposed to be angry with him. Then she didn't know what to feel. "What should I do to help?" she asked hurriedly, springing up from the pile of leaves.

"Feed and brush down Nubble," said Waxmelt. "And remember to curry him lightly, Clo. You bruised him the last time."

"I hear and I obey, Father, though I still say he put on a false mask of pain to gain unwarranted sympathy and a bite of honey from his indulgent master. Do I give the simulating beast oats and barley?"

"He deserves something better on such a beautiful day," said Waxmelt. "Why don't you mix in some honey mash, too?"

"You are an old softie," said Clovermead. She flicked a last leaf at her father and bounded away to the stable.

Nubble whinnied with wary mistrust as she entered, as if he thought it likely that Clovermead would tie knots in his tail or paint him white or put blinders on his eyes and tickle him mercilessly for hours. "Silly beast," said Clovermead affectionately to the roan pony. "I haven't done anything like that in years. Well, not since last year. Anyway, you ought to trust my great maturity and restraint. You're awfully silly to shy away from me—I'm here to groom and feed you. And guess what? Daddy said to spoil you rotten and feed you honey mash." Nubble's ears pricked up. He snorted and nuzzled up to Clovermead. "Now you love me! Mercenary beast. You don't deserve such delicacies." Still grumbling, Clovermead filled Nubble's feedbag full to overflowing with the sweet mash. While he ate, she gently curried and brushed his coat until it was clean and glossy.

A shadow fell across Clovermead. She looked up and saw a short, solid man at the stable door. A dusty black riding cape draped him from his shoulders to his knees. Beneath the cape he wore a brown leather shirt and trousers, both scuffed from long use. Muddy boots adorned with brass spurs swallowed his trousers just below the knee. He carried a short sword buckled to his waist. At his side stood a thin, elegant white stallion whose heaving flanks were flecked with bloody scratches. The man had a ready smile on his face, but it was cold. He had a square and balding head and a carefully trimmed brown goatee and mustache.

"Hello, missy," he said. "May I stable my horse

here?" He brought in the white stallion without waiting for a reply.

"Certainly, pilgrim," said Clovermead with bland courtesy that she thought marvelously disguised her great and sudden annoyance. "Ladyrest's hospitality extends itself to horses and men alike. It is particularly extended to horses who have to ride to Snowchapel this late in autumn, which is cold and unusual labor for a horse, particularly a skinny one like yours. I can see he's shivering. You can put him in the stall across from Nubble's. What breed is he? I've never seen the like."

"I'm not surprised, girlie. Featherfall's a racing horse, not one of your backwater drays." The man took a blanket that lay on a railing between two stalls, heaved it onto Featherfall's back, and knelt to check his horse's hooves. "He's pure Phoenixian—they're half greyhound and half lightning, and they cough their lungs out if you look at them cross-eyed. The breed's delicate. They don't care for cold, either. I didn't fancy riding Featherfall to this glacial sty, but I needed his speed. There's no one can beat him at the chase. Hah, he'd run himself to death if I let him. Is that your master or your daddy out back?"

"My father." Clovermead was repressing choice remarks with great effort. Waxmelt had given her many lectures about being polite to the guests, even when they weren't especially polite to her. *Grit your teeth,* Clovermead advised herself. *Remember your duties as a hostess.* "He'll be glad to welcome you, pilgrim. A penny will buy hot lunch for you and hay for your horse."

"Cold lunch will do," said the man. "I'll pay the same. Tell your daddy I'm in a hurry." He scooped a penny from his purse and tossed it toward Clovermead. It fell short of her, into the hay. Clovermead had to stoop low to pick it up. When she rose, the man was grinning nastily. "Sorry, girlie."

"Of course, sir. No problem at all, pilgrim." *I will spit into your sandwich, pilgrim,* thought Clovermead. *I will pour sawdust into your soup!*

The man swaggered out of the stall. "Don't call me pilgrim," he added sharply as he came to stand by Clovermead. "I don't worship the sky-crone." His fingers stroked his neck, and Clovermead saw that he wore a copper necklace, from which hung a long and yellowed bear tooth, stained blood brown at the tip. "I worship Lord Ursus."

Clovermead heard growling again. It shivered through the barn and echoed off the mountains. Nubble and Featherfall whinnied with terror. "The bear-priest is coming after you," Sister Rowan had said to Sorrel. "He brings blood with him." A claw had reached out from the puddle and struck the nun: "Ursus clawed me." The anger drained from Clovermead. Now she was afraid. "Who is Lord Ursus?" she had asked. "Blood and killing," the nun had said.

"You know my Master's name, girlie?" The man looked directly at Clovermead for the first time. "I see you do—there's knowledge and fear in your face. That's how it should be. I wonder how you learned of Him? I hadn't thought pilgrims would talk of Him much." His eyes flicked thoughtfully along Clovermead's cheeks and forehead and hair. "Strange," he said. "Your face is familiar. Now, where have I seen it before?" He absentmindedly ran his tongue along his teeth, as if his memory were a beast seeking something to bite, to chew, to swallow. Clovermead's knees swayed, and she wanted to run very far away, very fast.

The man shrugged, and the sudden relief left Clovermead limp. "It will come to me. In my line of work you see a great many faces. They blur together. Girlie, take me to your daddy. I've fed on jerky and stale cheese since I left High Branding, and I'm hungry for fresh food."

His black eyes bored at her, and Clovermead was dizzy and her head felt light. Her legs moved at someone else's command, and she led the man through the stable door. She heard his boots following behind her, unseen and horribly heavy, scratching in the straw. Ahead of her Waxmelt was sweeping the last of the strewn leaves into a neat pile underneath the beech sapling that grew by the midden. His hair shone like silver in the morning sun.

Waxmelt looked up at the sound of double footsteps and smiled with habitual ease. "Welcome, pilgrim! I thought I heard a rider on the Road. Will our guest eat, Clo?"

"Your guest will have the finest cold lunch you can offer, Master Innkeeper," said the man with scornful joviality. He stepped out of the stable's shadow. "Bring any fresh roast meats you have—"

And the man stopped dead in his tracks. Clovermead could move her limbs again. She turned and saw the stranger's mouth hanging open. "Waxmelt Wickward," he whispered. "Teeth and bones. Is this where you've been hiding?"

"Lucifer Snuff?" Waxmelt stood still and frozen. "Dear Lady, no."

"Lord Ursus, yes!" Snuff yelped with sudden, savage whimsy. His eyes slickly caressed Waxmelt's countenance. "Lucifer Snuff himself, Waxy. Lucifer Snuff, courier for His Eminence, the Mayor of Low Branding. Lucifer Snuff, who waited a long time in vain for you to deliver him a certain small package. Lucifer Snuff, who's searched for you these twelve long years. Don't be so formal to an old friend, Waxy. Call me Snuff. Everybody does."

Snuff cocked his head toward Clovermead. Biting mirth bubbled out of him. "Of course I know your face, girlie. You resemble your mother."

"You knew her?" Clovermead's heart thudded and her cheeks flushed red. She could not help asking, "Please, Mr. Snuff, who was she? What was her name?"

Snuff roared with laughter. The sunlight caught on his teeth. They were huge and rough, filed sharp and tipped with bronze. He laughed and laughed, and Clovermead found herself hating him with all her heart. Dear Lady, she wanted claws to tear him apart.

Snuff wiped tears of mirth from his eyes. "What do you call the girl?" he asked Waxmelt.

"My daughter's name is Clovermead Wickward," said Waxmelt. "She knows that her mother is dead. I've told her nothing else of the past."

"Such modesty, Waxy!" said Snuff. "You didn't tell her . . ." He turned to Clovermead. His glittering eyes caught her. "Did Daddy tell his little girl that he was a thief?"

Clovermead's breath was short. "You're lying. Daddy would never steal."

"Waxy, she doesn't believe me! Oh, you *have* taught her well. Tell her the truth, renegade. Tell her that you were a thief—a thief with no honor, a thief who stole from his fellow thieves. Tell her, Waxy. Or I'll tell her more."

"It's true, Clo," said Waxmelt. He stared at the ground, his hands trembling so badly that his broom shook. For a second Clovermead almost loathed him. He looked contemptible—the very picture of a liar and a thief. Her father.

"Very true, Waxy," Snuff sniggered. "You were a robber extraordinaire! A pilferer beyond compare! I never knew of so magnificent a purloinment. Girlie, it's really true? You know nothing of your mother? You know nothing of your father? You had no idea he was a thief? You have no idea what was stolen by the enterprising Mr. Wickward?"

"He's never told me anything," said Clovermead sullenly, her hand gripping her wooden sword. She urged her teeth to grow long and thick. She wanted to bite her father, Snuff, anyone at all. Her teeth stayed small and useless. "Will you?"

Snuff smirked. "No, girlie, I won't. There's no reason for you to know anything at all. It might be inconvenient. You won't say anything too particular to her, Waxy, will you?" he added sharply.

"I love her, Snuff," said Waxmelt. "Sweet Lady, I'd rather die than tell her."

"Oh, but she wants to know." Snuff drew his sword

smoothly from his belt and jauntily waggled it at Waxmelt. "Your poor little girlie's aching to know what Daddy did that's so bad. I hate to keep the young innocent. I've changed my mind. Tell her something, Waxy. In general terms."

"I'd forgotten how loathsome you are, Snuff." Waxmelt's hands clenched tightly on his broom. "Clo, I stole a gem. It was the most precious jewel in Linstock."

"Very good, old friend," said Snuff. "'Precious' is just the half of that stone's worth, Missy Clo. The owner would pay a royal ransom to have that wee rock back again. The plan was carefully laid out. Waxmelt Wickward would steal the jewel and hand it over to us once he had acquired it. Then we would contact the owner and arrange for payment. Ah, but Daddy got ideas of his own. He looked at the facets and took the jewel for himself. That was very selfish of you, Waxy."

"It tempted me as I held it in my hands," said Waxmelt. He smiled faintly. "The gem cried out to me and I knew I couldn't leave it with you. Old friend."

"The thief had a conscience! How remarkable." Snuff's nostrils angrily flared. "By His Jaw, Waxy, but you've put me to some pains since you disappeared on us. The Mayor had me scour the land for you. I looked for you under every rock in Linstock. His Eminence sent me to Queensmart, too, to every blasted one of the Thirty Towns, and down Loamrest River to Garum. Garum! I didn't think I'd find you by Lord Ursus' Great Temple, but His Eminence insisted. I'd given up all hope of finding you. You were very clever. I'd forgotten there was any life this way but those gabbling nuns up at

Snowchapel. Worm, robber, traitor, have you spent all twelve years up here in this glacial hole?"

"Worms know when to go underground," said Waxmelt. He shifted his grip on his broom and held it like a quarterstaff. "Didn't I choose my hiding place well, Snuff? I didn't think you'd look in Timothy Vale. Grizzle-worshipers like you don't come along Crescent Road."

"Waxy, you are disturbingly astute," Snuff said. He flashed his pointed teeth. "I would rather be skinned alive than pule with women at a moon-shrine. I absolutely refused His Eminence when he told me to go to Snowchapel, but he reassured me that I wouldn't have to pollute myself with the company of moon-biddies. Just a simple killing, he said—some Tansyard ragamuffin in Chandlefort service, sent off to Snowchapel by Lady Cindertallow to see what the nuns have to say about a new prophecy. You know how Lady Cindertallow is, always aflutter about one prophecy or another. Myself, I don't care what the fools babble, but His Eminence got it in his brain to get rid of the Tansyard." Snuff hopped forward abruptly, swung out his sword, and rapped it against Waxmelt's broom. Waxmelt stumbled backward and Snuff grinned again. "I wondered why Lord Ursus had condemned me to endure this frostbitten mission. Now I see the Bear has blessed me. Waxy, dear Waxy, I need to tell His Eminence where that gem is. You and the girlie are coming with me—"

The kitchen door banged open and a frying pan hurtled at Snuff. Snuff tried to duck, but the frying pan glanced off the top of his head and left a bloody gash. Snuff reeled backward, and Goody Weft sent a teakettle flying after him through midair.

"Miscreant wretch!" Clovermead yelled, ablaze with anger. "Ignoble paynim varlet!" She drew her sword, giddily delighted to find a release for her fury at last, and sprang toward Snuff as he woozily sidestepped the kettle. She roared and rapped him on the left knee as hard as she could. Snuff howled with pain, and Clovermead sliced upward against his sword hand. His short sword went flying and came to rest between two thick cedar logs in the firewood yard. Then Waxmelt was by Clovermead's side, pounding Snuff's chest and face with his broom. The broom end caught Snuff's copper necklace and snapped it. The bear tooth spun to the ground, and Snuff fell back against the stable wall.

"Take this, Mr. Wickward," said Goody Weft. Waxmelt dropped his broom and took a metal poker from her. Goody transferred her carving knife from her left hand to her right. "I'll skewer the blaspheming wretch," she vowed loudly. Her cheeks were purple with indignation. "How dare he talk that way about Our Lady's nuns? I've never seen such a villain in my life! Hanging's too good for him." She advanced menacingly on Snuff.

"The opinion is mutual," said Snuff. He put one hand to his bleeding forehead and with the other took a dagger from his vest. Goody stepped back hastily.

Snuff licked the blood on his hand and savored the taste. Then he bared his glittering teeth and laughed again, harsh and loud. "Waxy, what are the odds when a wounded man faces a woman, a weakling, and a child?"

"A child who knows how to fight," said Clovermead. "That Tansyard ragamuffin taught me, Mr. Snuff. Didn't he teach me well?"

"Well enough. I must remember to kill him slowly." Snuff grimaced. "Waxy?"

"Even odds," said Waxmelt. "If you want to ride back south, I won't get in your way."

"An interesting proposal," said Snuff. He shifted some weight onto his left knee and winced with pain. "The child is vicious."

"The child doesn't think much of your manners, Mr. Snuff," said Clovermead. "The child doesn't like being referred to in the third person when the child is present. The child thinks that you should be drawn and quartered and burned and espaliered and hung upside down in a waterfall and fed to the wolves, and then you should be killed until you're dead. I'd like to rip your guts out." She glared at Snuff in what she hoped was a sufficiently fierce manner.

"What an inventive little girl you are. I will have to punish you someday for your insolence." Snuff gnashed his teeth at Clovermead, and a thousand bears roared in her ears. She jumped away from him as gooseflesh ran up and down her arms. Clovermead looked around her—she saw nothing. Waxmelt and Goody Weft still had their eyes fixed on Snuff. They had heard nothing.

Snuff smiled derisively. "Little coward. Waxy, I think I must forego your excellent cold lunch. I accept the truce you offer. I swear by Lord Ursus' Pelt that if none of you harm me now, or interfere with me in any way, I will ride straight back to Low Branding and do you no injury along the way."

"You'll take no vengeance against Goody Weft?" asked Waxmelt. "Or against any Valefolk?"

"As you wish," said Snuff. "They are safe from me forever, by Lord Ursus' Pelt."

"Then, if you keep your oaths, I swear for all three of us by Lady Moon not to harm you or interfere with you in any way before you reach Low Branding." Waxmelt let his poker rest on the ground but kept a wary grip on it. "Go on, Snuff."

"Certainly, Waxy. But I'll be back with friends as quick as I can, never fear." Snuff put his dagger back in his vest. He jauntily saluted Waxmelt, blew a kiss to Goody Weft, and bowed low to Clovermead. "Farewell one, farewell all. His Eminence will have his jewel soon enough."

"I hid before," said Waxmelt. "I can hide again."

Snuff put one hand on the stable wall and hobbled along it, hissing each time he stepped on his bruised leg. "I will enjoy the hunt," he called over his shoulder as he limped into the stable.

Clovermead saw Snuff's bear tooth lying nearby on the pile of fallen leaves next to the beech sapling. It gleamed pale white in the sun. "A trophy of our victory," Clovermead said softly. She walked to the fang, stooped, and picked it up. A metal ring pierced through its center, through which the copper necklace had been strung. It was the work of a moment to string the tooth and ring on the same leather cord as her brooch. "Mine by right of conquest," Clovermead told herself. Nobody else had seen her pick up the tooth.

Snuff rode out on Featherfall, slashing at the Phoenixian with his spurs. The horse neighed wildly and galloped southward at breakneck speed. Man and horse passed from sight in minutes, south toward the Chaffen Hills.

Waxmelt let the poker drop and stumbled to Clovermead, hugging her tightly. Clovermead returned his embrace, then ran to hug Goody Weft. The Valewoman harrumphed, but she squeezed Clovermead close in her arms for a long minute.

Clovermead looked up solemnly at her father. "What do we do now, Daddy?"

Waxmelt stroked Ladyrest's log walls wistfully. "We pack today. Tonight we sleep in soft beds, and at dawn we leave Ladyrest. Then we run from the Vale as fast as we can and keep on running till we think Lucifer Snuff has lost our trail."

"We're leaving the Vale?" Clovermead asked. Her father was a thief and bears were roaring in her ears, and she knew she would feel unhappy and terrified soon enough, but right now she couldn't. A smile was tugging at her lips and a laugh was rumbling in her belly. "Oh, Father, I'm scared for us both, but this is wonderful! At last I will survey the wide lands of the world in all their infinite and strange variety. Dear Lady, I get to have an adventure at last!"

Chapter Five

THE GOLDEN CUB

CLOVERMEAD TOSSED UNDER HER WARM AND FAMILIAR blankets, wondering where she and her father would go and what he had stolen and what Sorrel would think when he found the abandoned inn, until weariness seized her and she drifted from the waking world.

The darkness growled and the innkeeper's daughter dreamed.

Clovermead was a golden cub with four stubby legs and a roly-poly torso who lay on the rocky floor of a cave blanketed by drifting snow. Her pelt was long and soft and warm. Beneath her skin effortlessly strong muscles smoothly bulged with the promise of power. Her gouging claws scraped half an inch into the compacted snow. She gnashed her teeth. They clacked loud and hard. If she bit down on a rabbit, she could break its neck.

Clovermead wobbled to her feet, clumsy as a baby, and looked out of the cave into the night. The world was an indistinct blur, where trees and boulders were brown streaks and gray smears, but her ears and nose were marvelously keen. Behind a nearby boulder the wind whispered to her of a sheer drop-off forty feet deep. Each swaying, unseen branch called out its location to her. The seductive scent of old honey wafted from a beehive high in a tree, and a school of trout tickled her nose from beneath the iced-over stream below the cliff. Clovermead inhaled bark and moss and grass and snow, and salivated when she smelled a distant doe. She was hungry.

Clovermead set off after the meaty smell. Her legs could barely hold her at first, but she learned to walk in seconds, to run in minutes. She made sure to stay downwind of her prey so as not to alarm the doe with the sharp musk of her own fur.

Delicious flesh, Clovermead hummed to herself. *Warm meat,* she sighed. *It's not as sweet as berries or nuts, but there are no berries or nuts in winter. It's not so smooth and swallowable as a good fish, but I'm too weak to break through ice. A stag's too strong to fight and the little fawns won't be born till spring, but a doe will do. A winter-hungry, winter-weakened doe to be my lunch. I'll gorge my fill and come back home. Then I'll sleep till spring.*

Clovermead licked her lips and roared for joy. The doe heard her and ran faster. Clovermead chuckled and swiftly pursued.

Clovermead padded through snowbanks and into a sloping forest of birch and pine and scrubby bushes. Crumbling limestone outcroppings rose from the thin earth, as teeth from receding gums. The hills were rotten with caves, and in each cave Clovermead smelled another sleeping bear. The underbrush was thin and black—a forest fire had raged here. The air was thick and wet, with an acrid tang.

This is how the pilgrims describe the land near Snowchapel, thought Clovermead. *Caves and bears and forests everywhere. I must be near the convent and Scrimshaw Harbor and the Western Ocean. So that's what salt water smells like! I never knew it would be so strong. Or is that my ursine nose at work? It's even colder than the Vale up here. I'd be a block of ice if I didn't have my pelt.*

The waning crescent moon, whose faint light scarcely limned the darkness, hung slack and pale and old in the hazy sky. A mocking owl hooted from above, swooped, and jubilantly seized some small rodent in its fierce claws. The victim squeaked, crumpled, and died. The doe's scent was getting stronger.

Clovermead heard other paws behind her. They chuffed into the snow slow and steady, with quiet weight on them that made the frozen earth throb. *Proom, proom, proom* came the inexorable paws of a huge old he-bear, unmistakably male from his sour perfume. *Proom, proom,* he came no closer to her, but he never fell behind. She heard his regular exhalations as they ran, and felt his warm, humid breath. She smelled fresh blood on his jaws. The scent made Clovermead's stomach churn, it made her mouth water, it was a horrible ecstasy beyond berries and honey and fish. She was terrified, and she would not turn to see who followed her.

Someone who wishes to make much of you, the old he-bear growled. His bass made the mountains tremble. *Perhaps your friend, Clovermead, if you will allow me.* His laughter charred the cold night. *Oh, little cub, your desire is sharp in the wind. Tell me your dreams. What do you want?*

Everything, said Clovermead. She nipped at the air. *I want to fence so well I could beat that Lucifer Snuff in a fair fight, all by myself. I want to be a thief for real and steal rubies from temples and present my loot to the Queen. I want to be grown up and not have anyone tell me what to do. I want to conquer the Empire and the far lands beyond. I want to tell lies to people and have them believe me. I want an army to bow down before me and hail me as their leader. I don't want to be the little girl who's sent away when trouble happens.* Misery and fury churned in her stomach, and she scratched at dead grass till it came up by the roots. *I want Daddy to stop keeping secrets from me. I want to rip the truth out of him.*

I can teach you, said the bear. *If you wish to learn.*

Learn what?

How to hunt, Clovermead, said the bear. *How to ambush and how to leap. How to be strong and how to be feared. All the necessary skills. I can teach you how to satisfy your hunger. Little cub, you are terribly hungry.*

I'm starving, said Clovermead. The scent of the doe came stronger and fresher to her, and she growled with hunger and the delight of the chase. Clovermead could not imagine adventure or glory sweeter than the taste of deer flesh. She wanted to kill—

A wave of nausea swept over her. *I don't want to be a killer,* she told the bear, told herself. What would she do? Bite down on a living animal? Crush it between her teeth? It was disgusting, bestial, degrading, tempting, and sweet. Her stomach turned, but still Clovermead ran after the doe. She didn't believe her hollow words. She wanted to kill. Let someone else feel pain, not her.

It isn't right to kill, she said, more weakly still. *Father told me . . .* Not to kill, not to hurt, not to steal, always to tell the truth. But Waxmelt was a liar. Was he a killer, too? She didn't know. Cruel, vicious Snuff had called her father his old friend, and maybe he was. Nothing her father had ever told her to do or not to do meant anything anymore.

Do you want to kill? the old bear asked.

I do! Clovermead howled. *I do! I do! Please, teach me!* She was weeping. Tears drenched her muzzle.

Then, chase, he urged, growling, laughing, smashing the mountainside beneath his paws. *Chase and I will guide you.*

I will, said Clovermead, and she ran. She heard the doe's footfalls, closer than ever. Clovermead could smell every inch of her—delicious, terrified, and tender. Clovermead roared, bared her teeth, and leapt up the ridge toward her waiting meal.

Go left of that stump, the old bear urged. *Extend your claws. Bite! Bite again. Prepare yourself to tear into your prey. Good, little cub. You learn well.* His bloodstained breath was hot on her fur. *We will hunt well together.*

Yes, teacher, said Clovermead happily. *Yes, Master.* The doe was just beyond the ridge and almost within sight. Clovermead was puzzled and she frowned. *Master, I don't know your name. What should I call you?*

Turn and look, said the old bear. His words were a harsh command that Clovermead eagerly obeyed. *Behold Me.* The mountains echoed his howling pride.

Clovermead whined submissively, let the doe race from her, and turned around.

The he-bear was immense. His shoulders were tree high and his great head veiled half the stars in the sky. He was as broad across as Crescent Road. His fur was satin black matted with blood, his rusty teeth were foot-long sabers, and his claws were sickles tipped with gore. His paws rammed through the heaped snow to the dirty moss below. He was horror and magnificence, strong enough to rip out the bowels of the earth.

I am Lord Ursus, he said.

No, said Clovermead, horrified. Her paws were weak, and the bloodlust had gone from her in an instant. Her hunger was gone too. All that remained in her stomach was coiling, trembling fear that grew and grew within her until Clovermead squeaked and moaned with shameful terror. She turned from Lord Ursus and fled.

She bolted down ravines and up crags and leapt over crevasses. Lord Ursus loped easily behind her. She swerved around a boulder and through a narrow gorge. She heard him spring over the obstacles, land on the ground behind her, and keep running. Clovermead smelled her own fear in the night air, and she heard Lord Ursus' breath grow deeper and faster as her panic reached his nostrils. He roared the delight of the hunt, and she could not escape. His stride grew faster. He was coming closer. His teeth grazed her tail.

Hunt with me or be hunted, he said. *You have no other choices.* He chuckled. *I would rather you hunted with me, Clovermead. You have my spirit in you, little cub.*

You're wrong, moaned Clovermead, but she was afraid he was right. *I'll never hunt with you! Never!* Her heart belied her: *I will hunt for you soon,* it said. It lusted still for blood, hungered still for power. *Give me your strength, Lord Ursus,* her heart whispered. *Give me your teeth and claws, and I will kill for you. Dear Master, let me hunt for you,* said her faithless, hungering heart. *Let me be your loyal servant. You will never deceive me, will you? Not like my weakling father? Tell me, isn't killing certain and true?*

I will never lie to you, said Lord Ursus.

Lady help me, Clovermead implored. Her legs collapsed under her and she tumbled to the ground. Ursus would kill her, or she would kill for him. She had no strength and she had no hope. *Sweet Lady, save me from him!*

Lord Ursus was gone. The night haze thinned and the moon shone bright. It lent a silvery hue to Clovermead's golden fur. She dared to look behind her and saw behemoth paw prints dug into the snow. Each print was four feet wide. Five claw marks nine inches long extended from the impress of each paw. Clovermead shivered. She was terribly cold. Her pelt had melted from her and she was a little girl in the snow.

Thank you, Lady, she said. *Lady, it isn't true. I'm not like him.*

Liar, whispered Lord Ursus. *We are alike, little cub. In the end you will hunt for me.*

Clovermead woke moaning in the darkness. The sheets of her bed were drenched with sweat. She clutched her bear tooth in her left hand. It was hot. Her right hand had clawed into her down quilt and torn feathers from its guts.

"Liar," Clovermead wept. "Liar," she repeated, but she didn't know whom she meant.

Chapter Six

THE CHAFFEN HILLS

THE SKY WAS GRAY OVER THE EASTERN RELIQUARIES when Waxmelt and Clovermead left Ladyrest. The trees on the slopes were dark silhouettes, the moon had set, and the stars were fading. Nubble, heavily loaded with their packs, nickered sleepily as Clovermead held him still. Clovermead shivered in the cold. Her hand patted the hilt of her wooden sword. It was safely cinched to her belt.

Waxmelt said farewell to Goody Weft at the door. "Leave for your family at once," he warned. "I think Snuff is a man of his word, but I don't want you to risk trouble. Stay away from Ladyrest this winter, Goody."

"I'll skewer the bear-boy if he comes sniffing around here," Goody said. She blew on her hands and spat at the ground. "A plague on the Lady hater! I'm not scared of him." She glanced unhappily at Clovermead. "I'd feel better if you left Clo with me. I can hide her well enough while you're wandering, Mr. Wickward. Valefolk won't tattle on her."

"It's too dangerous," said Waxmelt. "Snuff won't scruple to hurt Clo to get at me. He's persistent, too. You might hide her from him once, but he'd come back. We both have to disappear. There's no other way."

Liar, thought Clovermead. *I listen to you, Daddy, and I know you're marbling truth and lies together. I can't tell where the falsehoods begin, but I can hear them. Why don't you want to leave me in Timothy Vale? Are you afraid to go alone? Is that it? Then, I'll keep you company, no matter how dangerous the journey is. But if that's the reason, I wish you'd just say so.*

"Goody," said Waxmelt, "I'd be awfully glad if you asked Goodman Sawyer to look in on Ladyrest this winter. Come springtime, I think it would be safe for you to come back. You can run Ladyrest for me while I'm away and keep for yourself whatever silver you earn. Is that a fair bargain?"

"More than fair." Goody Weft's discretion wrestled with her curiosity and lost. "Where will you go, Mr. Wickward?"

"What you don't know, you can't tell," said Waxmelt.

"As you say, Mr. Wickward." Goody turned to Clovermead, kissed her full on the lips, and roughly embraced her. Clovermead turned her head so that her tears couldn't be seen. Wordless, she hugged the old cook.

"Tcha, enough of that, girl." Goody firmly thrust Clovermead away. "Enjoy your chance to gallivant. But you obey your father and don't flibbertigibbet. Good-bye, Clovermead. Good-bye, Mr. Wickward. Lady bless you both and keep you safe."

"Her blessings on you, too," said Waxmelt. Awkwardly he held out his hand. Goody snorted with amusement, crushed him close to her for a farewell hug, then retreated indoors. Clovermead heard her footsteps creak back to the kitchen.

Clovermead turned from her home, let go of Nubble's reins, and bounded to the Road. "C'mon, Daddy, let's go," she yelled. Waxmelt waved a last farewell to Ladyrest, followed his daughter, and whistled to Nubble. The pony trotted after them.

Waxmelt caught hold of Nubble's reins and turned south on the Road, leading the pony behind him. Clovermead walked quietly by his side. Soon they were past the first hill.

"Can I speak?" Clovermead asked. Her voice was startlingly loud in the silent morning.

"Softly," said Waxmelt. "No need to let everyone in the Vale know we're headed south. Snuff's sworn not to hurt the Valefolk, but he could trick them into telling which way we're going."

"I *am* speaking softly," said Clovermead with great dignity, but she lowered her voice. "Father, *why* are we going south? Low Branding and Mr. Snuff lie in this direction."

Waxmelt puffed out a cloud of air. Eastward the sky was turning pink. "The Road to Snowchapel is snowed in. The paths through the Reliquaries are murderous in winter. I don't like us following Snuff, but I think our best chance is to try to slip by him. It should take him eight days just to ride to Low Branding, and by then I hope we'll be through the Chaffen Hills. The Crescent Road's the only way through the Chaffens, but we can choose from a dozen roads once we get to Linstock. We'll have to leave the Crescent Road sooner or later—it leads straight to Low Branding."

"Do you prefer any particular road, Father?"

"I'd like to take the Tansy Pike, one way or the other. The Pike crosses the Crescent Road a day or two south of the Chaffens. The East Pike leads through High Branding to the Tansy Steppes. We'd have to stay in the northlands all winter long if we went that way, but we could ride south through the Steppes in the spring to Selcouth. The worst danger that way is Barleymill—the bear-priests menace the whole southern half of the Steppes from there. Or we could go south on the West Pike, along the western edge of Linstock. If we went that way, we could reach Queensmart by spring and not worry about bear-priests. On the other hand, that road takes us past Chandlefort. I don't know which way is better." He fell into a ruminative silence.

The Vale seemed abandoned in the early morning. As the shepherds ate breakfast in their kitchens the sheep baaed sleepily in their paddocks. A cow lowed at Clovermead and Waxmelt as they passed, but the rest of the world ignored their departure.

Nubble whickered mournfully as they started to climb another hill. With each slow step he reminded the world that he was more heavily laden than was right and just. He stared with liquid eyes at Clovermead, accusing her of complicity in this injustice. She soothed her conscience by patting his back till he was in a good temper again.

"Are you really a thief?" Clovermead said after a bit, when the sun had peeped over the Eastern Reliquaries. "Like that Snuff said?"

"May Snuff and his jabbering mouth spend eternity far from Our Lady," said Waxmelt. "I suppose I could lie to you again and tell you I'm not, but I've grown weary of lies. And I suppose you wouldn't believe me if I told you otherwise. I'm sorry, Clo. Yes, I am a thief." Waxmelt's affirmation shuddered harsh and flat in the air. Clovermead wanted to flail at Waxmelt with her nails.

A pale smile flickered across Waxmelt's face. "I think I'm a pretty good thief, Clo. Stars above, but I fooled them all a long time. I kept out of their way for twelve years. I'll swear they never dreamed that Waxmelt Wickward could do that."

I never dreamed you could fool me all this time either, thought Clovermead, but she decided to talk about something else, anything else, instead.

"Snuff said he was chasing after Sorrel," she said loudly. "He also said Sorrel worked for Chandlefort. Since Low Branding is at war with Chandlefort, why don't we look for refuge there? Why should we avoid the Cindertallows' scarlet citadel?"

"I never understood why they called it a scarlet citadel," said Waxmelt. "It always looked rosy to me."

"You've been there?" That was another secret he had kept from her.

"I stole the jewel from Lady Cindertallow's Inner Keep," said Waxmelt. "I wouldn't dream of going near Chandlefort, if Snuff weren't after us. Even he'd be chary of venturing near a Yellowjacket Guardsman, and Lady Cindertallow keeps a thousand of them in Chandlefort." Waxmelt looked thoughtfully northward. "Why did Sorrel stay so long at Ladyrest? He asked me where I came from in Linstock. I wondered at the time why he was so inquisitive. Ah, Clo, perhaps he was a Chandlefort spy."

He was frightened of the bear, Clovermead almost said. *He was my friend and he was resting on his journey.* Then she wondered if that was the truth after all. Maybe the Tansyard had deceived her, too—smiled at her and teased her and kept his eye on Waxmelt the entire time. Right now she could believe that the whole world was made up of liars.

They climbed into the Chaffen Hills, a land of sheer rock faces and rubble slopes, crumpled hills, and deep and hidden dells that pockmarked the high forests. Tiny streams curled lazily through the precipitous valleys and cut narrow slots through the crumbling rocks. Crescent Road ran boldly through this broken land. The Empire's engineers had cut into mountainsides to create a meandering, switchbacked, and almost gentle passage from Linstock to Timothy Vale that was passable by man and horse alike. But the road builders had departed long since, and rain and cold had loosened the Road's stones and left room in the crevices for grass to sprout.

At first Clovermead skipped up and down the hills, but the Chaffens' steep slopes quickly tired her. At noon Waxmelt took a sack of food from Nubble's back and put Clovermead in its place. Clovermead rode on the pony for an hour, nibbling a lunch of blueberry muffins and hard goat cheese, while Waxmelt carried the sack. In the afternoon he put the sack back onto Nubble, and Clovermead set herself to steady walking.

The sun lowered to the west, and Clovermead saw a black bear watching them from the entrance of a cave up a mountain slope.

"What's your name, Master Furball?" Clovermead

whispered. She listened intently. "Honeythief? A good name. Are you about to hibernate? Good sleep to you!"

Thank you, said Honeythief.

Clovermead looked sharply at the bear. His mouth hadn't moved. *Of course it hasn't,* she told herself, *this is just a daydream.*

She hissed with pain. The bear tooth under her shirt was blazing hot.

You shouldn't have that, small woman, Honeythief said. *You should throw it away. Or give it back.*

Not to Snuff! said Clovermead, without moving her lips. *He doesn't deserve it back. It's mine now. Go away, Honeythief!*

For a harsh second more the tooth was a burning knife cutting into her chest. Then the pain began to fade.

As you wish, said Honeythief. *But you have been warned.* The bear nodded to Clovermead, got to his feet, and padded back into his cave.

Clovermead felt cold, even under her layers of wool clothes. Her chest hurt. She reached under her shirt and felt blood. The tooth had cut her skin. An ugly pucker of a scar had already formed.

At dusk they found a hut in a low hollow, surrounded on all sides by hills that protected it from the wind. A few dozen yards behind it a clean stream bubbled down from the hilltops.

The hut was made of long, thin slabs of slate gray granite streaked with milk white whorls. Translucent goatskins had been stretched to cover the hut's small windows, but wind and rain had reduced the skins to flapping tatters. A small pile of logs lay by the doorway.

Clovermead saw a thin scattering of earth and small twigs on the floor inside the hut.

"One of the old Queens set up these Pilgrim Lodges every ten miles or so along the Road," said Waxmelt. "We should have a place to sleep every night."

"It's cold and it smells of squirrels and dirt and it's marvelous," Clovermead announced. "It's just the sort of place I'd expect to sleep in while I was fleeing through the wilderness. Look, Father, there's a broom by the hearth. I'll sweep up and light a fire. Can you bring in firewood?"

"After I feed Nubble," said Waxmelt. "Do you want to cook?"

Clovermead shuddered. "No, Father, and don't be cruel and resurrect memories of my culinary shame. I know full well that my strawberry goulash made poor Goody sick for a week. You may cook. I will bring water from the stream."

"She was only sick for a day," said Waxmelt. Clovermead rolled her eyes and swaggered over to the broom.

Waxmelt gathered a fistful of frost-rimmed wild mint, sliced it in with their beef jerky and hard cheese, and stirred up a remarkably tasty stew. Clovermead ate huddled up in front of the fire, swaddled in her blankets. Waxmelt sat by her side, swaddled just as thickly, nearer to the chill breeze blowing in through the window. Nubble, brought inside the hut to keep warm, slept a few feet away. When Clovermead finished her dinner, she smiled contentedly, closed her eyes, and immediately fell asleep. Waxmelt took Clovermead's bowl from her hands and for a few minutes quietly watched his daughter's peaceful face. He fed the fire with more logs when it threatened to go out, and looked through the window at the moon rising over the treetops' feathery profiles. Then he, too, slept.

They woke before dawn. Clovermead splashed stream water on her face, Waxmelt cooked them a hot breakfast to get the night chill out of their bones, and Nubble refreshed himself with a nibble of grass. They left the hut before the sun had time to burn the mist out of the hollow.

They spent four more days climbing through the forest, rising through hills where short, squat trees interwove their gnarled branches to form a dense canopy that cast the forest bottom into a deep and somber shade. Roots swelled under the Road itself. Then the trees grew shorter and sparser still, and thick brambles took their place on either side of the Road, forcing them to walk single file. The huts where they spent their nights were badly decayed.

Clovermead's dreams were half-remembered jumbles of full moons and dark fur. Sometimes she woke smiling with the memory of silver light. Sometimes she woke with her fingers dug tightly into the blankets, her mouth stretched into a snarl, and her bear tooth throbbing with heat.

The next day the sun never came out. The morning mist thickened into marrow-freezing fog and spattering sleet. Waxmelt and Clovermead reached the summit of the Chaffens, where Crescent Road ran flat over a high, treeless moor studded with spongy patches of bog and leafless blueberry bushes. Sheets of muddy water inundated the Road. The whistling wind cut cruelly through Clovermead. She rode half the day on Nubble, with her arms thrown around his warm neck.

"It's not the cold," she said irritably. "You know I'm used to cold, Daddy. It's this mucky, marshy, truly awful spongiferous climate. It's never this clammy in Timothy Vale."

"Hush," said Waxmelt. "Save your strength."

Night came and they found no hut. Waxmelt hacked them a shelter under a blueberry bush on a rare patch of solid ground. The bracken was dry enough to sleep on but too wet to set alight. In pea-soup darkness they ate a supper of cold cheese, and Clovermead fell asleep in Waxmelt's arms as the pelting sleet turned to a gentle fall of snow.

The Road was a sheet of ice the next day. Snow and more snow fell on the Wickwards as they skidded southward through the bog. An arrowhead of honking snow geese flew south, half seen through the whirling snow. Mid-morning they passed what had once been a hut—a gaping ruin of cracked stones where snow had piled three inches thick on the floor. At sunset they camped in the lee of a boulder. Waxmelt piled leaves over Clovermead and himself and held his daughter in his arms again.

The next two days were a little warmer. Cold drizzle fell on the bog and melted the ice and snow. Occasionally the sun, pale and milk white, shone through the clouds. The Road began to descend from the high moors, and the land around them grew drier. Small oaks and elm trees reappeared. The air ahead of them smelled strangely lush.

"It smells like all the spices of the Jaifal Archipelago steamed into milk," said Clovermead dreamily. "I didn't realize that different places have different scents. Now I know Timothy Vale smells dry and sharp. I wouldn't have known that if I hadn't come south."

The day after dawned clear and sunny and almost warm. The bright yellow leaves still clung to the trees on these southern slopes, ignorant of winter's imminent onslaught. A stream ran alongside the Road, exultantly babbling as it fled the northlands. Here the Road was in better repair. Its stones, though abraded, fit together tightly. No weeds grew in the cracks.

Clovermead caught glimpses of Linstock through the screen of yellow leaves. The little she could see was staggeringly immense. South and east of them stretched a limitless expanse of dry fields of short grass, manicured yellow-and-brown orchards, puffs of smoke from far chimneys, and a slice of rippling silver Clovermead was sure must be the Whetstone River. Far, far to the east the Harrow Moors, which hid the Tansy Steppes, were no more than a patch of gray.

"How much does it snow here, Father?" Clovermead asked.

"Down in Chandlefort we hardly ever got more than three or four inches at a time. Once when I was a child, twenty inches fell. That doesn't seem like much in the Vale, but we stared at the drifts of snow as if they had fallen from the moon. The castle looked as if it were made of silk and icicles."

"I'd have spent the whole day sledding among the pinnacles and parapets." Clovermead looked sharply at her father. "You were a child at Chandlefort?"

"Did I say that?" Waxmelt shook his head. "I'm getting careless. Though I suppose there's no reason now why you shouldn't know. I was born in Chandlefort, Clo."

"What were your parents' names?" asked Clovermead.

"Mother's name was Primrose. Father was Hivefinder. We were servants, so we lived in Lackey Lane. We had a garden in back where Mother grew tomatoes, radishes, spinach, and a pear tree. . . ." Waxmelt's face went blank. "No more questions, Clo."

Clovermead said nothing more the entire day.

It took four more days to leave the Chaffen Hills. Each night they spent snug and warm in well-repaired stone huts stocked with huge piles of dry wood. The Road wound down progressively wider and gentler valleys and met a baby of a stream that grew rambunctious and joined forces with other rivulets to form a rowdy river. Waxmelt told Clovermead that the river was called the Tallowspume.

They passed a burned farm nestled in a flat hollow, where the Tallowspume interrupted its skittering descent to laze for half a mile. A house, a water mill, and a barn had been charred to a skeleton of timbers. In the barn a rooster and three chickens nested within a broken yoke. The grass grew lank and wild, and a thousand saplings sprouted up in the fringes of the abandoned fields. A half-wild herd of cattle grazed at the far end of the meadow. The patriarchal bull gazed at Clovermead and Waxmelt with angry suspicion.

"Twelve years ago I bought milk for you here," said Waxmelt. He looked around with sadness and wonder. "This was the last farm in Linstock on the Road. It was a bustling place. The owners did well by the pilgrim traffic. Dear Lady, I hope they were able to flee."

"Are all the farms in Linstock burned?" Clovermead asked.

"Linstock is much bigger than Timothy Vale, Clo. It has thousands of farms. No one could burn them all. You'll see."

Yet they passed nothing but charred ruins as they descended. The hills had been swept clean of human life. Clovermead saw old hoofprints, slashing dents, and splashed mud on the blackened timbers. Boars grunted in the forest. Once the Tallowspume broadened into a lake, and Clovermead saw a herd of mustangs grazing in the yellow grass on the far shore. But for the stone huts, the hills were desolate.

"We should reach the Tansy Pike tomorrow," said Waxmelt that evening. They ate stew by a blazing fire in a cozy hut. "I think we should head east, to Ryebrew and the Steppes. I want to avoid as much of Linstock as possible. All this destruction terrifies me."

"No Chandlefort?" Clovermead pouted. "No rose parapets and silk icicles?"

"No Chandlefort," Waxmelt said firmly. "Safety before sightseeing. Cheer up, Clo. There are supposed to be walls ten miles long around Ryebrew, from when it was the Queen's main garrison in the north. They say that the soldiers guarded the walls in three shifts of eight hours each, and that there were five thousand men in each shift."

"I'd still rather see Chandlefort," said Clovermead. She looked moodily into the fire and tossed a twig into its heart, to ignite, blaze, and die in ashes. "It seems I won't, ever. You stole a jewel and now it isn't safe for me to go near the place. It isn't fair."

"Not in the slightest," said Waxmelt almost cheerfully. "You aren't missing so much. It's nothing compared with Timothy Vale." Clovermead scoffed. "Truly, Clo. Don't you know how beautiful the mountains are?"

"Maybe to you. I've seen them all my life. I want to see fine buildings. I want to see cities. I want . . . everything." She arched her fingers into claws that ached to rip at the earth and the moon and the stars. Then her arms fell to her sides. "But I won't get it. I'm a thief's daughter, and that means I'll be on the run all my life." Clovermead released an exorbitantly loud sigh. "I wish you'd never stolen that jewel. Lady's Veil, what possessed you to do that?"

Waxmelt bowed his head. His face was a chiaroscuro of glowing orange and long shadows in the firelight. "At first I didn't want the jewel itself," he said. "I decided to steal it when Snuff offered me gold for it. More gold than I could have earned in a lifetime."

"But you took the jewel instead?"

"I decided I wanted the jewel after all," said Waxmelt. He smiled. "Ah, now, that was the best decision I ever made. I'll never regret that, no matter what happens."

"Tell me what happened," said Clovermead.

"I can't," said Waxmelt. "I've told you, Clo. It's not possible."

"You don't have to tell me everything. Tell me as much as you can. Please, Father. Tell me some of the truth."

Waxmelt saw tears in his daughter's eyes. He winced. "I'm sorry I've hurt you, Clo," he said. He hesitated a second, ten seconds, half a minute. Clovermead saw him come to the decision. "I'll tell you as much as I can."

Chapter Seven

THE TALE OF THE THIEVING SERVANT

"I FIRST SAW LUCIFER SNUFF STANDING IN THE DOORWAY of the Periwig, the tavern on the uphill end of Lackey Lane where we indoor servants drank. He wore the livery of the Mayor of Low Branding and a wine steward's ruffled silk shirt with mother-of-pearl buttons. Mr. Pellitory, who owned the Periwig, told his man to let Snuff in. We didn't see servants from Low Branding every day in the Periwig, and we didn't feel so friendly to Wharfrats, as we called them, but they came often enough that we had a tradition of courtesy toward them. They were polite to us, too, when we were sent on Chandlefort business to Low Branding and wanted a friendly place to drink in for an evening.

"Inside of a minute Snuff made us sore pressed not to forget our courtesy and tell him outright that we loathed him. Just the way he sauntered into the Periwig, as proud as a Guardsman in his yellow jacket, was enough to start a fight. So was that sneer on his face when he looked us over. The blood brown tooth around his neck was the worst of all. We'd heard how bear-priests scoffed at Our Lady, how they whispered sedition and rebellion into the Mayor's ear, even rumors that they did away with people at their altars and plunged those teeth they wore into their victims' hearts. That browned fang made us believe that everything we'd heard was true and that the best thing to do with a grizzle-worshiper was to kill him, fast. Anyway, that's what I was thinking, and I'm pretty sure we all felt the same.

"'I don't much care if you want to crucify me,' Snuff said loudly, as if he'd read my mind. I suppose he didn't need to. He could have read our faces easily enough. 'My name is Lucifer Snuff, gentlemen. I work for His Eminence, the Mayor of Low Branding, and I follow Lord Ursus. If any part of that is a problem, try your worst. I don't mind dying.' He gave us a ferocious, half-crazy grin to make us know that he spoke Our Lady's own truth. He patted the short sword at his side. 'Be advised that I'd take a few of you with me. Gentlemen, I didn't come here to fight. I want a drink and a game of cards. Does any man here mind?'

"We did, but nobody said a word. I was scared of Snuff, of course. I'd have been insane not to be scared of a berserker bear-priest. I think I admired him too, though. It took guts to stand up to a whole room.

"Mr. Pellitory showed Snuff to a booth near the Periwig's back door and brought him a flagon of Ryebrew ale. Snuff slung himself down, pulled out a pack of cards, and upended a pouch of money on the table. Dozens of silver shillings rolled around the table and glinted in the torchlight. Mixed in among them were heavy, lustrous gold sovereigns. 'Who'll play with me?' Snuff asked. He laughed contemptuously as he watched us turn and stare.

"I'd never seen so much silver coin in my life, Clo. I counted five gold sovereigns on that table—I'd seen sovereigns before only when I served sherry to wastrel Milords and Miladies gambling in Chandlefort's back parlors. With those sovereigns a man could buy his son an apprenticeship with a lawyer or pay a poor knight to marry his daughter. He could sail to the Jaifal Archipelago and let his children go hang. With that much gold a man could stop being a servant. Snuff had no cause to sneer at us. He'd dropped dreams on that table, not money.

"Most men in the Periwig turned away from that blinding sight. It hurt to look at those coins and know you could never have them yourself. Only six of us could bear to join Snuff at his booth. I couldn't stay away. Dear Lady, that gold pulled me right out of my chair.

"'Well, boys,' said Snuff, 'do you have coin to wager?' He asked as if he was sure that the answer was no.

"'I have money,' said Andiron Grinder, and 'So do I,' said Charfennel Comb, and 'I do too,' said the others, and I just jerked my head up and down while my heart raced and my shirt itched and sweat trickled down my eyebrows. We poured our coins on the table. I took out two silver shillings, twenty-odd copper pennies, and a few half-coppers and quarter-coppers. That was my entire life's savings, bar the house my parents had left me. I always kept my money on me, to guard against the burglars of Lackey Lane. My home had been broken into twice since my parents died.

"We all put about the same amount of money on that

table. Our piles of dull copper were dross next to his glittering coins. He could have bought and sold all six of us with one gold sovereign.

"'Penny-ante players,' Snuff said. He caught my eye and smiled so I could see his filed teeth. I—I saw bones in his pupils, Clo. The gnawed bones of men. I heard a bear roar. I was afraid for my life, and I nearly ran out of the Periwig then and there. I stayed where I was. I could not leave that gold.

"'They'll never believe me back in the City,' Snuff said. 'The smallest bet in the Mayor's cellars is a shilling—don't blanch, children! We'll play for good old copper here. Who'll be rich tonight?' The cards were hummingbirds as they fluttered between his hands.

"Snuff toyed with us poor fools. Silver sloshed back and forth across the table at his command. When one of us was tempted to leave, Snuff would take the man's money away or give him more—whichever was more likely to keep him at the game. We were entranced. The other servants left for their homes and families, but we stayed. Mr. Pellitory usually closed at two in the morning, but a silver piece dropped offhand into his palm kept the Periwig open. Snuff treated us to ale, beer, wine, whatever we wanted. We didn't need the liquor. We were already drunk with the game and the play and the shining, dazzling coins.

"Snuff talked while we played. 'It isn't easy to labor for the Mayor,' he said. 'His steward's a tough man and there's no shirking under him. I emptied chamber pots before I came to work in the cellars, and let me tell you, an Alderman stinks as much as you or I, or maybe more, from all that rich food he eats. I've scrubbed floors till I was bone weary. I spent six solid months scrubbing floors. I felt my strength go out from me, and friends, if I may call you friends, I was sure I'd be scrubbing floors for the rest of my life, weaker and weaker, till I was a pale husk of an old man who could only look back at a life of drudge work for a man too proud to know my name. Is it also like that here in Chandlefort?'

"He looked around with those terrible, bone-filled eyes of his, and I heard myself babbling words. 'It's just like that,' I said. 'My mother was a scullery maid. She scrubbed pans all day long and her hands were hard as bricks. Father was servant to the horse doctor in the stables. He'd hold mares still while the doctor birthed them, work like that. A horse kicked Father in the head and he died. Mother wore herself out in the kitchens.'

"'Chandlefort used them up and spat out the husks, yes? I know how it goes, boy,' said Snuff with a sort of sympathy that tore at my guts. 'Chandlefort is a machine, just like Low Branding. The laborers serve the upper servants, the upper servants serve the lords and ladies, and the lords and ladies serve Lady Cindertallow. Lady Cindertallow, bless her callow, highborn heart, never knows the names of the laborers who work themselves to death for her pleasure.' Snuff smiled lazily. 'But it need not be that way for us, hey? Fortune smiled on me, the way it appears to be smiling on you at the gaming table, friends. I was transferred to the wine cellars, and now life is sweet.'

"The others didn't say anything, but I did. I knew I was going to lose all my money, but I wouldn't let him insinuate that I had no dreams or hopes besides his sneering coins. 'I won't just scrub floors,' I said. 'Before they died, my parents bought me a place as an indoor servant. I'll rise. I'll make them proud. I'll become understeward before I'm done.'

"'A noble ambition,' said Snuff. He said it almost gently and that was even more cruel. I heard my own words echo in my ears and I saw more than ever that my life was small and dreary and bleak. 'Well, life is sweet. It's a pity about the arguments between His Eminence the Mayor and your Lady Cindertallow. Have you followed the nub of the dispute? In the pride of her youth, having succeeded her venerable grandmummy to the Ladyship, Lady Cindertallow has renounced her allegiance to those weaklings down in Queensmart. His Eminence argues that the city of Low Branding owed its allegiance directly to the Queen and that Low Branding's obedience to Lady Cindertallow was due to her solely as representative of the Queen. Therefore, though Lady Cindertallow claims that her rule over Linstock survives her declaration of independence from the Empire, His Eminence argues that Low Branding is now independent of both Queensmart and Chandlefort.

"'Lady Cindertallow is not indulgent of this argument. She is perhaps foolish to be so stubborn, since her Yellowjackets have become lamentably disorganized since Lord Cindertallow's death in that unfortunate hunting accident. Such a lot of accidents happen to the Cindertallows lately! Parents gone when their boat ran onto those rocks on the Whetstone River, husband gone; Lady Cindertallow must be feeling awfully lonesome.

Overworked, too—I gather Lady Cindertallow is hard pressed to run Chandlefort without a Lord Cindertallow to help her out. She should remarry, but she will insist on staying a mourning widow. Silly woman.

"'Well and well, a fine mess. But despite this dissension within Chandlefort, Lady Cindertallow won't compromise an inch with His Eminence. There are sharp words and mutual threats of force, and the nuns of Our Lady run about clucking and preaching peace and praying to that dead whiteness in the sky—pardon me, that's a partisan effusion. I meant no disrespect. Clearly I think His Eminence is in the right, since I am his man, but I don't think so terribly hard. What do you think of the matter, friends?'

"By then I must have been half crazy with greed and drink and despair. 'Why should we care?' I asked. 'We work and die without honor in Chandlefort. If war comes, the Yellowjackets will fight with the Mayor's soldiers, taxes will go up, my house will be burned, and nothing will change. I'd have fought for the Empire. My parents told me the Queen's justice was fair and swift when they were young, before the legions went back to Queensmart. I'd die for Our Lady, but Lady Cindertallow's nothing to me. I wouldn't move a finger to save her.' That was the first time I'd ever dared say out loud what I felt. The other servants moved a little away from me, but none of them contradicted what I'd said.

"'Is that the truth?' asked Lucifer Snuff softly. He chuckled and the tide of play turned for good. His pile of silver grew, ours dwindled, and Andiron Grinder, Charfennel Comb, and the others fled the table one by one, clutching what paltry profits they had eked out of the night.

"I had as much money on the table as I did at the start of the evening. 'Play,' I said. I knew I would lose all my savings and I wanted to play anyway, for the hope of wealth and freedom. I wanted Snuff to run me through with his sword and gnaw on my bones. I didn't care to be a servant anymore. I pushed everything I had to the center of the table. 'Double or nothing.'

"Snuff looked at me thoughtfully. 'Are you sure?' he asked. 'Are you quite sure, Mr. Waxmelt Wickward?'

"And then I wasn't sure at all. I was only a foolish young man who'd almost lost his future. 'I can't,' I said. I scrabbled for my money and I started to cry. 'Dear Lady, I can't. I want to be more than a servant, but I can't. My wife's pregnant with our first child. I want our children to be more than servants, but I don't dare gamble their future away. My children will be servants all their lives, and their children too. It's stamped in our souls, Mr. Snuff. We're small, and we're scared, and we'll never be free.'

"Snuff accompanied me down Lackey Lane. I was too drunk and exhausted to make it home by myself. I lived in the far end of Lackey Lane, among the stinking hovels built up against the east walls of Chandlefort, downwind of the castle privies. My wife was waiting at the door, angry at me and frantic with worry. Snuff took a long look at her. 'The mother of servants,' he whispered in my ear. He dropped me in my doorway and stalked off, laughing, into the night.

"He returned five months later. Your mother had just

died in childbirth. I held you in my arms and fed you cow's milk. I was clumsy and dribbled the milk on your cheeks, and you cried. I should have farmed you out to a nursing scullery maid down the way, but I couldn't bear to part from you. You were the only family I had left.

"Snuff opened my door without asking and sat himself down on my best chair. 'I heard about your loss, Mr. Wickward,' he said. 'I'm sorry to learn of it.' He couldn't have cared less and he didn't mind that I knew. 'I have an offer to make you, old friend,' he said. 'I think you'll be interested.' He opened his hand and there was gold in it.

"He was pain and mockery and something bloody and corrupt, and I should have thrown him out of my house and into the night. But I didn't. Ah, Clo, I wanted that gold. I wanted freedom from a servant's life for us both. I listened to his offer.

"'I am not a wine steward,' said Snuff. 'I serve His Eminence, the Mayor of Low Branding, but not in a menial capacity. I provide . . . special services, shall we say. Of an irregular nature.' He grinned. He had bronzed the tips of his teeth since the last time I saw him, and the metal glowed red in the firelight. 'Right now my duties bring me here, to make certain preparations before war comes. War will come, Mr. Wickward. His Eminence wants to be his own master, and Lady Cindertallow will not see reason about the matter. As you said so eloquently, soldiers will fight, farms will burn, and what does it matter to us below? Nothing. But work is work and I have mine. I am here to steal the Cindertallow Ruby.'

"The Cindertallow Ruby. Do you remember those silly stories you read about robbing temples, Clo? All that nonsense about strange priests who'll fight to the death to keep hold of a magical jewel? Well, it isn't all nonsense.

"The Cindertallow Ruby was dug out of the ground from the very first ruby mine in the Salt Heath, long before Queensmart sent its legions up into Linstock. That was in the time of the first Lady Cindertallow, who built Chandlefort's walls and trained a rabble on horses until they had become the Yellowjacket Guardsmen. Her miners found the Ruby, and her jewelers polished it and made it the center of her coronet. The second Lady Cindertallow wore the coronet as she led the armies of Chandlefort toward the Whetstone River. Each Lady Cindertallow wore it into battle thereafter, and the Ruby became the talisman of Chandlefort's power during the two hundred years it took for them to conquer Linstock. Even after Chandlefort submitted to the Empire and we Fortmen came to believe in Our Lady, we still reverenced the power of the Ruby.

"Every Lady Cindertallow was crowned with the Ruby, was married with the Ruby, and died with the Ruby. She was supposed to wear the Ruby when she led the Yellowjackets into battle. Servants, Guardsmen, and lords all knew that Chandlefort was doomed to fall if it ever lost the Ruby. We were superstitious fools to think so, but still we believed that our fortunes were linked to the Cindertallow Ruby. The Cindertallows knew how we felt, and they guarded the Ruby very well. Which is why I laughed in Snuff's face.

"'Nevertheless,' Snuff said imperturbably, 'I will have the Ruby. I'll pay you ten gold sovereigns if you help me. You don't even have to lead me to the Inner Keep. You can go alone. I'll distract the Guardsmen from somewhere else while you take the Ruby from the Treasure Room.'

"'I'll be chopped to bits if anyone finds me within three hundred feet of the Treasure Room,' I said. 'I suppose you think servants wander all around Chandlefort unnoticed. That's true of some areas, but not of them all. There aren't any chamber pots to empty in the Inner Keep. Mr. Snuff, you can't distract every Yellowjacket Guardsman in the Keep. There are dozens of them. I'd be very obvious and then I'd be very dead.'

"Snuff smiled and rubbed his brown tooth. Old blood flaked onto his fingers and he licked their tips clean. 'Call me Snuff, Waxy. Everybody does. The Guardsmen are not a problem, old friend. You won't need to do much. I'll give you directions through the Keep to the Treasure Room. Just walk there quickly. The Ruby is in a glass case in the center of the room. Break open the glass and take the Ruby with you. Then walk out again. Once you've returned to the Outer Citadel, you'll be just one servant in the crowd. Leave through Menials' Gate. I'll wait at the end of Lackey Lane with a spare horse. I'll pay you for the Ruby, and then you and your daughter can ride with me to Low Branding. From there you can flee Linstock and make yourself a new, better life, somewhere very far away.'

"I knew I was a dead man if I said no. Snuff couldn't let me go after he'd told me his plans. Maybe if I got the

Ruby for him, I'd be a dead man anyway—corpses tell no secrets. Just then you whimpered in your sleep. I wondered if he'd let you live.

"I thought about informing on him. I supposed I would be given what the lords and ladies called 'a handsome reward, for someone of his station.' Lady Cindertallow would have an upper servant thank me for her and pay me some shillings. Then I would return to my servant's life and you would follow me in your turn, Clovermead. We would never be anything more.

"Snuff offered me a dream of yellow gold. I knew he'd most likely kill me, but I thought I'd take the chance. My wife was already dead and part of me with her. I didn't think you had anything more to lose than a servant's life.

"'I'll do it,' I said.

"Snuff gave me two gold pieces and seven silvers that night, as an advance payment.

"A week later, at the time Snuff had arranged, I put my scouring rag behind a marble statue of Our Lady and walked to the Inner Keep. I heard a bear roar, and I shuddered in my bones. I smelled putrid flesh and felt a thickness in the air. Somewhere ahead of me men screamed in terror.

"I came to the entry of the Inner Keep and I saw Guardsmen sprawled on the ground, still screaming. Their arms jerked and their mouths foamed and they looked at some horrible shadow. No one saw me. The lucky ones had fainted. Beyond, I heard more screams, and more, and more. The roaring was louder than ever.

"I kept walking through the Inner Keep and saw

servants and Guardsmen mad with fear. Their noses bled and their eyes rolled up and some Guardsmen swung their swords at phantoms before they turned and ran. The bear roared again and the air was thick with madness. I wanted to go mad myself. I heard the bear huffing in my ears, barely leashed from clawing at my mind. I heard Snuff laugh and I knew he was protecting me. I wanted to pray to Our Lady, but I would not dirty her with my filthy prayers.

"I finally reached the Treasure Room, where five more Guardsmen lay trembling and moaning on the floor. I stepped over their bodies and looked down at the Ruby. I—I fell in love, Clo. I had seen the Ruby before, but never so close. It was perfect—dazzling and beautiful. It was as large around as a baby's hand, faceted, and set in a filigree of gold and pearls. Its color was half scarlet and half a summer sunset. I almost wept to see it. I looked at the Ruby and I knew that I couldn't give it away. Not to Snuff and Low Branding and that thing that was killing those Guardsmen. I didn't care what happened to Chandlefort and Lady Cindertallow, but I couldn't give the Ruby over to that sort of enemy. I would have become something foul if I'd done that.

"I looked at the Ruby, Clo, and the thought gleamed in me that I would take the Ruby for myself. I would steal from Chandlefort and Low Branding alike. I felt giddy, and astonished at my own daring. I was anything but a servant now, for Snuff or Cindertallow. I smashed the glass case with a hammer I had secreted in my clothes, and I picked out the Ruby from the glass shards. I also picked out a brooch engraved with the Burning Bee of Chandlefort, though it didn't look so valuable. I dropped the Ruby and the brooch into my pocket and walked out of the Treasure Room. All the way back to the Outer Citadel I stepped over screaming Guardsmen musky with fear.

"I went to my house in Lackey Lane, picked you up from your cradle, and put the money Snuff had given me in my pouch. Then I walked over to the horse market and bought a gray nag for a silver piece. I got onto the nag with you and turned north, onto the Tansy Pike. I had only a hazy idea of what lay that way. I'd heard of Snowchapel, though, and it seemed as good a place to go as any.

"I waited for Lord Ursus to strike me down as he'd struck down the Guardsmen. Later that day I felt something in the air, roaring, sniffing for me, sending out fear, but I had already come many leagues from Chandlefort and the fear was weak. The thing passed me by and it never came again. Afterward I began to think I was safe from Snuff.

"And sometime later, when I'd had time to think about matters, I decided that I didn't need to keep the Ruby with me. That would have been too dangerous for you. I was happy as long as neither Chandlefort nor Low Branding had it. I hid the Ruby. But I kept the brooch. I . . . made changes to it. Clo, to people who know how to look, that brooch is a map to where the Ruby is."

Clovermead took out her brooch and peered at it. "It doesn't look like a treasure map."

"It isn't supposed to be obvious," said Waxmelt. "I told you before to keep it hidden. Now do you understand why?"

"Not entirely, Father. You're still lying to me. I can't tell what was true in your story and what wasn't, but I'm certain that something important was false. Or a number of things."

"A few things," Waxmelt said.

"I didn't expect better," said Clovermead. A tear trickled town her cheek and inside she roared. "How did Snuff summon Lord Ursus?"

Waxmelt shuddered. "I think he killed a man. Killed more than one man. Killed them slowly. I've heard since that Lord Ursus gives more power if his sacrifices hurt while they're dying. I've also heard the power he gives is strongest while the blood is fresh. I've had some time to think about it, Clo, and I think that's the reason Snuff wanted help to steal the Ruby. He had to kill his victims somewhere private, where he wouldn't be interrupted, but that would have to be far from the Chandlefort walls. The blood-power would have gone stale before he reached the Treasure Room. He needed an indoor servant, like me, to get to the Ruby while the blood was still fresh and the summoning was still strong."

Clovermead shuddered too. "What happened to the gold sovereigns?"

"I used them to buy Ladyrest from old Granny Mendloom. Her children had died and she wanted to become a nun at Snowchapel. She used the two sovereigns to dower herself into the convent."

"How lovely, Father! Mr. Snuff would gnash his teeth if he knew his money had ended up in Our Lady's chapel." Clovermead laughed. "Serves him right. Father, what if I find myself in a tight situation and have no choice but to deliver up the brooch to either proud Chandlefort or sinister Low Branding? To which of these warring powers do I give it?"

"To Chandlefort," Waxmelt said, unhesitatingly swift. "To your sharp-eyed friend Mr. Sorrel and to Lady Cindertallow and to the whole lot of them. Though it will tear me apart to give her back the Ruby. Remember that if they get hold of it, Clo. It will tear me apart." Those words were urgent and filled with pain. "But far better them than Snuff and Low Branding."

Chapter Eight

AMBUSH

THE DAWN WAS COLD AND FOGGY. TREES A HUNDRED FEET away faded to shadows in the white mist. Tiny droplets of rain floated in the air and crept inside Clovermead's hood no matter how she arranged it. The thin skeins of ice that covered the puddles on the Road cracked wetly when Clovermead stepped on them. A light, chill wind blew from the northwest.

Midmorning they reached the Tansy Pike. It was a straight gray cobblestone road that demarcated the northern boundary between the flatlands and the hill country of Linstock. A cairn of red rubble marked its intersection with Crescent Road. A little back from the intersection a wooden inn cheerily radiated light from its windows and smoke from its chimneys. It was built in much the same style as Ladyrest, though it was larger. Inside the attached plot of fenced-in, withered grass, a black billy goat tied to a post curiously watched Clovermead and Waxmelt and bleated contentedly. Clovermead heard mist-hidden cows low in the distance.

"Can we stay for lunch, Father?" she asked wistfully.

Waxmelt shook his head. "I'm sorry, Clo. Snuff's sure to stop and ask if we've been there."

They turned east on the Pike. The mist swallowed up the inn, the lowing of the cows, and all sounds but the steady *clop-clop* of Nubble's hooves on the cobblestones. The wind blew colder against the three of them, and the droplets of rain turned first to sleet and then to snow. The snow melted on the ground but left a white shadow behind.

The Pike passed through a dreary land of scrub forest, ponds, and isolated farms huddled on either side. The farms would suddenly loom up out of the mist and just as suddenly vanish into the mist behind them. Clovermead thought that the roofs were strangely flat—*Evidently,* she told herself, *they do not fear blizzard as much as do we hardy northerners of Timothy Vale.* The farmers had painted their farms white, yellow, or pale blue. Most had also painted a crescent on their doors, but a few hung bear-tooth necklaces instead. From the barns came the muffled sounds of clucking, quacking, neighing, oinking, and mooing. Guard dogs loured at Clovermead and Waxmelt from inside fences, trotted alongside as the Wickwards passed by, and growled angrily until the two travelers disappeared from sight.

"Where is everybody?" asked Clovermead. "I thought Linstock was so full of people that you tripped over a dozen of them between the back door and the outhouse. These houses look like people are living in them, but they don't come out. Do Linstockers hibernate like bears?"

"Maybe they're scared of strangers after so many years of war," said Waxmelt. "I was in the Vale five years before I stopped being afraid when pilgrims knocked on the door."

A few minutes later Clovermead heard horses neigh

ahead. There was one, three, a dozen of them, galloping on the Pike. "Is it Snuff?" she asked. Her legs were tensed to send her bounding into the underbrush.

"I don't think so. The straight route from Low Branding is up the Crescent Road. This way leads to High Branding and Ryebrew. It's someone else." But Waxmelt put his hand to his sword as the troop of horses approached. Clovermead put her hand to her wooden sword too, but it didn't make her feel much safer.

The horsemen burst into view and grew rapidly from distant manikins to nearing giants. They wore armor made of green leather and chain links, carried lances and shields, and rode immense, furious warhorses that seemed to be another species from placid Nubble. Each of the riders' shields bore a different escutcheon on it—a green fox, a red fish, a silver honeycomb, a pair of crossed brown axes. Each steed's blanket had been embroidered with the same escutcheon as his rider's shield.

The leader reined in his horse and the other riders halted with him. "Stay for the Borderers of High Branding," the leader cried out in a low, reedy voice. He looked the Wickwards over as they stopped obediently. Waxmelt kept his eyes to the ground, but Clovermead boldly examined the leader's features. He was a thin man with a long face, wispy blond hair, and oiled mustachios. His expression was mild and matter-of-fact.

"Travelers," he said with an air of formality and flourish that was both pompous and bored, "you have entered the Purlieus of High Branding. Please state where you are from, where you are bound, and what your business is."

"From Ryebrew," Waxmelt said. "Returning there from pilgrimage to Snowchapel. Sir, can you tell us how the roads are ahead?"

"I regret to tell you that the road through the Harrow Moors is washed away," the horseman said without any particular sympathy in his voice. "The autumn rains have been strangely fierce this year. The Pike has been an impassable mire for a month."

"Darkness and eclipse!" Waxmelt swore. "Are you sure there's no way through? How are the southern Moors?"

The horseman shrugged. "The Moors are flooded for a hundred miles. Farther south there are brigands. There will be no passage to Ryebrew till spring. Of course, the Moors are never easy to traverse in autumn. As any traveler from Ryebrew knows." He cast a skeptical eye on the Wickwards. "You were unwise to return this late in the year."

"My niece fell sick in Snowchapel," Waxmelt said. "I had to wait till she had recovered. Sir, we may need to stay awhile in High Branding. Can a visitor find work here for a few weeks?"

"Ah," said the horseman. "An excellent question—it is strange you do not know the answer, since you must have passed through High Branding on your way from Ryebrew to Snowchapel. Everyone who passes through High Branding knows that work is scarce in the town. We are a byword for generous hospitality, travelers, and we have opened our city these twelve years to refugees from all Linstock. There are far more people than jobs in High Branding. We are charitable, travelers, but it has become necessary to reserve all new jobs for our native citizens. It has even become necessary to close our borders against those unfortunates who flock to High Branding with hopes of feather beds to sleep on and gold coins to spend." The horseman smiled thinly. "I regret to inform you, sir, that travelers suspected of vagrant intent are not allowed inside the Purlieus of High Branding." The troop of horsemen drew closer to the Wickwards.

"Can I prove to you that we're not vagrants?" Waxmelt asked, holding his hands flat and open, standing very still.

"Entry fee to the Borderers is a shilling from each traveler," said the horseman. "You must also prove possession of at least one sovereign per traveler."

"That's an outrage!" Clovermead burst out. "No one has that much money."

"You'd be surprised, miss," said the horseman. "Some do. They are honored guests at High Branding. Sir, will you be able to be our guest?" Waxmelt shook his head. "Alas, sir. You'll be returning westward, then?" The horseman extended his lance past Waxmelt's forehead and pointed back toward Crescent Road.

"So it seems." Waxmelt bowed low. "Good fortune attend you, Borderer."

"And you, refugee," said the horseman. He waited until Waxmelt had turned Nubble around and started the pony away from High Branding. Only when the Wickwards had left the troop far behind did Clovermead hear hoofbeats and halloing and a jangling diminishing to the east.

"They are coldhearted rascals," said Clovermead. "An opossum knows more of courtesy and welcome. And they're certainly not knightly! Sir Auroche in the *Heptameron* shares his last food with a hideous crone, though of course she turns out to be a beauteous maiden the next morning. And his boon companion Sir Plateous welcomes seven snoring merchants into his forest cave, and they all stink of rancid horse grease, but Sir Plateous never complains, though he does pray to Our Lady to make them snore less, and she grants his wishes. Even you, Father, you let that smelly pilgrim from Selcouth stay at Ladyrest for a week last summer, and you didn't charge him a penny. I'd like to tell High Branding what I think of their nasty little city! I . . . I . . . I'd blow the Tansy Horn and down would come their walls, *bzam, blam, boom*! And that would show that bored Borderer what is what."

"'Even you, Father,'" Waxmelt repeated ruefully. "You think more of your blessed Sir Auroche than you do of your own father. This is a lesson to me: I should never have let you learn to read."

"You cannot mend what is broken, Father, as you said when you saw me with that shattered tureen of candied apples. I believe it was then that you agreed to let me learn my letters, so as to keep me out of mischief. You were very wise, Father. I didn't break nearly as many dishes afterward. Should we try to slip around these horsey knaves and scuttle through the Purlieus of High Branding? We don't have to stay on the Pike."

"Too dangerous. The land around here doesn't have enough places to hide—it's too flat and open. And those

Borderers won't just threaten us if they catch us again." Waxmelt sighed. "I suppose we must take the Pike past Chandlefort after all. Lady preserve us."

The snow fell harder as Waxmelt and Clovermead returned west on the Pike. Great, shuddering northern gusts chilled the air and sliced through their coats as the pale sun fell before them. Now the farms were not even shadows by the roadside, but only hints of color in the swirling white. The animals were quiet in their warm barn stalls. A lone dog growled at Waxmelt and Clovermead as they passed, but low and dispirited. Nubble groaned in the harsh cold.

"I do hate retracing our steps," said Clovermead as they ate a late lunch by the roadside. "I wasn't worried before, but now I fear an ironical coincidence. Do you suppose Mr. Snuff will have arrived with his henchmen at the crossroads? I see him now, searching for us with villainous intensity. He will bare a hideous grin and his eyes will light up with gratified malice as he sees his victims approach. He will laugh so poisonous spittle flies from his jaws. I can see it distinctly. If you want, Father, I can describe his features in even greater detail."

"Please, Clovermead. Your poor father is eating. Don't upset his stomach." He tousled her hair and looked anxiously at the soft whiteness underfoot. "We were slow going through the Chaffen Hills and we've lost time today, but I think we've outrun him. I'm more worried about the snow. Snuff might see our tracks and follow us. If he finds us—if he does, I'll try to hold him. You run and don't come back for me, don't try to save me. Go down to Queensmart by yourself, or to Chandlefort as a last resort. I'll meet you if I can."

"I absolutely refuse," said Clovermead. "I'll stand and fight. I'm not afraid. How could I leave you?"

Waxmelt laughed. "You've never been frightened in all your life, Clo. I know that. But sometimes it's no shame to run." He looked at Clovermead as she stood there, defiant and uncertain. "Don't any of your books tell you that?"

"No," said Clovermead sullenly. "But I'll run if you say I have to. I'll leave you." But behind her back she crossed her fingers.

"Good," said Waxmelt. He opened his purse and counted out half his coins to Clovermead. Clovermead stuffed them down her stockings. "Don't go running to spend that. You'll need it all if you want to get to Queensmart."

"Couldn't I go back to Timothy Vale?" Clovermead asked wistfully.

"Too dangerous, Clo," said Waxmelt. "There are bears all through the Reliquaries. By now Snuff must have sent word to them to watch the Vale. We don't dare go home."

They passed the Crescent Road again a few minutes before dark. The Wickwards squinted southward and saw only whiteness falling. The snow was already three inches deep. The fog was thicker than ever. Now houses only fifty feet away vanished in the haze.

The Pike angled southwest through a wilder country of undulating hills sparsely clothed by scrawny trees, fallen brown leaves, and haggard bracken. The farms grew more scattered here—a few had been burned and abandoned, and the rest were poorer and smaller than the farms in High Branding's Purlieus. These homesteads were defended by stone walls.

They walked another hour before the last light faded. Then Waxmelt turned off the Pike, walked half a mile into the gullied bracken, and found a rock-strewn hollow formed by fallen trees. He cleared the snow from the ground and lit a fire behind a broad tree trunk, where it couldn't be seen from the road. Waxmelt had Clovermead snap off a pine branch and whisk snow over their footprints all the way back to the Pike. She enjoyed spreading the snow so as to fill the faintest dimples their boots had left behind. When she returned, she found that her father had turned a blanket into an impromptu roof and had made ready another stew. The taste was drearily familiar, but she wolfed it down.

The moon shone terribly bright in her dreams, glaring warning and danger, and Clovermead woke in the velvet darkness of the late night. Waxmelt huddled underneath his blanket, snoring and shivering close by the fire, his face careworn and exhausted. The fire had burned low and the fog was thick as coal smoke, dank and hungry to swallow the last heat of the burning logs. All around Clovermead snow fell out of the darkness into a sphere of dim light.

Something scuffled, something cracked a branch, something hissed, and something hooting pretended to be an owl. There were many somethings padding and scratching and arranging themselves around the Wickwards. They shuffled and slunk, never fell silent, and never went away. The noise was a throb and an itch. The tooth on her neck bit at her, but sleep numbed its insistent, sharp alarm. Languidly, Clovermead pinched her arm. The pain was dull and a long time coming. *I'm still dreaming,* she told herself. *This is a fear-dream, nothing real. When I cry out, Daddy will tell me not to worry and to go back to sleep.*

Clovermead heard a growling laugh. It bit into her sharper than frost and her tooth was a bonfire on her chest. She was wide awake and she was paralyzed with fear. Cold pumped out from her chest to her guts and lungs and head and limbs. Her fingers were nerveless slabs of flesh.

A bear limped into the firelight. Old Bonegrinder was mangy and scarred from many battles. His left ear had been torn off and his small yellow eyes gleamed nastily. He grinned at Clovermead, saying, *I have you now, little prey. You've given us a hard chase.* Clovermead smelled rotting meat on his breath.

Bonegrinder cast an enormous shadow that pierced the white mist and made it bleed darkness. The shadow-bear scraped at boulders and bit trees, pacing back and forth on yet darker hills. The shadow moved when Bonegrinder was still, and roared silently. A black and oozing trail followed his progress.

Bonegrinder drew closer to Clovermead. His back left leg was twisted out of kilter. His tongue ran across his blood-lined yellow teeth. Clovermead followed his tongue with her eyes, but she could not move, could not cry out, could only whimper deep in her throat. She despised herself for her helplessness.

Waxmelt tossed in his sleep, frowning, and Bonegrinder's ears twitched. He snarled and extended his three-inch claws. Clovermead screamed, but no sound came out of her mouth. She ran, but she lay quiet and still. Waxmelt jerked the blanket higher over his face. Bonegrinder's teeth were notched and splintered, and some were stumps. His melon-large muscles rippled under his scabby hide. *I'm hungry,* he said, and he leapt and grew huge and the air whistled past his enormous, nearing jaws—

And a shadowy figure at the edge of the clearing whipped a knife through the darkness to slam into Bonegrinder's eye and pierce his brain. The bear howled with surprise and indignation, slumped in midair, and fell whimpering between Waxmelt and the fire. Waxmelt jerked awake and fumbled for his sword, but the bear was already dead. The bear's shadow growled contempt for his unlucky servant and melted into the outer darkness. Clovermead felt Bonegrinder die and she cried out loud at last. The corpse began to smoke and burn as sparks from the logs set its fur ablaze. The somethings around them were yelling and clattering and moving, and the deadening ice was gone from Clovermead. She sprang to her feet. All around them the somethings had become visible, turned into neighing horses, cursing horsemen, and loping bears. They rushed at the Wickwards from all sides.

"Run!" yelled Waxmelt. He charged at the nearest horseman, who swept at Waxmelt with a cruelly sharp sword and hit a low-hanging branch. From the darkness the shadowy figure hurled a handful of pebbles at the horseman's head. While the horseman cursed and raised his hands to cover his face, Waxmelt hacked at the horse's belly. The creature shrieked, tossed its terrified rider high into the air, and crumpled to the ground. The horseman landed heavily on a protruding boulder, and Clovermead heard his neck snap. Waxmelt gulped and looked nauseous, but he turned to face the next horseman.

Clovermead seized a long branch, thrust it into the fire, and waved the burning brand at the three bears hurtling toward her. Nuthoarder, Rootswallow, and Comblick were smaller than Bonegrinder and not half so fierce. They whimpered at the light and fell back uncertainly.

Lucifer Snuff charged into the clearing on Featherfall. Sweat gleamed on Snuff's balding head, and sharp branches had tattered his black cape. He wore a new bear tooth around his neck. He laughed exultantly and kicked deep into his horse with his spurs. Featherfall sprang forward with redoubled speed, his eyes huge and red with fear. "Take care of the man, boys!" Snuff called out. "Keep him alive. My pets will deal with the girl." He raised his sword, rode straight at Clovermead, and smashed the branch from her hands. The blade passed an inch in front of Clovermead's eyes, and her torch guttered out in the snow.

He could have killed me, Clovermead thought. *He let me live.*

She hated Snuff more than ever for his contemptuous mercy.

The bear tooth scratched her chest. Clovermead drew her wooden sword in her right hand and pulled the tooth from under her shirt with her left. She gasped at its charring heat.

With her torch extinguished, the bears had regained their courage and now they boxed her in, growling, their teeth bared and their claws full out. Nuthoarder snapped at Clovermead. She fell backward and stumbled over the corpse of the first horseman. As she fell her hand jerked the tooth loose from the cord.

The tooth twitched in midair and fell point-first into the bleeding corpse.

The tooth glowed. Bloodred light filled the night. The bears looked confused, almost afraid. They stopped snarling and took a step back from Clovermead. The tooth . . . drank. The corpse whitened and withered, and the tooth glowed brighter and brighter, pulsing, a crimson heart in the darkness. At the other end of the clearing the soldier fighting Waxmelt flung his arm up against the glare and Waxmelt stabbed him in the leg. The soldier screamed and fell backward. Another soldier ran up to Waxmelt, and Waxmelt turned to face him.

"So that's where my tooth went to," said Snuff, cackling. "The girlie picked it up! Thank you kindly, missy. I missed my old friend. You just give him back." He held out his hand. He was sweating more than ever. For the first time Clovermead thought she saw fear in him. He snapped his pointed teeth at her. "Give it now, chit, or I'll hurt you. I'm not allowed to kill you, but His Eminence won't mind a few bruises on you. I won't warn you again."

Clovermead scarcely heard him. Her eyes were pinned to the tooth's red glow. Her fingers caressed the tooth's slick enamel. She heard roaring inside her, a message, an invitation. *Do this,* the tooth whispered. *Do this, and this, and this.* She heard the dead horseman cry out. His death was in the tooth along with his blood, and the tooth was savoring his pain.

"Go away," Clovermead whispered to the bears. They took another step back. The tooth blazed brighter than ever. Clovermead laughed with the delight of power. She pulled the tooth from the horseman's body and lifted it high in the air so that the red light filled the rocky hollow. She looked the bears straight in the face. "Go away, Rootswallow. Depart, Comblick. Never return, Nuthoarder. I command you all—leave me alone!"

The bears obeyed her. *We meant no harm,* said Comblick, and she was cuffed by Rootswallow for her obvious, stupid lie. *One tooth says come, another says go. We are dutiful. Tell Lord Ursus we followed every order. Don't punish us, great mistress.* They bowed their heads before the blazing red light, whined, and crept away.

"Most impressive," said Snuff. He clapped his hands, ironically and slowly. "You have blood-talent, girlie. Those three won't stop running for a year. If you were a boy, I'd say you should be a bear-priest. You need to work on your control, though. Such a waste, Miss Clovermead. You've already used up that fool's blood."

"Used up?" Clovermead asked, but the answer was in front of her. The bloodlight had faded. The tooth was small and dry and cold again, with just a tinge of brown on its tip.

"All gone," said Snuff. He idly whirled his sword and kicked Featherfall forward. "That game's over. Give me my tooth." He held out his hand. Clovermead looked for Waxmelt, but he was desperately fighting two soldiers at the far end of the clearing. The shadowy figure dashed out from behind a tree and heaved a clod of earth at one of the soldiers, who stumbled but did not fall down. Firelight silhouetted the figure, and now Clovermead could see that the figure was a man. The man turned, looked at Snuff standing by Clovermead, and slipped away from Waxmelt. He ran through the darkness toward Clovermead.

Clovermead snarled and rapped Snuff's knuckles with her sword. He cursed and jumped back. "All right, if that's the way you want to play." He leapt lightly from Featherfall's back and landed catlike on flexed knees. He jabbed his sword toward Clovermead. His smile was an ugly, lopsided wound. "His Eminence will be very understanding about your injuries."

"I'll kill you," Clovermead growled. She swung at Snuff and he leapt back. "I'll hack off your limbs, bear-priest. I'll gnaw on your guts." She lunged at his chest.

Snuff easily parried her thrust. "What a vicious cub you are. Do you think you're grown enough to hunt? You're wrong, little one. Don't bare your claws at your elders." He slashed at Clovermead and she barely brought her wooden sword up in time. The metal dug half an inch into her sword, and the force of the blow nearly dislocated Clovermead's arm. "Give up, girl."

"Never!" Clovermead yelled. She pulled her wooden sword from Snuff's blade and leapt at him again. Her sword whirled madly and she swung at him with all her might. She grazed Snuff's ribs and he grunted with pain. He snarled and fell back and parried desperately hard. She pressed her attack again—and was parried again.

Now Snuff grinned. He stood his ground as Clovermead attacked. His sword flashed and flashed, and splinters of wood chipped off from her wooden blade. Clovermead's lungs were on fire and her legs were lead and her arms were numb from the force of her attacks, but she would not stop fighting. She swung and swung, and once she raked the side of his head, but Snuff scarcely flinched. He fought on. His blade smashed hers until at last her blade snapped in her hands.

"Teeth and claws, you do fight well!" said Snuff, nodding respectfully at her. He was breathing heavily. Then he raised his sword. "Will you give up now? Or do I have to knock you out first?"

"I'll claw your eyes out," said Clovermead. She lifted up her hands against him. Snuff giggled and came toward her.

A stone flew out of the darkness and hit Snuff in the stomach. Breathless, Snuff staggered back and grabbed his middle, his sword falling to the ground.

"This way, Clo," said Sorrel from his hiding place in the gully behind her. Snuff looked wildly around him and scrabbled for his sword. Still stunned, he caught at pebbles and dirt. "You must hurry!" Sorrel moaned anxiously as Clovermead gaped at the astonishing, impossibly present Tansyard. He threw another stone at Snuff. Snuff batted it aside. Clovermead saw her disarmed father surrounded by three horsemen. Two horsemen more were cantering toward her. *I'll kill one,* she thought, *and use his blood to call the bears. The bears will eat the rest of them.*

Above her the clouds parted. Moonlight shone on Clovermead from a waning crescent moon, and she sobbed in horror at what she was thinking. *I'm sorry, Father,* she thought, and weeping, she ran as fast as her aching lungs would permit to join Sorrel in the gully. *I can't rescue you that way. I can't save you at all. I'm sorry.*

The clouds closed once more and the moonlight faded. Clovermead tied the bear tooth back on to her leather cord as she ran.

"This ravine will take us all the way to the Pike," Sorrel whispered. He wormed a hundred feet farther on into the darkness. Clovermead followed him close behind. No one else was pursuing them yet, so Sorrel stopped a second and smiled at Clovermead. "You fight well, Miss Clovermead—I have taught you skillfully, yes? As they say, you have come up to Snuff." He chortled. "Say thank you to your heroic double rescuer, Miss Clovermead; be gracious to your bear stabber and Snuff startler, who is master of tossed stones and of air-slicing daggers!"

"Thank you," Clovermead replied mechanically. She looked backward. "My father—"

"Will not be killed," Sorrel said. He pressed his hand awkwardly to Clovermead's shoulder. "You heard what Snuff said, did you not? I believe that monster and so should you. I am sorry. I tried to help your father in this ambush, with flung stones and earth, but I could not save both of you. We can think later what to do for Mr. Wickward. Now we must keep ourselves alive and unpunctured and free. Will you come with me?" Clovermead nodded reluctantly. A horseman halloed behind them and Sorrel blanched. "Did I attack an entire troop of the Mayor's men? This was the most amazing folly. I shudder and I praise Our Lady in advance for keeping us alive—you hear, Sweet Lady? Miss Clovermead, follow me."

They bolted along a curving fissure just steep and narrow enough to prevent the horsemen from following them directly. It was fringed by trees that forced their pursuers to circle widely around. Snuff jumped after them into the gully, but he slipped on a rock while Clovermead and Sorrel raced ahead. They swayed around more curves. The commotion and light faded behind them.

Brown Barley was waiting at a fir tree a few feet in from the Pike. "Good-bye, dear companion," said Sorrel. Sadly he stroked Brown Barley's face and loosed her from the trunk. "Off to Chandlefort you go. So they will learn that the Tansyard is alive but in trouble, and maybe they will send someone to help him out. Do not let those bearish murderers catch up with you, and you will rest yourself at home in your own dear stables and stall. Eh? Good-bye, good-bye." He slapped Brown Barley's rump. The horse neighed, reared, and galloped southward.

Sorrel burrowed into the snow and brought out his backpack, a steel dagger, which he handed to Clovermead, and three pairs of skis. He sighed as he brought out the third pair. "I had also hoped to bring out Mr. Wickward. I am most sorry that your father is not here. You know how to ride skis?"

"Of course," said Clovermead. "There's nothing but skis and sleighs in the Vale once winter's settled in." She slid the dagger into the scabbard where her wooden sword had lain, and smiled as she realized that she had a real weapon at last. Really, she ought to be knighted as a reward for her epic battle with Snuff. She quickly tied a pair of skis to her boots.

"Most rapturous. Then can you show me how one uses these ridiculous devices?"

"You don't know how?" Clovermead asked, appalled.

"Not very," Sorrel said sheepishly. "The plan came to me before the skill. They will chase Brown Barley and her tracks, and we will slip-sloop-slide away west, into obscure hills, on these skis that the Snowchapel nuns assured me I would need to have, and they were most correct. But I did not practice on them more than an hour in my life, Miss Clovermead."

"Lady bless us," Clovermead fervently prayed. "It isn't hard, Sorrel." She crouched and put his skis on for him. Then she was busy giving him instructions and helping him slide across the snowed-over cobblestones and gliding for the far trees before the horsemen came out onto the Pike. She told Sorrel how to make a smooth slide, how to turn to avoid trees, how to brake himself, and soon they were speeding through the darkness. The world grew silent behind them and the falling snow covered their faint tracks. Each passing mile lashed Clovermead's heart as they fled farther and farther away from her abandoned father.

Chapter Nine

In the Mill

NEAR DAWN CLOVERMEAD AND SORREL FOUND A deserted water mill while trying to ford an ice-coated stream. Rime covered its plank walls, but the frosty mill seemed summery to them after their night speeding through the snowstorm. They made beds of the chaff and flour that coated the floor, untied their skis, and fell asleep.

Clovermead dreamed of Timothy Vale and buckwheat pancakes and mutton lunch and beating the laundry with Goody Weft. She dreamed of her father bringing a basket of apples to her room, she dreamed of him mopping the floor at Ladyrest, and she dreamed of him trussed up and slung over Featherfall's back. Clovermead whimpered. She was afraid for her father and she was afraid for herself. She had never been so alone before, and she tried to dream of something else, anything else. Then she dreamed of an old granny bear walking in the moonlight, her fur mottled gray and white. The bear smiled at Clovermead and told her, *Don't worry, little one, it will all turn out for the best. Hush you, hush you, don't cry.* She sang a gentle, rumbling song to Clovermead till Clovermead's fears drained from her and she woke with a smile.

The sun shone through the roof. An arrow of light

pierced through a crack in the timbers and fell on Clovermead's face. "That was a nice dream," said Clovermead, yawning. "I don't see why it should cheer me up so much, but it does. It will all turn out for the best! Oh, I hope so." She squinted at the sunbeams. "The sun is high. Are adventurers allowed to be late risers?" Clovermead looked over to Sorrel. He was still asleep, smiling delicately as he dreamed. A light brown curl fell over his forehead. "And thus I discover that my rescuer is not as heroic as he claims," said Clovermead sadly. "Heroes scowl ferociously in their slumber. I consider myself to have been rescued under false pretenses." She yawned and stretched, and her stomach rumbled. "I wonder if Sorrel can cook? I mean, anything more than fried horse steak and hoof pudding and mane-and-tail pie, and other such delights of Tansyard cuisine. Perhaps he has brought dried horse jerky with him for the journey south. I hesitate to take the risk." Clovermead rose and poked around the mill. A pigeon fluttered away from her nest in the rafters. Clovermead climbed a ladder and looked in, but there were no eggs.

"I am daunted, but I do not despair. Appetite will put an edge to my wits. Think, Clovermead! What would Sir Auroche do? Besides lament his hunger, that is." Clovermead fell silent, pondering the wheres and wherefores of breakfast, and wondered ruefully if Waxmelt's full meals had atrophied her ability to forage. Beneath the mill the cold stream slowly rippled, not yet completely frozen through.

"Fish!" Clovermead exclaimed. She ran down to the mill cellar and found a net, loose planks on the floor, and an old weir underneath. Clovermead peered down at the water swirling in a muddy cul-de-sac at the stream's edge. Silvery glimmers darted back and forth in the murky water. Clovermead waited till she saw five flickers beneath her, then swiftly lowered the weir gate.

Clovermead dipped the net and came up with a wriggling foot-long trout. "I suppose I shouldn't say so, little meal, but I feel most like unto a bear," Clovermead said conversationally to the fish. "I wouldn't say so at night, but I can't feel so scared in broad daylight. Mind you, the comparison doesn't exactly comfort me. Alas, alas, it should cheer you still less." She cut the trout's head off with her knife. The fish jerked once more and fell still. "I told you it was an ominous comparison, dear breakfast. Dear lunch and dinner, while we're at it. Oh, oh, I'm sure that Sorrel is a growing boy who can't be stopped from nibbling. He certainly liked Daddy's stews back at Ladyrest. You won't last us till tomorrow. Ah, little fish, the auguries are all so very dark. I prophesy massacre amongst your brethren. Woe, woe!" She dipped her net in twice more and came up with another trout and three perch.

The smell of roasting fish woke Sorrel. His nose twitched and his eyes flew open. The Tansyard gazed delightedly at the spitted fish above the fire Clovermead had lit. He sat up, drew in his breath sharply, and smiled helplessly. "Clovermead, you must pinch me. I want to know that this paradisial scent is not a dream. You would not be cruel and deceive a poor Tansyard?"

Clovermead giggled and pinched Sorrel hard. He yelped and swatted at her. Clovermead jumped out of range and handed him a bowl of river water. Catlike,

Sorrel tasted it with the tip of his tongue first, then drank deeply. "Most delicious, Miss Clovermead. Fresh water and trout-taste were a delicacy of my youth. The first time I fed on them, I was a six-winter boy, or maybe seven-winter. In late summer we wandered on the north edge of the Tansy Steppes by those slopes of the Reliquaries where the mountain streams trickle into the grasslands. My father most bravely stumbled into the water, though he could not swim, and he seized a knee-high silver monster, a true flapper. Father struggled greatly and defeated it, and that night we ate cream-soft trout—strange, tempting water-flesh on a steppe boy's tongue. I have not had fish more than three times since." Sorrel licked his lips. "How much can we eat? I finished the biscuit I brought from Snowchapel yesterday morning, and I was too busy tracking you to get new supplies. I am very hungry."

"We'll split one fish," Clovermead said. "The rest we save for later." She cut into the shining scales with her knife and appraised the white flesh. "It's ready," she said, and prayed to Our Lady that she had remembered how long fish was supposed to roast.

Clovermead took the spits off the fire and cut the first fish in two. Sorrel speared his half with his knife, bit into scales—and spat them out. "Egh," he said, wrinkling his mouth. "I do not remember water-flesh so."

"You're eating it all wrong, Sorrel," said Clovermead. "Do it like this." She scraped off the skin and scales and nibbled carefully around the bones.

Sorrel imitated her cautiously, then smiled in delight. "Ah, yes! Fishy-flesh should be just so. Dear Lady, I am in raptures! Lovely, Miss Clovermead. You are a heavenly cook."

"Father's much better than I am," said Clovermead. She took a small bite. It wasn't at all bad. Father would be proud of her when she saw him again and told him how well she had cooked on her own.

If I see him again, thought Clovermead. The comfort of her dream had faded in the clear day, and she almost cried as the realization of Waxmelt's absence sank into her. She ate the rest of the fish in silence. Sorrel saw the unhappiness take hold of her, and he also kept quiet while they ate.

Clovermead swallowed the last bit of her fish and dropped the skeleton on the floor. Sorrel belched politely and licked his fingers. Clovermead turned to gaze steadily at her rescuer. He looked mild and sweet and harmless.

"What are you doing here?" asked Clovermead. "I didn't have time to ask you questions in the rush last night, and then you were sleeping and eating, and I didn't want to interrupt you, but I'd like to know how you happened to find us in the middle of the wilderness. I'm very grateful, you understand, but I'd still like to know what brought you after us."

"That is a long story," said Sorrel. "I do not know quite where to start."

"Snuff said he was hunting you," said Clovermead. Sorrel paused a second with his fingers in his mouth, then continued to clean them. "When he found us at Ladyrest. He said you were working for Chandlefort. I think that must be true. I heard you send Brown Barley there. What are you doing for them?"

Sorrel gave her a level, cautious look. "I chase prophecies," he said after a bit. "A dubious task, yes? You never can tell which foretelling will come true the day after tomorrow, and which will take a thousand years. And even if you know it is about the day after tomorrow, they are most inscrutable. 'A great empire will fall,' you are told before a mighty battle, but which great empire will fall is not elucidated. 'The man who has married his mother must be driven from the Horde and made blind,' the seers command, the Horde Chief assents, and then, *hoopla,* it is himself who by strange coincidence is the mother marrier. It is all tragic, fated, ironic, unhelpful. And as we say in the steppes, no seer ever made the future come more quickly. Miss Clovermead, do you know exactly why that bear-priest Snuff was chasing you and Mr. Wickward?"

"Father wouldn't tell me," Clovermead said. "He did something to make Mr. Snuff angry a long time ago, back in Linstock. That was why he fled to Timothy Vale. When Mr. Snuff found us again, chasing you, he wanted to get revenge on Father. We were able to chase him away"—she interrupted her story long enough to tell the details of the fight, with due emphasis given to her heroic feats of swordsmanship and to Goody Weft's adroit use of a frying pan—"but we had to run from the Vale before Snuff came back with reinforcements from Low Branding. We were still running when you and Mr. Snuff found us, but I guess we didn't run fast enough." Clovermead's brooch seemed very heavy against her neck. Her bear tooth was cool. She fancied it approved of her closemouthed suspicion of Sorrel.

"Is that so?" asked Sorrel softly. His eyes bored in on hers—and he blinked, shrugged his shoulders, and smiled. "Well and all, Miss Clovermead, I am sorry to have brought the ferocious Mr. Snuff upon your father's hideaway. Snuff's reputation in Chandlefort is very bad, very deadly. He is not a good man to have for an enemy. I wonder how your father got on his bad side?" Clovermead shrugged her shoulders just as the Tansyard had. He laughed. "You have grown a shell around your tongue, Miss Clovermead. Well, I am still talkative, and I will reward your silence with tales of derring-do. Chandlefort is indeed my employer since—for three years. I am a messenger boy for occasional and extraordinary purposes. Sometimes I am wanted to ride with words or papers or parcels, very swift, very inconspicuous. They also have Yellowjackets to do these things, but they are fight-fight boys, heavy and slow. I am Tansyard and we are the wind's children." Sorrel smiled ingenuously. "Besides, there may be spies among the Yellowjackets. So I am sent to carry most secret things. What I carry, what I do, I do not always know. That way is safer, yes?"

"Safer but frustrating," said Clovermead. "I'd peek at any letters I was carrying."

"Well and so, I will not recommend you to succeed me at my position," said Sorrel. "Curiosity killed the cattle, as we say in the Steppes. As Our Lady ordains matters, I cannot read. I think that is one reason I have my job. Anyway, Miss Clovermead, my latest assignment is to ride to Snowchapel. A rush-rush prophecy comes from the nuns in Queensmart, uncalled for and dumbfounding. What exactly it says, I do not know, but they whisper around Chandlefort that a long-lost stolen something was not destroyed after all and can be found again. What is stolen? Who has stolen it? In Chandlefort everyone is strangely pursy-lipped. My curiosity is frustrated. I wonder, has your father perhaps told you something of this subject?"

Clovermead blinked her eyes most innocently. "Father was very uncommunicative. I blame him profoundly for my unconscionable ignorance."

"He most assuredly should be censured," Sorrel agreed solemnly. "Well-a-day, this prophecy flummoxes and perplexes. If this missing something still exists, where is it? How can it be found? The nuns of Queensmart say they cannot help us, they have done quite enough already. They advise Lady Cindertallow to seek out others of Our Lady's Vision Meres. So messengers are sent out, quiet as can be. Snowchapel is the farthest of the Meres from Chandlefort, but its reputation is the best. It is a great compliment to his horsemanship that Sorrel the Tansyard is told to fly on the Snowchapel route—but carefully, so as not to attract attention.

"I go north. It is an unsettling journey. Bears follow me and I begin to suspect that Low Branding knows something of our news. I become fearful of being eaten one fine night. I ride Brown Barley very hard so as to escape my four-footed followers—and it is with great relief that I take a few days' rest to teach a little girl sword fighting on a hillside pleasantly free of any animals larger than a sheep. It is a lovely interlude, attention avoiding, and a respite I need after a month on the road. Or so I tell myself. Perhaps I am a little irresponsible. My superiors have accused me of this flaw before." Sorrel's face turned pink.

"I don't see that I'd be a worse messenger than you," said Clovermead. "At least I'd get things to where they were supposed to go on time. Better to have your mail read than not delivered, I say."

"You saw what passed with Sister Rowan," Sorrel continued hastily. "I go most briskly on to Snowchapel and deliver my message. I expect to be given papers to take back to Chandlefort, but the Abbess comes back to me with a cry when she has looked in the Pool. She tells me, 'The Innkeeper at Ladyrest is pursued by a bear-priest from Low Branding. You must hurry, Sorrel, to try to rescue him and his daughter—they have fled south. You must bring them back to Chandlefort.'"

Sorrel coughed and looked straight into Clovermead's eyes. "The Abbess says, 'If you must choose between father and daughter, save the daughter. Ask her and she will show you the reason.' So off I rush and spend many long days—I will pass quickly over a tedious story of a miserably cold Tansyard struggling through endless blizzards. I finally find your trail north of the Tansy Pike, and then at the crossroads I see horsemen's tracks coming north from Low Branding. I shiver with fear, I see you and they have loop-the-looped toward High Branding and back, and I follow you all most carefully on the Chandlefort road. The ambushers do not expect any lone, crazy-bold Tansyard to follow them, so I am soon in sight of the Low Branding brigands and lurk unseen quite close to them. Then at last they approach the sleeping Wickwards, I make my hasty skiing plans, and I throw most wonderfully accurately daggers and stones when their attack begins. I try to save both of you, but it cannot be done. So, you are rescued and your father is not. Miss Clovermead, why should the Abbess say to rescue you first? I do not think you have been forthright with me." Now there was a trace of anger in his face. "There is something you should reveal."

"I hate prophecy," said Clovermead. "Father told me not to say anything. He had something that came from Chandlefort, and he gave it to me for safekeeping." She reached under her sweater, untied the leather cord, and held the brooch out toward Sorrel. She hid the tooth in her hand. "I suppose the Abbess meant I should show you this." *Now it will come out,* she told herself. *Sorrel must know about the Cindertallow Ruby. He'll look at this brooch and he'll know Waxmelt stole both the brooch and the Ruby from the Treasure Room.*

Sorrel reached out trembling fingers. He stroked the bee, the flames, the sword. He looked at Clovermead with astonishment. "Lady Above," he said in wonder. "I think I begin to understand. No, no, it cannot be. I am wrong. I must be wrong." He slapped his forehead. "That would be just like a prophecy—circuitous and unlikely."

"What are you talking about?" asked Clovermead.

"I do not think I should tell you," said Sorrel after a long minute.

Of course you don't, Clovermead thought sourly to herself. *No one will ever tell me just what is going on! No one,* she repeated bleakly.

"I may be wrong," Sorrel continued slowly. "Others

should decide. You and that brooch must go to Chandlefort."

"Must?" Clovermead lifted an eyebrow. "I don't want to go. Father said I should avoid both Low Branding and Chandlefort. He said Chandlefort was better than Low Branding, but he didn't make either place sound appealing."

"Ah and so," said Sorrel. He blinked rapidly, and his dagger was in his hand. "I am somewhat larger than you, Miss Clovermead, and I did not teach to you all I know of sword fighting."

Clovermead wished her father and Goody Weft were there to defend her. She was afraid of Sorrel, she was angry, and the tooth spoke to her. *I know how to deal with that jackanapes,* it said. *Let me speak in you.*

It will all turn out for the best, an old white bear reassured her, but Clovermead would not listen to her foolish counsel. *Speak away,* said Clovermead inwardly to the tooth. She smiled as blood-thoughts entered into her and her fear drained away. *The Tansyard is presumptuous, isn't he? Trying to frighten me. Show me how to be powerful, tooth.*

Clovermead roared. The sound boomed through the empty mill. Sorrel turned white and his hand shook till the dagger fell to the floor. When he had picked it up again, the tooth lay revealed in Clovermead's hand.

"I have this," said Clovermead. "You saw what I did with it last night?"

"I thought you had dropped it. I think it would be better if you had. Bear-priest gear is vile, Miss Clovermead. It fouls you to use it." Sorrel looked at her mouth and her grinning teeth and Clovermead saw that *he* was afraid now. "Miss Clovermead, did you have fangs a second ago?"

"Perhaps." Clovermead spread her lips savagely wide and bared her teeth. "If you're in a rush to return to Chandlefort, I won't detain you. But I prefer not to accompany you, Sorrel."

Sorrel scratched his head and rose slowly to his feet. He showed his open palms to Clovermead and paced backward and forward a few times in the small room, carefully distant from Clovermead and her waiting, hungry tooth.

He is a lovely morsel, said the tooth. *A nice plump prey, full of blood.*

"And yet," Sorrel said thoughtfully to Clovermead, "I do not think Lady Cindertallow will be happy when I confess to her that I have muffed up prophetic commands. She will think worse of all Tansyards if I fail, speak slightingly of their abilities, never hire any further steppe lads down on their luck, suggest to every lordling in the land that Tansyards are an idle, shiftless lot. I owe it to my people to bring you to the Rose Walls."

"Go away," said Clovermead.

"That is a harder command to enforce," Sorrel said. "Unless you want to kill me."

"You ran from a bear in the mountains near Snowchapel."

"So I did," said Sorrel. "I had stopped in a cave to rest, and a bear woke from its sleep and came out. Most naturally, I ran. How do you know?"

"I saw you in a dream at Ladyrest. Through the bear's eyes. You ran like a rabbit." Clovermead laughed.

"I was the usual coward," said Sorrel. "Still, I will not go. I repeat, to make me go you must kill me."

You would be safer with him dead, said the tooth. *He looks delicious.*

Clovermead sweated and trembled. "The tooth wants me to kill you. I don't want to. I like you, Sorrel, when you aren't pulling a knife on me and scaring me half to death. I just don't want to go to Chandlefort. Please, go away before the tooth bites you."

Sorrel made the crescent sign. His eyes were wide. "The *tooth* wants to kill me? Miss Clovermead, I entreat you in Our Lady's name to rid yourself of that thing." Clovermead shook her head and the tooth howled its joy. Sorrel retreated a step from her, then stood his ground, his eyes fixed on the tooth. "I do not think your bear-magic is all powerful, Miss Clovermead. It occurs to me, you cannot use it while you sleep. I am thinking of the possibility of sneaking up one fine dark hour and—*thunk!*—rendering you unconscious. Then I would truss you up and bury that tooth. The possibility seems most attractive."

"I can ski faster than you," said Clovermead. "You'd never catch up to me."

"I learn most swiftly," Sorrel replied. "Besides, you would not run that fast. Life is full of unfortunate coincidences, and as you speedily fled doubtless you would come across Mr. Snuff again. Then where would you be?" He wiped sweat from his forehead, but more sprang up. "Miss Clovermead, a compromise occurs to me. I could accompany you awhile southward and swear to Our Lady that while we traveled, I would not harm you or hinder you or make any effort to take you captive to Chandlefort."

"Or I could kill you now," said Clovermead. She could. She could. All she had to do was call on the tooth.

Do it, the tooth urged. *Do it now.*

"Then, kill me," said Sorrel. "I will not run from you." He stood and waited.

Hungrily Clovermead ran her tongue across her teeth. Her bear tooth throbbed in her hand. For a moment the world was red. She saw Sorrel bleeding before her, saw herself lean in to bite and crunch—

Dear Lady, no! Clovermead made a convulsive crescent over her sweater and prayed for the Light. She gasped out her thanks as the dark, murderous desires slowly receded from her. She put the cord around her neck again and thrust the tooth back into her shirt. Her heart was hammering. "Swear what you said earlier. Come along with me till we're two days south of Chandlefort. Then you leave me free to go and you head back to Chandlefort. Is that a deal?"

"To this I swear," said Sorrel. "It is not a very good deal, but I think it is better than none. We are travel companions?"

"We are," said Clovermead. She stood up and firmly shook his hand.

He is so plump and full of blood, said her tooth.

Chapter Ten

HORSE THIEVERY

CLOVERMEAD WRAPPED THE ROASTED FISH IN BURLAP bags Sorrel found in a corner of the mill, and slipped the bags over her shoulder. Sorrel put his backpack on, crept furtively out of the water mill, and hailed Clovermead outside. They were alone in an austere, snow-draped land. Their tracks had been erased by the night's snow. Endless matchstick-slender trees pierced the rolling white hills, save along the meandering curve of the stream. The sky was pale blue, cloudless, and crystal clear.

They skied south through the remainder of the short day, skimming away from the stream. Swathes of frozen grass poking through the snow became more common and trees more infrequent. Where wind had blown away the snow, a half-parched, sandy soil was revealed. What snowmelt there was ran over the rejecting earth toward the steep ravines and etched them deeper still. Glaring sunlight reflected from the snow.

"Look at the sky and trees, Sorrel," said Clovermead. "Don't look at the snow."

"Why not?"

"You'll go snow-blind if you look at sunlit snow too

long. All that whiteness is hard on the eyes. You won't be able to see for hours. Maybe not for days."

"You possess the wisdom of the northlands," said Sorrel. "In the Cyan Cross Horde we spent our winters in the south Steppe. There it was cool, but there was no snow. Now I know the wisdom of my ancestors, who ordained that the hordes always avoid this terrible season. Why did Our Lady make snow?"

"Winter is part of the natural balance," said Clovermead. "The earth rests beneath a blanket of snow. Barns feel useful when they can keep snow away from horses and sheep and chickens." She knelt and scooped up a snowball while Sorrel watched her uncomprehendingly. Her eyes were alight with mischief as she hurled the snowball at Sorrel. The snow splattered over his chest and under his tatterdemalion shirt, and he yelped with cold and shock. "Also, it's fun. Catch me if you can!" Giggling, she fled as the satisfyingly outraged Tansyard chased after her, pitching snowballs as he went. He had learned to ski quite well, and he surprised Clovermead by staying even with her. They ran for half a mile before Sorrel was able to paste her back with a well-thrown snowball.

Clovermead slewed around and raised her hands. "I surrender! You have won the combat of the snow! Please don't hurt me! I'm a small and weak child." She batted her eyes at the Tansyard.

"I have never heard such nonsense in my life," Sorrel grumbled, but he let the snowball in his hand drop to the ground. Then he grinned. "You really have played this way? It must be most delightful."

"It is very most delightful," Clovermead assured him. While they skied on, she regaled him with the epic saga of the snow fort she had built two winters before and how she had single-handedly defeated the Merrin boys in snow warfare. The story was almost true, if you didn't count the fact that Sweetroot had been in the fort with her or that Card Merrin had turned traitor at the last minute and started lobbing snowballs at his brothers. She had rewarded him with a kiss, which was a mistake because he had started to be soft on her afterward.

Then they continued in silence. The few farmhouses they passed were clustered along the occasional streams through the plateau. The farms were ramshackle affairs, half sod and half timber, with small, feebly irrigated stream-valley gardens. What wealth these farmers had was in the shaggy ponies and gaunt cattle that paced moodily in their split-rail corrals.

Cowherds armed with spears stood sentry at the corners of their farms. Clovermead and Sorrel kept out of their sight as they wended south. Clovermead had the impression that if soldiers should attack these farms, the inhabitants would hide with their precious animals in some nearby ravine and let their flimsy houses burn.

"They seem like Tansyards," she said to Sorrel. "They look like they'd rather live on horseback than in these huts."

Sorrel nodded. "Most astute you are, Clovermead. I have spent a night or two here, while traveling, and I have listened to their tales. These cow catchers are descended from Tansyard mercenaries who fought for Chandlefort, before the Empire came. As payment for their service to her, the tenth Lady Cindertallow settled them here on the north fringes of the Salt Heath, where there is some water. They are strange to me—Sweet Lady, Tansyards who farm! On the Steppes it is unthinkable. But they are kin. I can talk with them, though we must speak slowly to one another. They left the Steppes two hundred years ago and their language has changed. Their grammar is very odd."

"Like pilgrims from the Thirty Towns," said Clovermead. "I can hardly understand some of them. Are these cousins of yours still loyal to Chandlefort?"

"More or less," said Sorrel. "They say they are, but they do not pay the taxes they owe to the Lady Cindertallow. They are most lackadaisical subjects."

They spent the night in a ruined farmhouse. Its back wall had been smashed in, but it kept the worst of the night wind away from them. Sorrel lit a small fire from stray pieces of timber, and Clovermead reheated a fish for dinner.

"I hadn't realized how peaceful Timothy Vale was," said Clovermead after she had finished her meal. "Valemen don't carry weapons with them. They aren't foolish—the men drill with their axes and bows in case soldiers should come north one day. But no one really thinks the soldiers will come. Everybody I've seen here in Linstock seems to carry a weapon. I knew there was war down here, but I somehow thought that was just soldiers fighting one another. It isn't. Everyone's fighting."

"You are very lucky up in Timothy Vale," said Sorrel. "I envy you your years there. I am sorry you had to leave."

"And the Tansy Steppes? What are they like?"

"We say that before she left for the sky, the Tansy

Steppes were Our Lady's last resting place on Earth. It is a blessed land and we are blessed who may roam its leagues." Sorrel stared into the fire and frowned. "It is not as blessed as it used to be." He lapsed into silence then, and Clovermead shrank from asking him any more questions about his home.

Early next afternoon they came through a patch of woods to the back of a barn. One hundred feet away a cowherd walked idly back and forth, whistling a lugubrious tune and tossing pebbles at a tree. Soft neighing drifted out of the barn.

Sorrel's eyes shone. "An undefended barn," he said gleefully. "Oh, it is too much of a temptation. The horse you do not guard becomes my horse, as we say on the Steppes. Surely they are Tansyard enough to know that?"

"Sorrel," Clovermead said sternly, "are you contemplating larceny? From poor defenseless farmers?"

"It is much safer to steal from the defenseless than from the defended," Sorrel pointed out with mild logic. "Also, they owe taxes to Chandlefort. And I have grown tired of this slide-slide-sliding, Clovermead. I am not a Valeman, whose feet take naturally to skis. My toes long for stirrups. My calves tingle to press horseflesh."

"These reasons are specious," Clovermead declared. "And you may keep your tingling calves to yourself, thank you very much. Sorrel, my father was right when he said that Tansyards were natural horse thieves." *My father the thief,* she thought to herself, and half her resistance broke down at once.

"Calumny, Clovermead," Sorrel said in an elaborately shocked tone of voice. "The truth is, our neighbors are unusually careless of their property. Many horses wander onto the steppes. How can we tell which horse belongs to which man? All we know is that there are abandoned horses. It is disinterested kindness to rescue a horse from abandonment. We Tansyards are a kindly people." A shadow of a smile flickered across his face. "I feel sorely my recent lack of opportunities to bestow benevolence."

"Oh, dear," said Clovermead. "Sorrel, this is wrong."

"Are your legs tired?"

"Yes. But it doesn't matter. Or—tell me, is thievery adventurous?"

"It is a most profound and dangerous thrill," Sorrel solemnly assured her. "It is the greatest and noblest excitement."

"Oh," said Clovermead longingly. "Oh, my. Have you ever stolen anything yourself?"

"Two or three times," said Sorrel. "For a young man I am very kind to poor lonely horses, my father said."

"Then, let's do it!" Clovermead grinned suddenly. "It isn't temple robbery, but it sounds almost as exciting. Though I do feel awful taking something from these poor people. Sorrel, leave them this." She took a silver shilling from her stockings and gave it to Sorrel. "They deserve some recompense."

Sorrel blinked at Clovermead. "I do not think you have quite grasped the point of thievery," he said delicately. "Traditionally, one does not pay for what one has stolen."

"I am not a robber," said Clovermead. "I'll howl and I'll scream and I'll yell 'Stop, thief!' if we don't pay." *I'll be better than Daddy was,* she thought. *I won't be a thief like him.* "Anyway, isn't the chance to steal worth the money?"

"Ye-es," Sorrel admitted, "but . . ." He looked at Clovermead's implacable gaze and sighed. He took her shilling and rolled his eyes. "Never mind, Clovermead, it is not worth the argument. I will leave the shilling behind. Walk to the south end of the field, and I will meet you under the elm tree there."

"All right," said Clovermead—and she was talking to no one. Sorrel had disappeared.

Clovermead scampered cautiously behind the first line of trees, took off her skis, and hunkered down by the elm. From there she could see the farmhouse itself, where another farmer was drawing water from his well. Nearer, the barn door creaked back and forth and a shadow flitted inside. A horse neighed briefly, then went silent. The barn was quiet for a long five minutes. Clovermead chewed her fingernails.

A large black stallion, saddled and reined, ambled out the barn door. He hardly seemed to know he was moving. Sorrel crouched on the stallion's right side, invisible to both the cowherd and the farmhouse. His left hand crept a little over the stallion's mane and guided him with a tug on the reins.

The farmer looked up, saw the stallion out of the barn, and cursed. He shouted at the cowherd, who came out of his whistling trance a moment later and called to the horse. The stallion tried to turn toward his master, but Sorrel pulled him back. He pressed the horse's flanks, and the beast began to trot toward Clovermead.

The cowherd began to run and the farmer yelled back at the farm. Sorrel vaulted onto the horse's back and spurred him hard. As the horse galloped toward her

Clovermead saw half a dozen men boil out of the house. She dashed out from her hiding place and ran as fast as she could toward Sorrel.

"Whoa, Shilling," Sorrel cried out to his newly named acquisition. The stallion came to a sudden halt. Clovermead scrambled up behind Sorrel and gripped his waist in her arms. "No more draft work for you, Shilling," Sorrel exulted. "I will show you the open road." He spurred Shilling with his heels, and the horse galloped south into the woods.

Clovermead looked behind her. Farmers with rakes and pikes chased after them. One farmer dashed into the barn and came out on a black colt, galloping after them. Another fumbled with a rusty crossbow.

"They're coming after us, Sorrel! Can we go faster?"

"Shilling was the fastest horse in the barn," Sorrel said cheerfully. "We have nothing to worry about."

A crossbow bolt zinged over their heads. Clovermead whimpered and clutched tight to Sorrel's waist.

"Oh, dear," Sorrel said. "Clearly he did not see that shilling. The beast is paid for!" he yelled back. Their pursuer kept on coming. "My father always said I was impetuous. Clovermead, please do not hold me so tight. You are hurting me. Yah, Shilling!"

More farmers chased after them, but soon only the first remained in sight. Hunched over the neck of his black colt, he tailed them relentlessly through the scrubby forest. Freed from a plough at last, Shilling stretched his legs and galloped from sheer joy. The snow was thin enough here that his hooves could punch through and catch on the cold ground. He neighed and raced with all his might—and the pursuing farmer's colt kept pace with him. After a while he began to inch closer to them.

"He's gaining," said Clovermead. "I have an awful feeling that Shilling was the second-fastest horse in the barn. He's energetic, but that other horse is marvelous steady." Another crossbow bolt sliced through the air.

"It is an old Tansyard skill to ride and shoot at the same time," said Sorrel ruefully. "They have forgotten less of Tansyard ways than I thought. At least he cannot shoot accurately. We must thank Our Lady for small blessings, eh?"

A third bolt whipped close overhead. "Small and getting smaller," said Clovermead. "Can we stop, give Shilling back, and let them keep the silver shilling for their trouble? We could say that we are very sorry."

"There are other Tansyard customs, about how to deal with captured horse thieves. I would not like to see if they also have been preserved. We must ride faster, Clovermead."

"Sorrel, there must be something we can do to get out of this mess." Sorrel shrugged grimly and spurred Shilling harder.

I know a way, the tooth whispered. *Give me horse blood. Give me boy blood. I am power for the taking. If you choose to use me.*

I won't, Clovermead told the tooth. *I don't want to grow fangs. I don't want to be turned into a killer.*

Do you think I gave you the urge to kill, little girl? All I've done is show you your true self. You are destined for strength and power. Haven't you always dreamed of that? Take up the challenge, Clovermead.

A bolt sliced the edge of Sorrel's jerkin. He hissed with pain, and red droplets whipped out into the wind. He kicked Shilling again, but the horse could go no faster.

What a waste of blood, said the tooth.

He's not yours, Clovermead thought fiercely. *I won't let you touch him.* But her stomach squirmed as she imagined the different ways Tansyards might deal with horse thieves, and as the *clip-clop* of their pursuer drew closer still, she loosed one arm from Sorrel's waist and took out the bear tooth from her vest. It was hot and sharp and throbbed eagerly as she held it in her palm. Clovermead squeezed it tighter and her lips curled away from her teeth. Her teeth stretched at her gums. Her nails thickened. She was hungry and she bit the air. Sorrel smelled like roast lamb, his bleeding arm like divine nectar.

Not him! Clovermead repeated. With all her power she clamped her mouth shut. Her teeth shrank to human size. She pressed the bear-tooth against her thumb. *Take my blood, monster,* she whispered. *I'll use up myself if I have to. He lives.*

The tooth bit deep into Clovermead. She gasped as the sudden, burning hunger devoured her. She groaned with the delicious taste of her own blood. Pinkness trickled into the tooth.

Pathetic, said the tooth. *What sort of weakling bites herself?*

I do, thought Clovermead. *Never mind the name-calling. Bring me . . . bring me Boulderbash, that huge bear from the valley. I want her to scare away that farmer. Bring her to me.*

I need more blood, said the tooth, and it reached deeper into Clovermead's flesh. She gasped but let it bite. She bit, she was bitten, and she felt a strange and horrible mixture of pleasure and pain. She called for Boulderbash.

Clovermead felt weak and closed her eyes. She gripped Sorrel even more tightly with her free arm to keep from falling off Shilling. In the darkness of her skull Lord Ursus appeared, large as a mountain. He growled, low and terrible as an earthquake. Clovermead's bones danced to the rhythm of his roar.

Behind them the colt screamed. Clovermead tore her thumb from the tooth, let the fang fall back within her vest, and whirled around. White Boulderbash was there, half invisible against the snow, bounding in from the eastern woods with mouth agape. The farmer yelled his terror too and dropped his crossbow into the snow. The colt screamed again and fled westward into the plain.

Boulderbash growled contentedly and leapt forward to pace Shilling. Sorrel looked back once, blanched, and tightened his grip on Shilling's reins. The stallion nearly went into a frenzy, but Sorrel's strong hand kept him in line. He made the horse continue galloping.

"Clovermead," said Sorrel in a small, tight voice, "I think I see the bear who followed me to Timothy Vale."

"Her name is Boulderbash," said Clovermead. Her hand ached and she looked down to see an ugly scar stretching across the ball of her thumb. It was already old and long since mishealed. Swollen purple lines scored her flesh far beyond the scar. Her veins had broken from her thumb tip to her wrist.

Sorrel laughed high and fearful. "Ah, good, you are on a first-name basis. How marvelous. I am pleased to make your acquaintance, Boulderbash. Clovermead, can we get rid of dear Boulderbash now that she has served our purpose?"

He isn't very polite, said Boulderbash. *You'd think he'd be grateful.*

"He is grateful," said Clovermead. "He's just upset."

"To whom do you speak?" asked Sorrel.

"Boulderbash. I'm sorry, I didn't mean to confuse you. I'll talk to her in my head from now on."

"That would gratify me," Sorrel said, shuddering. "I wish I could say that you were mad, or I were mad. I do not like to imagine a conversational bear."

Yet we have lived with talking humans for a long time now, said Boulderbash. *I suppose we are a more tolerant species.* She huffed laughter. *Tell me, Clovermead, whom should I kill for you?*

You don't have to kill anyone, said Clovermead. *All I wanted was for you to give that man a scare. He was trying to kill us.*

Is that all? Boulderbash was incredulous. *Every human asks us to kill someone. Or to capture them so that they can do the killing themselves.* Boulderbash roared with disgust, and Shilling bucked in terror. Then she looked quizzically at Clovermead. *You really don't want me to kill anyone?*

Really, said Clovermead. *No one. You might rough up Lucifer Snuff a bit, but you don't have to kill him.*

I would bite that one's head off, said Boulderbash. *Uhrr. I think you are telling the truth. How extraordinary. Truly, I had come to think all humans were murderers. I had not thought it mattered if we bit a few of your kind. This is most upsetting news.* She loped on in silence a little more. *Are you the small human who made Nuthoarder and the others flee from Snuff's ambush?*

I am, Clovermead said proudly.

Hrrooom. You had a companion there?

My father.

I am sorry to hear that, said Boulderbash. *My own cub is . . .* She fell silent. *Never mind that. Snuff has sent word to the bear-priests that your father will be sacrificed to Lord Ursus.*

WHAT?!?

Snuff spoke to the bear-priests with the power of a tooth in him, and his words echoed through all Linstock. He did not care if we bears heard too. Your father will be sacrificed before the walls of Chandlefort. Can you do anything to free your parent, little cub? If so, I would advise you to do it soon.

I don't even know where he is. Has Snuff already taken him to Chandlefort?

Snuff has summoned the bears of Linstock to join him and his men. He is due east of here and heading south. Boulderbash grunted. *Your tooth has run out of blood. Good-bye, little cub. I hope you find your father in time.*

"No, wait," Clovermead called out loud, but it was too late. Boulderbash had already swerved and headed east, into dense forest. Shilling ran south alone.

"Praise Our Lady that we survived," said Sorrel. He was weak with relief, but he kept Shilling galloping, increasing the distance from the bear. "I never want to undergo that again. Clovermead, I do not like a great monster by my side and a witch-child behind me telling me she is chatting about the weather and cookery and Lady knows what. I do not wish to know the subject of the conversation. The different ways to nibble Tansyards, most likely."

"She said Snuff was going to kill Daddy," Clovermead said. "She said the bears of Linstock are coming to join Snuff, and he's going to sacrifice Daddy at Chandlefort."

"Most kind of her to inform you," Sorrel chattered fearfully. "Indeed, most solicitous. I am afraid there is nothing we can do. We are two and Snuff leads many, and we will say prayers to Our Lady for kind Mr. Wickward's soul. I am sorry, Clovermead, but I will not face an army of bears. I grieve for your loss."

"You needn't grieve yet," said Clovermead, suddenly full of anger and determination. "We're going to rescue him."

Sorrel giggled hysterically. "Please, do not joke."

"We're going to rescue him," Clovermead repeated.

"You are silly and stupid," said Sorrel. "If Snuff says your father will die, he is as good as dead. If you can, you should save your own life. Do not fritter away your safety in a futile attempt."

Put me to his throat, the tooth whispered to Clovermead. *Tell him to ride east or be slashed. Give me a drop of his blood to make him know you're serious. Make him know you're not silly, not stupid. Make him do what you want. Make him do what is right.*

Clovermead's fingers quivered to take the tooth out from her vest. She bit her lip and clung tight to Sorrel's ribs with both hands. The tooth laughed and roared.

"Not so tight, please," Sorrel complained. "I won't let you fall, Clovermead." Clovermead forced her hands farther apart. Viciously weak, they scrabbled at Sorrel as they loosened. "Ouch! Be careful."

"I'm sorry," Clovermead whispered. Hot tears burned along her cheeks. "Please, Sorrel. I'll go by myself if I have to, but please help me. Snuff's going to sacrifice him.

It sounds slow and painful and awful. Daddy told me to leave him behind, but I'm sure he didn't mean I should let him be tortured. He couldn't have meant that. And it doesn't matter what Daddy said, I can't just run and leave him to be butchered. He's given up everything to save me. I'd be a monster if I didn't do anything to try and save him." He was a thief and a liar, but he was still her father.

"But he did mean to save you," Sorrel said more gently. "Clovermead, think what it will do to him if he discovers his sacrifice was in vain."

"I know it'd be terrible," said Clovermead miserably. "He'd feel hot and cold and like crying, and not caring whether or not he died. Same as I do now."

"Ah? You are not just playing at being the heroine? Perhaps you are playacting a tale of derring-do, Clovermead. Perhaps this is a fancy from your books?"

"Maybe it is," said Clovermead. "I don't know. It isn't any sort of fun and it doesn't feel like an adventure. I feel miserable. I feel like I have to try to rescue Daddy, and I feel like I don't have any choice. Some ways, I'd rather ride off to Queensmart and tell myself he was going to come join me someday and that Snuff was just an evil dream. I can't.

"And also"—this was the hardest to say—"I didn't know about this brooch, or that Daddy knew Snuff, or anything, till after you'd left Ladyrest. Then when I thought about it, I realized I don't know much of anything about Father. And he won't tell me anything either. I've been so angry at him. I always trusted him. He was a rock, and I could be silly and wild because he was a rock. If I went into Gaffer Bolts' land to tickle his sheep, or I pulled Card Merrin's hair, or I broke a pot, or, you know, slipped into a pilgrim's room, I could always come back to him. He might be stern and he might punish me, but he was always there and I knew I could count on him. Now if I try to lean on him, there's nothing there. And I know Daddy loves me, but still I feel so angry at him. The anger comes and goes, and when it's in me, I feel like I could let him die.

"I think—I'm afraid—if I don't even try to rescue Father, if I just let him die, it'll just be because I'm so angry with him, and that would be about the lowest thing I could do. Don't you think? If you were me, wouldn't you still try to rescue your father, Sorrel?"

"A fascinating and terrible question," said the Tansyard. "One to answer another day." He fell silent again. "I will help you," he said abruptly. "I will be a fool and I will dare even an army of bears." He laughed sourly. "How quickly my service to Chandlefort disintegrates! I am a bad servant to Lady Cindertallow."

"You aren't the first bad one she's had," said Clovermead. She slumped and felt exhausted. "Turn east. Boulderbash said we'd find Snuff in that direction, heading south."

Sorrel turned Shilling's head away from the setting sun.

Chapter Eleven

STEPPE TALES

SORREL AND CLOVERMEAD RODE DOWN FROM THE SALT Heath into a land of flat marshes, ponds, and the occasional low and cedar-covered hill. They saw a half dozen villages scattered among the ponds, each a cluster of high-roofed log cabins that perched on stilts in shallow water a careful twenty or thirty feet from the shore. Clovermead watched enviously as laughing children skated on the iced-over ponds near the cabins. Farther out brawny men with iron-spiked clubs skated sentry around their villages. Sorrel kept a healthy distance from the villages and rode Shilling along the snow-capped crests of the hills, looking from each summit for signs of Snuff's passage.

They found the wake of Snuff's horsemen at day's end. They had left a trough through the snow ten feet wide, smashed and dirtied by half a dozen horses. The horses had been galloping, and their hoofprints were far apart. Their trail seemed to Clovermead a filthy wound on the snow-clad world. It slashed south through open country, and to either side Clovermead saw the occasional tracks of foxes and rabbits. Their footprints never crossed the muddy furrow. No animal walked where Snuff had ridden.

They followed the trail south the next four days past more iced-over ponds and distant villages and over hills that lengthened into long ridges. The ridges grew higher and higher, till they became palisades that heaved toward the sky. Full-grown and stately cedars and oaks crowded thickly on every height. Far away Clovermead heard wolves howling. Dark, snow-laden clouds of the north grew closer and more huge. The nights were dark; the moon was gone.

On the fourth night the new moon rose in the sky, a hair-thin sliver that lit the snow to gleaming silver. The stars shone in a jet black sky, and the air was bitter cold. At the edge of a pond Sorrel and Clovermead huddled around their fire. Sorrel's lips were frozen purple, but Clovermead was quite comfortable. She had grown a light pelt of fur underneath her clothes to keep her warm. It seemed very natural to her, more familiar than her skin. They heated a perch in the flames. Clovermead bolted her portion, wishing it were still raw.

By the firelight Sorrel touched Clovermead's golden tresses with his finger. "They are so very pretty," he said musingly. "But they make you conspicuous, Clovermead. If we are Snuff hunting, it occurs to me that we ought to take countermeasures and disguise you."

Clovermead curled her fingers through her hair. "How?"

"We must cut off your hair," said Sorrel.

"My hair?" Clovermead let her claws grow long. She sliced her paw through her locks and the hair whispered off. Twenty inches of golden hair suddenly lay in her palm, and she snarled with joy at the power of the stroke. "What else, Sorrel?" asked Clovermead.

"Dear Lady, help me," Sorrel whispered. His eyes were round and large, like prey. His teeth chattered and his Adam's apple bobbed up and down in his throat. Clovermead longed to catch it in her teeth and bite down. "Clovermead, what is happening to you?"

"I'm growing up," Clovermead said. She growled and flung the hank of yellow hair into the fire. It flared up, charred, and was gone. The sudden stench of her locks wafted into her nostrils, and as they burned Clovermead could smell summer days and Goody Weft doing the laundry and herself sneaking outside to climb a tree and Waxmelt chopping wood at Ladyrest. She smelled her past blacken, and suddenly she was crying, her body racking with sobs. Her fur vanished and she was left cold and shivering. She could not move and was limp as Sorrel awkwardly put his arms around her. She buried her face in his shoulder and bawled till no more tears could come. His arms warmed her.

"I'm sorry," Clovermead gulped. "I'm not usually like this. I'm brave and resourceful and bold. I'm not a weeper."

"Nor am I usually scared out of my skin," said Sorrel. "You terrify me, Clovermead. Even crying and huddling. You are not just talking to bears, no? You have a bear nose and bear claws when you want them?"

"I didn't want them," Clovermead whispered. "They just came to me."

"Oh, dear," said Sorrel. "Will more bearish body bits just come to you? Will I wake one morning and find no Clovermead at all by me, but just a bear?"

"No!" cried Clovermead. But the bear tooth laughed. "Maybe. Oh, Sorrel, I don't know. I'm scared. I think I want a little bit to be a bear. I think I want it more the longer I have the tooth. The tooth wants . . ." she fell silent.

"It desires that you should be a bear?"

Clovermead nodded.

"Miss Clovermead, perhaps this would be a good time to throw away your tooth." Sorrel cleared his throat. "While you still can. We told stories of such transformations on the Steppes. It is easy to become an animal. It is harder to regain human form."

Clovermead reached for the tooth. It would be easy. She could bash a hole in the ice and drop the tooth down into the waters below. She would ride away and leave the fur and fangs and claws behind.

How will you rescue your daddy without me? asked the tooth. *You can't, little girl. Think about that.* And then it said: *The little girl weeps. The bear will never cry. Do you want to weep all your life?*

No, thought Clovermead. *Yes,* thought Clovermead. *No,* thought Clovermead. *I don't mind being a bear for ever and ever, just so I never cry again.*

"I have to keep it," Clovermead said to Sorrel. "Just a little bit longer. I'll get rid of it when we've freed Father."

Sorrel gazed for a long minute at Clovermead. She tried to meet his gaze, but she could not. She softly growled her discomfort.

"I would not take the risk myself," Sorrel said at last. "I would try to rescue my father, yes, but without the tooth." Clovermead said nothing and Sorrel shook his head. "I have told you what I think. Well and so. Clovermead, you are still familiar, chop-shanked and all. I think we must disguise you further. Please wait here." Clovermead stared moodily into the fire while Sorrel walked into the darkness. Her tears dried on her cheeks. She licked her tongue against her teeth, and her claws clacked against the ground.

After fifteen minutes Sorrel came back with a handful of mossy bark, dark clay, and roots. "Hair and skin dye," he explained. "I will get a pot of water and bring it to a boil. We often do this on the Steppes, on raids, to camouflage ourselves against the grass, and then to leap up and whoop, and shock our enemies. No one will know you when I am done."

Sorrel blended the ingredients in a small pot of water, then stirred and heated them. When the mixture was ready, he gently bent Clovermead's head upside down and lowered her hair into the pot. His fingers teased out and rubbed stain on each strand, and then on her face and hands.

Clovermead leaned over the pond's still waters and looked wonderingly at a strange boy reflected in the firelight. His hair was black and his skin had been tanned in a ferocious sun. Only his sky blue eyes remained from the familiar girl she had seen in Ladyrest's mirrors.

"You are very like a boy of the Green Spike Horde," said Sorrel. "Sometimes we meet them in winter, in the southern Steppes. They sing that their ancestors came from the far south, beyond the Loamrest valley and the Astrantian Sands, from a land of lions and hideous horned beasts and striped horses. You can remember that? That you are of the Green Spikes?"

"A boy of the Green Spike Horde," Clovermead repeated. "I've always wanted to wander in disguise. Sir Auroche in the *Heptameron* disguised himself as a blind beggar and was very convincing in the role until he triumphed at the archery contest of the Bailiff of Silkweavery, which, as the Bailiff said, 'Hathe notte synce there were bowes and Bailiffes / Beene ever wonne by eyelesse caitiffes.' Do you think no one will recognize me?"

"So long as you do not grow fur," said Sorrel. "Nor claws."

The bear tooth howled with laughter. "Don't worry, Sorrel," Clovermead said with a chuckle. "I won't show my teeth till the time is right." Sorrel made the crescent sign against her and Clovermead grinned at him. She settled down again by the fire and Sorrel sat down by her—not too near. Clovermead looked to the southeast. "Why did you leave the Steppes, Sorrel?"

"I had no choice," said Sorrel. He swallowed the last of his fish.

"Did the Cyan Cross Horde exile you?"

"This is not your business," Sorrel said.

"I'm always curious, and nothing ever is my business. Father and Goody Weft said that to me all the time. Sorrel, I wasn't asking just to be nosy. I want to know why—why you work for Chandlefort. And why you're willing to stop working for them to help me find my father. And why you're scared all the time, but not scared enough to leave me. I'm terrified of me, of the tooth, but you don't go. Why?"

Sorrel smiled faintly. "Our Lady's Judgment must be like this. She will ask me, 'Why, why, why? Justify your life, young Tansyard,' or perhaps old Tansyard if I am lucky. I will have to answer her. But you?"

"Me you don't have to answer," said Clovermead. "Whatever the reason, I'm awfully glad you don't run and leave me alone."

"I ran before," said Sorrel. He looked in the fire at nothing. "From the soldiers of Low Branding. From the bear-priests. From the bears."

"What happened?" asked Clovermead quietly.

Sorrel looked at Clovermead long and steady. His eyes glittered with sorrow. "Much."

"Tell me," said Clovermead. Around them the snow began to fall again.

Sorrel laughed unsteadily. "If you wish, Clovermead. I will tell you of the destruction of the Cyan Cross Horde."

"When I was a boy, too young to ride alone, there were only two places in the world for me. The world itself was much larger—there were mountains and hills and moors on all sides of the Steppes and on the Steppes themselves the endless plains and rivers—but there were only two places. One was holy Bryony Hill. The other was Barleymill, where demons dwelled.

"The Cyan Cross Horde would spend the winter in some southern stretch of land, camped under the Farry Heights. Then we would trade with merchants come from the Loamrest River towns. Summer we spent lazing along the slopes of the Reliquaries, where Ryebrew merchants would come to engage us in other buyings and sellings. Spring and fall we spent in constant motion in flat land wider than the sky, riding and hunting and joyfully whooping to be free men and women in Our Lady's Garden. We were the Cyan Cross Horde, seven hundred fifty families strong, the proudest Horde upon the Steppes. Gray Bar and Green Star and Red Diamond and White Crescent and Yellow Square each thought itself the proudest Horde, but they were incorrect. Cyan Cross had Bryony Hill.

The rest of the Steppes were not *places*. Grass grew tall one year and was burned in prairie fire the next. Poplars flourished, then were struck by lightning. Rivers flooded, their banks burst, and they set themselves down in new courses. Back and forth we wandered, and where we had been, where we were, where we would be, we did not exactly know. We did not care to know. In our forgetting, the Steppes were always new and doubly to be enjoyed for each surprising rediscovery.

"But Bryony Hill was ours. It lay on the western edge of the Steppes, due east of Low Branding, with only a small strip of grassland to separate it from the southern end of the Harrow Moors. It was a perfect hill—an even cone, the only hill in the world fashioned by Our Lady's own hand. No tree grew on Bryony Hill, just the long, lush grass. The first and last building ever built by Cyan Cross stood upon the summit. It was a temple, an amphitheater of white marble the Horde had bought and pilfered from Low Branding centuries ago and laid in the earth with their own hands. We would spend spring equinox and fall equinox at the white marble temple of Bryony Hill, to watch the sun by day and to watch the moon by night. We prayed to Our Lady to preserve for us fresh wind, healthy horses, and the Freedom of the Horde. We conducted songs and rites of which I should not speak. At dusk our Shaman-Mother would look into the clear blue pool in the center of the amphitheater and foretell the future of the Horde.

"Cyan Cross had fought against the other hordes for Bryony Hill ages ago, in the time of legends, and none ever took it from us. Then Queensmart had tried to lay claim to Bryony Hill and to all the Steppes. Cyan Cross gathered the Hordes for war, spearheaded the assault that slew four legions, and by our own hands and our own blood captured the Imperial banners. Cyan Cross still had those tattered, yellowed banners four generations later, when I was a child.

"Barleymill was the place where we Tansyards did *not* go. It nestled in the southwest corner of the Steppes, beneath the curve where the Farry Heights broke from the earth, strode farther south, and wheeled eastward to bound the south end of the Steppes. For centuries Barleymill had been reputed an evil place. Before the Empire came, when Ryebrew and Barleymill were Linstock trading posts, Barleymill men took Tansyard boys and girls and sold them as slaves to Low Branding. The Empire ended the slave trade, Our Lady be praised, but it brought terrible things to replace slaving. In the hills by Barleymill the delving miner men of Queensmart found a vein of *hwanka-velika*—what do you call it? Liquidburn, lungpoison, quicksilver, mercury—what magpie farm-dwellers use to refine silver ore into silver, for your jewels and coins and other glitter-trifles. The Empire sent prisoners, debtors, and poor fools who thought they were immortal into the mines to hack out quicksilver. Many went in, few came out alive. Their bodies were buried haphazard in the plains around Barleymill. The corpses stank of acid, and the poisoned grass did not grow above their graves and we shied away from the evil place.

"It was always a place of pain and death, and when the Empire grew feeble, it became a place that worshiped pain and death. A new religion sprang up there, a dreadful heresy. Its priests came from seaside Garum. They worshiped bears and they cursed Our Lady. Then little Queen Almargent came to the Imperial throne too soon, when her mother died of plague—a cradle-child, not even walking—and there followed many civil wars in the Empire. Those years we were busy raiding Ryebrew and into Linstock, and bringing home many farmers' steeds and cattle. When we looked again at Barleymill, the bear-priests ruled. They mined more mercury than ever and once more brought slaves to the city, from Linstock and the Thirty Towns and Selcouth. It was said they sacrificed some slaves to their bear-god. We would have erased these monsters from the Steppes, but already they were too strong. And they did not enslave Tansyards. So, grudgingly, we let them stay in peace, and we fled farther from the city's charnel stench.

"Those were the stories that I heard as a child. As I grew up new tales came to us. It was said that Barleymill and Low Branding had allied in war against distant Chandlefort, that the bear-priests marched in Linstock, that the claws of Lord Ursus stretched far. The Elders said to one another that this was a great evil, but at least the bear-priests were far from the Steppes. Perhaps they would come to a bad end somewhere else, as Our Lady willed it.

"Then three years ago, the day before the fall equinox, we came to Bryony Hill and found a score of strange soldiers camped between the slopes of the Hill and the Harrow Moors. They had not touched the Hill itself, for that would have been intolerable desecration, but they had come insultingly close to its slopes. Their stinking, square camp was a scab on the plains, an ugliness to mar Bryony Hill and ruin our equinox festivities. The young men of the Horde wanted to attack them at once. I myself would have ridden alone to their pickets and sent a spear sailing, for I was the youngest of the young men, scarcely tattooed with man's colors and eager to prove myself in battle. The Elders restrained us. 'It is always good to talk first,' they said. 'We can kill them later. There is no honor in slaying so small a band without a parley.' We young men yelled our frustration to the sky, but we obeyed our Elders.

"The Elders talked with the soldiers, then came back to tell us that the strangers were from Low Branding. They were infantrymen, slow and stolid, with no horses, who must have marched on foot all the way across the Harrow Moors. They apologized for coming so close to our sacred lands, but they had known no other place and time where they could be sure to find us. They had come to make us an offer. As Chandlefort had hired whole hordes eight generations before, now they wished to enlist as much of the Cyan Cross Horde as would serve in the cohorts of Low Branding. They would pay us well for a summer's service—they showed us a chest full of gold ingots that would be our advance payment.

"'I do not trust these soldiers,' Horde Chief Centaury said, scowling, to the gathered Horde. 'Their captain has a bear-priest by his side, whispering in his ear. The Barleymill men have no love for us. I think they use Low Branding to disguise their plots. I think they plan to play some trick on the Steppes when our fighting men are far away. Or perhaps they want to throw away our warriors' lives in some useless battle.'

"'Traders say Low Branding's war is weary and long,' Elder Weld said. He was a white-haired, toothless man who wore smooth leather breeches from Garum and a necklace of copper disks that hung low on his chest. He had gone traveling for years among farm folk when he was young, and he had acquired some of their taste for soft and shiny things. 'Perhaps they really need us? I think we are better than any farm-folk soldiers—they would be wise to hire us. We can buy more horses with the gold.'

"'We can steal what horses we desire,' the Horde Chief replied contemptuously. We all knew that he had little love for Elder Weld and his foreign ways. 'Gold is nothing. This is a noose for a rabbit. Are we foolish enough to enter it?'

"'We are strong,' Elder Weld said. 'If they try to betray us, we will kill them—for we are the Cyan Cross Horde, who gathered the Hordes and defeated four legions, and we are a match for any army in the world. If they are honest—well, I do not despise gold. Gold can be made into jewelry. Gold can buy dyed cloths. We will be the pride of the Steppes when we have earned those ingots with our mighty deeds.'

"Back and forth the argument went among all the men and women, and no agreement appeared. We warriors of the Cyan Cross professed disdain for farm-folk trinkets, but we dearly loved the way the ingots glinted. The history-singers said that Cyan Cross had once earned whole pounds of gold from Chandlefort—that was how we had built the temple on Bryony Hill. But to work for bear-priests? That would degrade the Horde. But to worry about danger from farm folk? That would also degrade the Horde. Elders and young, men and women, were all equally split. We wrangled till long after sunset.

"'Enough,' Horde Chief Centaury at last commanded. 'We cannot make the decision tonight and we do not need to. The Shaman-Mother looks in Bryony Pool at the equinox tomorrow, and Our Lady will grant her a vision to guide us in our wrangles. We will continue this debate the day after the equinox, with Our Lady's wisdom as our aid. Let us go to our tents now: We must wake early for the equinox rites, and we will commit disrespect to Our Lady if we say them yawning. But this decision I have made: Whether or not we take the gold, we will stay here long enough to purify the Hill of these outsiders' polluting presence. Some of you warriors, keep watch over the Low Branding soldiers.' He waved a hand in my direction. We drew lots for sentry duty. It fell out that my father, Dapple, drew picket duty, and I was sent back to my tent to sleep.

"I still slept in the family tent with my mother, Roan; my younger brother, Clary; and baby Mullein, my parents' only daughter and my mother's favorite. My older brother, Emlets, was already married, with a tent of his own and an infant son. I had my eyes on—well, any number of sweet beauties, but I would get no kisses from them till I had been blooded in battle. I did not entirely mind. I was young yet, and I confess that the prospect of kissing was still terrifying.

"I suffered bad dreams. Nightmares assaulted me of screaming and blood and roaring, and I tossed and turned. Bears trampled across the world and there was a greater roaring than ever, and I was no longer asleep, it was not a dream. There were screams throughout the camp, and flames, and the terrible growl of bears.

"I stumbled through the flap of the tent. The moon had set, but there was enough firelight to see by. There were soldiers everywhere, hellish horsemen in Low Branding livery, with burning brands to torch our tents and set our poor horses afire, and swords to slash at any man they saw, and at any woman or child. There were not twenty soldiers, but hundreds, thousands perhaps. They had been hiding—where? I have thought long about this. I think they lurked in the Harrow Moors. They would have ridden forth at sunset, reached us at moonset, and then the slaughter could begin. They must have killed every picket at once, for we heard no warning. My father must have died in the first minute of the assault.

"Bears raced among us, tearing, biting, mauling, scratching. They growled and roared, and ice ran through my blood. If not for the bears, I think we could have fought back. The Horde would have been hurt, grievously hurt, but we could have survived. The bears turned us from warriors into mewling cowards. I trembled and cried, and I could not grasp my spear and sword. I saw others likewise, shaking statues too terrified to fight. The bears displayed no mercy. They slew my friends before my eyes. They killed Emlets. At least my brother had a sword in his hand and killed one horseman before the bears butchered him.

"My mother, Roan, slapped my cheek with the flat of a blade and shook me roughly from my terror. She had Mullein in one arm, a dagger in the other, and Clary at her side. He blubbered as I did and clung to her leggings. 'Sorrel, follow me,' my mother shouted fiercely. Then she ducked and wove into the chaos, among the carnage, and I chased after her. I was a helpless boy, no warrior. I fled at my mother's heels.

"She took us east through the dying Horde. Other families fled, while bears and soldiers pursued us all. My family was lucky, not brave. The soldiers did not see us in the flickering patches of darkness between the raging fires, and the bears found other prey. We lived.

"Then we came to the outer lines and there was no escape. A further ring of horsemen waited around our camp. Other refugees ran for freedom and horsemen came to cut them down. Some of the Cyan Cross still had their steeds, but they were no help. The soldiers rode Phoenixians, and they could outpace even our steppe ponies. They killed and they killed, and I knew they meant to destroy all of the Cyan Cross Horde. It was slaughter for slaughter's sake.

"We had no choice—death behind us, death in front of us—we had to run. And we were lucky again. Some other family ran a second before us, and the horsemen near us bunched up by these first refugees. Only one laggard remained to keep the line.

"He saw us, of course. He raised his sword and galloped toward us. He thought we were easy prey. He was almost right. He thought I was the dangerous one and he charged me, but it was Mother, with Mullein in her arms, who leapt under his horse's belly and hamstrung the beast. I ducked his first swipe and then I did not need to worry. The horse collapsed, screaming, and the soldier fell. His leg was crushed underneath his steed.

"'Run!' Mother shouted, and indeed we ran. I was a fleet-footed rabbit, a dazzling coward, and I ate up the dark turf. Horsemen and bears came after us, but I did not turn to look, for fear they would catch up with me. Mother and Clary and Mullein fell behind—then I did turn. I thought to take Mullein in my arms. My mother howled and gestured to me to go. I think I should not have obeyed her, but I was afraid to die and I fled. Once more I turned my back on my family and I ran till I splashed into a stream. Then I stumbled upstream, hoping the water would hide my scent from the bears. At last I came to a wet thicket, girdled with thorns, and I embraced it as my only hope. I wriggled between the branches and felt their sharp tips score my arms and legs and body. Only when I was at the heart of the thicket did I cease my flight and look for my family.

"I heard no one nearby, only far roaring and crackling flames. I saw only darkness and the bonfire that had been the Cyan Cross Horde.

"Somehow in the red dawn I fell asleep. I woke at noon in the cool muck, terribly weak. Through my bars of branches I saw that I had not come very far at all, less than half a mile from the camp. My thicket was on a little rise of ground, so I could see all through the desolated campsite and up Bryony Hill. I expected there would be men beating the earth for me and the other refugees of the Cyan Cross Horde, but they did not bother. I think there were no other refugees but me and that the soldiers did not realize they had lost me.

"The soldiers had finished their killing and their looting. They sat among our dead and cooked themselves lunch and gambled with one another, with our paltry possessions as their stakes. I remember smelling roasted horse meat and how my mouth watered. The soldiers did not seem discommoded by the carnage around them.

"The bear-priests had chained together the few remaining of Cyan Cross—all women and children, a few dozen at most. They wailed, but the bear-priests only tied the chains tighter. I recognized the Shaman-Mother among them by her white robes. I looked for my family, but I could not make out faces at that distance. The bear-priests cracked the whip and their prisoners, their slaves, began to march toward Barleymill.

"Up on Bryony Hill the bears were pulling apart our temple, stone by stone. Soldiers were setting up a log fort beside them. Where our white marble had shone, bear-priests erected an obsidian altar. I feared, I knew, that it would soon be stained heart red, heart brown.

"So the day passed. The next day most men and bears departed, bar a small garrison busy carpentering. I remained in my thicket, too fearful to realize that I was starving. That night I squirmed out of my refuge and fled into the steppes, more dead than alive.

"What happened after is very strange. I had thought the bear-priests had destroyed us so as to begin a conquest of the Steppes, but no further armies came eastward. The bear-priests have built a temple to Lord Ursus on Bryony Hill, and around the temple they have built a fort, which they garrison strongly, but the Steppes are still free and Tansyard. The other Hordes do nothing, only now they shy clear of both Barleymill and Bryony Hill. They do not want to risk destruction.

"Why the bear-priests attacked the Cyan Cross Horde and no one else, I do not know, but I think they wanted Bryony Hill very much. Why else would they try so hard to kill us all? They must have had some reason to destroy the Cyan Cross Horde. I cannot accept that it was death for death's sake. That would be too horrible.

"There was no place for me on the Steppes. The Hordes would say, if I were a warrior, I should have died that night fighting. The Hordes would say, if I was a coward, I deserved to die. I thought so too, perhaps, but I still wanted my revenge. And so I left the Steppes for Chandlefort—arrogant Chandlefort, callous Chandlefort, but unmurderous Chandlefort, that still follows Our Lady and does not worship death. There I found employment as messenger boy. I am still no warrior, but I have been of some use in the fight against Low Branding and the bear-priests.

"And now I help you, Clovermead, because you try to save your father from the bear-priests. I think you are braver than I was when my family died. I very much want you to succeed. I will risk accompanying a bear-child, in hopes of saving her father.

"I miss my family very much."

Clovermead was crying. "I'm sorry, Sorrel. I had no idea. I shouldn't have asked you to talk. I never dreamed—it isn't like that in the *Heptameron.* I never read of anything so awful."

"I could not have imagined it either," said Sorrel. "Sometimes I try to forget that massacre, Clovermead. I owe it to my family to remember how they lived and how they died, but it is often tempting to let them slip away, like a dream. That would hurt less."

"I wish I could make it so it had never happened," said Clovermead. "I'm so sorry."

"Our Lady is in your heart," said Sorrel. He made the crescent sign and gripped Clovermead's hand thankfully in his. "I will always remember that of you."

"There shouldn't be such things," said Clovermead. "People shouldn't hurt so." Sorrow for Sorrel filled up her heart and for a while there was no room in her for the whispers of the bear tooth.

Chapter Twelve

THE ARMY OF LOW BRANDING

THE SNOW WAS TWO INCHES DEEPER THE NEXT MORNING. High cirrus clouds filled the morning sky and hid the sun. Their wispy billows glowed brilliant white with the sun's refracted light. Underneath the glaring sky Sorrel and Clovermead rode around a wide, ice-capped lake filled with whirring sleighs traveling across the ice and edged all around with little villages and farms. Armed patrols on sleigh and horseback watched them pass and shook their spears at Shilling when he came too close to the lake edge. Here and there Clovermead saw burned houses through torn-off gates.

"Those destructions are not recent," said Sorrel, pointing to some blackened ruins. "I have heard from Yellowjackets that there was much fighting in the Lakelands the first year of the war. Yellowjackets and Low Branding men wandered across the Lakelands, and each pillaged what they wanted. The peasants formed a militia next winter and fought against both sides that spring. They were inexperienced fighters, but they became better quickly, and they achieved most excellent skill at boat fighting. Yellowjackets, at least, no longer care to come to the Lakelands."

"Who do they think rules them?"

Sorrel laughed. "That is an excellent question! I am told that Lady Cindertallow often asks it in the most nettled of tones. I suspect the Mayor of Low Branding makes similar queries. In the Lakelands they answer these questions politely but most vaguely. They assure each questioner that they are loyal. To whom? The reply is noncommital, evasive. Chandlefort has not pressed them on the issue lately."

In late morning they left the Lakelands. The south edge of the lake curved away to the east in a flatland covered by a low, thick forest of leafless beeches, maples, apples, and elms. Some miles later the trees thinned out, and soon Sorrel and Clovermead were riding along the borderlands between the forest and the plain. The dry plain was enormous, featureless, and almost bare of snow. The sere cold crackled into their lungs, and a keening wind whipped through the plain's brown stubble of dead grass and flung frozen dust into their eyes.

"This is the edge of the true Salt Heath," said Sorrel. "The farm where we took Shilling was also on the Heath, was also dry land, but that was the north Heath, not one smidgeon so harsh a place. Chandlefort occupies the largest oasis in the true Heath. That beautiful castle is easy to defend, for thirst is always its ally."

"Does anything beautiful ever grow here?" Clovermead stared at the rocky rubble that littered the thin, scabby soil of the plain. "This is a feeble excuse for grass, which would disgust a sheep."

"Orange poppies bloom during the spring rains, the years that it does rain. While they bloom, this grass is lemon yellow, and together they make the Heath look handsome." Sorrel grimaced. "I would not live here by choice. The Steppes are lush; this is withered. Even your Timothy Vale, mountainous and closed in, I like more than the Heath. Only natives praise the Heath—and they are sometimes halfhearted."

"It's horrible," said Clovermead firmly. "It's as if—"

As if a great tooth had sucked the blood out of the land? said the tooth. *You are right, Clovermead. I like this place. In time I will make all Linstock look like this.* The tooth growled with quiet anticipation. Clovermead shuddered.

In early afternoon they came to a road. A few hundred feet west of the forest's edge, by a small pool no more than ten feet wide, Snuff's trail intersected the broad stone highway that ran from Low Branding to Chandlefort. A rose granite spire twenty feet high marked the intersection.

The earth around the pool had been churned to mud by hoofprints, footprints, and cart tracks. The begrimed water roiled with dark clouds, and the few plants at the water's edge had been gnawed to the nub. Charred logs and scattered mutton bones straggling for hundreds of yards along the road back toward Low Branding bore further witness of a recent encampment.

"The Army of Low Branding was here," said Sorrel. "It contains four, five, six thousand men, by the size of these garbage heaps. They were here no longer ago than yesterday—I see the embers still glowing in their fires."

"I can't smell Father or Snuff," Clovermead said angrily. "The stink of the army is too strong." She snuffled at the air. "I smell bears. Hundreds of them."

"I hope they are far ahead of us?" asked Sorrel.

Clovermead shook her head. "They were here today. Bears and men and horses all jumbled together. And I smell the stink of blood. Sorrel, can you make Shilling go faster? I'm worried about Father."

Shilling galloped west on bare stones stripped of snow by tramping feet. The sun set with wintry speed, a pale blaze ahead of them all through the brief afternoon. The land sloped upward toward a high plateau. Clovermead saw a pair of falcons soar in high updrafts, but otherwise the Heath was bare and lifeless.

As twilight deepened the slope began to gentle. Clovermead heard tramping and neighing and trumpets echoing faintly over the rocks. Sorrel groaned something in Tansyard, half a curse and half a prayer, and made the crescent sign. Clovermead recoiled from the intensity of the stench ahead of them. They rode over the crest of the slope and onto the plateau itself. Spread out before them, a little ways distant, was the Mayor's army.

The soldiers plodded in a thin line half a mile long. A thousand guttering torches clawed back the darkness and illumined the marching army. The standard of Low Branding, crossed golden scimitars over a silver fish thrusting up from a sapphire river, fluttered weakly at the army's head. A score of smaller regimental banners followed behind that first standard, each emblem emblazoned in gold, silver, and sapphire. Each regiment in the line marched in a tight, distinct clump.

The first and last regiments were cavalry, from whose ranks outriders regularly parted to ride up and down the army's flanks, halloing from sheer joy at their own speed. The horsemen wore silvery gray jackets, navy blue trousers, and tall black shakos, all liberally besmeared with mud. The steeds were tired, and their heads drooped, but they still raced with pride and fire when their masters spurred them forward.

Between the regiments of cavalry marched the multitude of infantry. Pikemen and swordsmen and archers all dressed in the ragged remnants of dark blue uniforms. Some still walked, but more limped and hobbled. A few sang marching songs, but most concentrated on the task of putting one foot in front of the other. Their thin clothes flapped in the feeble breeze.

In the very center of the army, drovers in muddy brown coats whipped and cursed at the black oxen who dragged hundreds of creaking carts. By their side, in an island of coiling silence, a hundred fur-clad bear-priests manned large ebony wagons draped with black curtains. The soldiers kept as far from the bear-priests' grim wagons as possible.

An oval of bears encircled the Mayor's army. They padded on dust and stones, sniffed the air, and constantly licked their lips. They looked hungrily at the men they guarded and growled softly to one another. Clovermead tried to eavesdrop on them, but they were too far away to be heard distinctly.

"Will you turn from here?" asked Sorrel grimly. "Or must we ride into an enemy army surrounded by toothed demons?"

"We go on," said Clovermead, though her stomach squirmed and she had more than half a mind to run screaming. Only her tooth was brave—savage and hungry, but fearless. It gave her courage when she clutched it to her. "We have to. Father's here."

"Evidently I was born under a short-lived star. Now I understand most viscerally the phrase *the jaws of death*. Dear Lady preserve us," Sorrel prayed, and he kicked Shilling forward.

The Army of Low Branding rushed up before them. A few soldiers idly watched them approach, but no one made any great fuss. The bears at the back of the army parted easily to let Clovermead and Sorrel inside the oval, then sprang back into position. Clovermead had a feeling that it would be harder to leave the ring of bears than it had been to get inside.

A redheaded cavalry officer cantered up to Clovermead and Sorrel as they left the bears behind. He yawned as he came to their side, and covered his mouth with a hand that was missing three fingers. "Messenger or commissary?" he asked. He swayed in his saddle and his breath stank of alcohol. "I hope commissary," he confided, leaning low toward Clovermead and Sorrel. "We need fresh food. Huh, you're young. You must be commissary—the Mayor wouldn't send messages with children!" He hooted with laughter.

"We were sent by the quartermaster into the Lakelands to procure rations," Sorrel said with sudden, cringing humility. Clovermead hastily imitated his servile crouch. "We could not extract food from those farmers."

"Course you didn't," said the cavalryman. He hiccuped. "Those Lakefolk have teeth—if he'd asked me, I'da told the quartermaster that myself. They don't take to requisitioning. You didn't get anything?" he asked mournfully. Sorrel and Clovermead shook their heads. "In you go, then," said the redhead, waving them forward. His hand wobbled as he waved. "I should ask you the password," he confided, "but I'm ab-so-lute-ly soused, and I don't remember it myself. Doesn't matter. Ain't a spy stupid enough to come through all these bears. Have to be mad to let bear-priests surround you with monsters. Or drunk. I'm not mad, so I got drunk. I'd go mad otherwise," he concluded with a serene smile.

"Can you tell us where the quartermaster is?" asked Sorrel. "We must report to him."

"Dunno. Somewhere by the carts," said the soldier. "That's where you commissary slaveys work, ain't it? Not the prison carts, I guess, unless you're serving the bear-priests dinner. And they'll eat you for dinner if you get too close to them!" He bubbled over with terrified laughter and slapped his horse's neck.

"Thank you, sir," said Sorrel. He bowed deeply, then led Shilling into the heart of the Mayor's army. "We will hide in the commissary, yes?" he muttered to Clovermead. "Evidently we will attract less attention there."

Thousands of men marched along and hardly spoke, only glanced surreptitiously from time to time at their ursine escorts. They were unshaven and shivered with cold, and their uniforms hung loosely on their too thin bodies. The tramp of their boots was louder than their words. A great many of them were drinking, slowly and steadily. The few whom drink got fighting mad were quickly knocked unconscious by their fellows, before their shouts might attract the attention of the bears.

"I feel sorry for them," said Clovermead. "They look like condemned prisoners on the night before the execution."

"They deserve execution," Sorrel said savagely. "They are butchers." He looked around him again, sighed, and shook his head. "Ah, Clovermead, I am mistaken. These are scarecrows, not butchers. Perhaps they once were butchers, but no more. I wish they did not look so miserable and pathetic. Now it is hard to hate them properly." His mouth set into a thin line. "Still, I will not object if the bears swallow these murderers. It will be justice."

They came to the commissary at last. Harried men, women, and boys ran back and forth, digging out barrels from the bottom of the moving carts, sorting the contents, and dashing off with them to other parts of the army. Within each cart was a jumbled mess of cooking pots, rock-hard biscuits, barrels of flour, and casks of wine.

Clovermead shuddered fastidiously at the sight of the mess. Goody Weft would never have allowed this sort of hugger-mugger confusion in the Ladyrest kitchen.

Sorrel and Clovermead tied Shilling to a cart where other horses were already tethered and then walked boldly among the commissary boys. Immediately a harried old woman grabbed them, put empty casks into their hands, and screamed out an order to fill the casks with water. She shoved Sorrel and Clovermead toward a small oasis by the roadside, crammed with commissary boys on the same errand, all in a hurry to fill their casks and buckets before the army had marched on. The oasis was drained dry when the boys were done. Afterward they were called to hold up a provisions cart while the wheelwright repaired its broken axle. By the time the cart was fixed, the crescent moon was high in the sky and the army had made camp. Then Sorrel and Clovermead carried armloads of rancid beef and cheese to the stew pots, where fifty men cooked supper for the army. When that was done, they carried water and wine to infantry regiments camped in the treeless mud.

Past midnight, sitting by Shilling's side, they wolfed down bits of stew the soldiers had left at the bottom of the pots. They were too tired and hungry to care about the taste.

Sorrel smiled. "I am proud of myself. Am I not excellently nonconspicuous?"

"Extremely nonconspicuous," Clovermead agreed. "I don't think anyone knows we're here."

"No one but Our Lady," said Sorrel. He made the crescent sign. "She favors us with her blessing."

And Lord Ursus knows we're here, thought Clovermead bleakly. *I think he favors us too.*

The next afternoon Clovermead took a bucket of water to the bear-priests' prison carts. She made as if to water the oxen—and a bear-priest strode up to her and slammed her bucket to the ground. He struck at Clovermead, but she ducked under his blow and scrambled backward.

"Keep away," the bear-priest growled. His teeth had been filed as sharp as Snuff's, and he wore a bear tooth around his neck. "Next time you come, I kill you."

"Yes, sir," Clovermead squeaked. She bowed low

and scrambled away. Her tooth itched at her chest and she dreamed of clawing the bear-priest. She would pay him back for his insolence to a true servant of Lord Ursus! Once she had rescued her father . . .

The next morning Clovermead and Sorrel were ordered to bring firewood to the Mayor's entourage. Clovermead stole long glances at the Mayor as she dashed back and forth with armfuls of logs. He rode on a surprisingly small and tame gray mare, who looked uncomfortable beneath the weight of her silvered leather saddle and the Mayor's plump body. The Mayor himself was a greasy man of about sixty, with thin white hair combed vainly over his balding dome. His arms and legs stuck out like matchsticks from his soft dumpling stomach. His face was a stoat's, and his probing eyes, alive with harsh intelligence, darted suspiciously all around him. As he spoke to his accompanying aides Clovermead heard a golden voice that commanded, complimented, and chastised with equal facility. His aides obeyed him quickly, some even with the appearance of devotion.

Half the ranks of the Mayor's honor guard were patricians of Low Branding—tall, slender, laughing young men perfumed and exquisite in a rainbow of cloaks and finely ornamented suits of armor. They rode Phoenixians with arrogant style, heedless of the common soldiers and servants they forced to leap out of their way. The other half were bear-priests. They had wolves' heads for caps and blood-spattered bearskins for capes, and they imperturbably exposed their bare flesh to the cold. Each had a necklace with a bear tooth. All the bear-priests were huge—more than six feet tall and thick with muscle. Their unsheathed broadswords were Clovermead's height and thicker across than her leg. Their cheeks and scalps were matted tangles of black wire and gray grizzle. Their fingernails were long and thick, and their mouths twisted into rictuses of hunger. Their eyes were black holes that thirsted for blood. While the patricians chattered, they rumbled like beasts, or were silent.

Clovermead looked gingerly among them. "I don't see Snuff," she whispered to Sorrel.

"Thank Our Lady for small favors," Sorrel whispered back. "He would spy us at once and deliver us to the tender mercy of his compatriots."

"Maybe. But we have to find him sooner or later. How else will we find my father? Or should we go peeking at each prison cart tonight?" Sorrel's only answer was a low moan.

But when they skulked to the perimeter of the sable-blanketed prison carts that night, they found a blazing circle of torchlight and dozens of patrolling bear-priests. The bear-priests' eyes were cat large, and they sniffed the air hungrily.

"Don't they sleep?" asked Sorrel.

"Sleep is for weaklings," said Clovermead. "Lord Ursus grants sleeplessness as one of his gifts." Her voice was low and guttural; she whispered Lord Ursus' name with fear and love.

The following day the army traversed a rubbly wasteland of sharp rocks and ripped-up flagstones that sliced boots to tatters and wedged horseshoes off of hooves. The Mayor ordered a special ration of wine for all the soldiers, and Sorrel and Clovermead carried sacks of wine to every regiment. The soldiers clapped their wine bearers hard on their backs, teased Clovermead for her beardless youth, and spoke to them with rough kindness.

At evening they camped by a shallow creek that Sorrel identified as the last stream in the Heath east of Chandlefort. The whole army gathered by its banks to drink. Sorrel took a small sip of muddy water and filled his canteen. Clovermead knelt by the creek and dipped a finger through the skein of ice to the water beneath. She brought the finger to her mouth and wrinkled her nose. "Ugh, it's filthy. How can you drink this?"

Sorrel shrugged. "Fill up. If you take no water now, you will regret it later." Sullenly Clovermead followed his advice.

In the morning the army marched through a parched plain, monotonously flat but for the regular row of teardrop-shaped pillars along the road. Each sunset red column was fifteen feet tall and tapered to a point on the west side.

"Lady Cindertallow's great-grandmother put those up," said Sorrel. "There are hundreds of them. Every taper points to Chandlefort."

"Doesn't that make it easy for invading armies?" asked Clovermead.

"There were none then. They showed the way for merchants. That proud lady did not know how greatly the world would change."

"She was a fool," said Clovermead. Her tooth approvingly echoed her words. Clovermead circled around the nearest pillar. The flaming bee and sword that emblazoned her brooch had been engraved on the pillar's far side. She reached her hand up to trace the deep grooves a century of blowing sand had etched in the stone. The cold rock chilled her fingers to the bone.

Snow swirled in again that night. Soldiers shivered close to the fires, denuded the sparse bushes of the Heath for fuel, and roasted a few desert rats unlucky enough to be caught outside their burrows. Sorrel and Clovermead copied the other commissary boys and stole a slab of salt beef meant for a cavalry regiment for their dinner.

"Do you have ideas about how to rescue your father?" asked Sorrel.

"Just one." Clovermead had been working out the details of a rescue operation all that long day marching through the Heath. Her tooth liked it. The plan required blood, and that would bind her even further to Lord Ursus. Clovermead was afraid of what she would be after she rescued her father, she looked forward to her transformation, she felt both at once. "I don't like my plan. Have you thought of anything?"

"No," said Sorrel. "I am sorry."

"Me too," said Clovermead. "I guess we'll have to use mine. Soon. Daddy will be sacrificed when we reach Chandlefort. We have to hurry."

"Hurry and we make mistakes," said Sorrel. "Then we die too."

"We don't have a choice," said Clovermead.

Late the next afternoon the Mayor's army marched into Chandlefort's fertile demesne. Between the fields stretched eight immense irrigation canals, stone-bottomed spokes that thrust two miles from the castle. Smaller canals threaded out from the great eight, and tinier ones from the small, till they laced a circle around the castle four miles in diameter. The canals had gone dry. The fields between them were dotted with the stumps of chopped-down trees, and some had been burned black from old fires. Drifts of sand encroached on the fertile land.

Clovermead peered forward to where the castle of Chandlefort sat at the hub of the canals. The castle's outer walls, made of smooth, rosy granite, a dozen feet thick and a hundred feet high, rose with massive grace over the Heath. They formed an eight-pointed star, with high, round towers at the end of each point. On each tower scurrying figures pounded drums and blew trumpets in derisive welcome to the Mayor's army. At the pinnacle of each tower a huge, polished ruby glowed in the winter sun.

Within the walls were a forest of high turrets, tipped with small and glinting rubies, and beneath the jeweled turrets a masonry bestiary of gargoyles, phoenixes, owls, and unicorns. Rubies encrusted the central pinnacle, which soared two hundred feet above the high walls and blinded Clovermead with its dazzling red glare. Near the pinnacle's top a cloth-of-gold flag fluttered proudly in the breeze, emblazoned with a bee wielding a burning sword. Above the flag stood a solid sphere of milk white crystal three feet across, irregularly freckled with rubies—a map of the moon whose rubies represented Our Lady's dark seas. Surrounding the ruby tower, twenty haughty marble figures gazed out with possessive pride at the land below.

"Those twenty statues represent the Ladies of Chandlefort," said Sorrel. "From the time of the first Lady Cindertallow, a statue has been sculpted at each Lady Cindertallow's inauguration. There is only room for twenty-one. There are prophecies that claim that the twenty-first ruler of Chandlefort will be the greatest of them all. There are also prophecies that she will be the last ruler of Chandlefort. Rumors whisper of further prophecies known only to the Ladies Cindertallow. Prophecies abound, some true, some false, and among silly humankind, who can tell the bramble from the grass?" Sorrel glanced sideways at Clovermead. "Have you heard of such stories in Timothy Vale?"

Clovermead shook her head. "Father never talked of Linstock, and the pilgrims never talked about that sort of prophecy. Lady Cindertallow's heir must be awfully full of herself."

Sorrel laughed nervously. "She has no heir. Her nobles mutter unhappily of her barrenness. Who will succeed her? The Mayor is full of hubris, we hear, and he boasts that he will succeed to the throne of Chandlefort. Perhaps it is even true that he swore in the Mayor's Palace that the twenty-first statue will be of him. I have heard it said that he has already made the statue."

"Do you think he brought it with him?" asked Clovermead.

Sorrel laughed. "I would not be surprised. That man is arrogant enough."

The oval of bears split and extended itself to surround the castle. When it had reformed, it had become a circle around both besieged and besiegers, a half mile distant from the walls. Then the army oozed and expanded into an inner ring around Chandlefort, cautiously distant from walls and bears alike. The infantry set themselves to digging trenches, while the cavalry methodically explored every rock and canal for hidden tunnels, ambushers, and traps.

The Mayor sat on his gray mare, watched the preparations with an unblinking eye, and smiled with satisfaction when his army had finished girdling Chandlefort. He whispered some words to an aide, and soon messengers went around the camp to announce a special bonus of a shilling to every man in the army. The soldiers loudly cheered His Eminence, and cheered even more loudly when the silver actually appeared and began to be distributed.

The prison carts halted in the southern quarter of the besieging army, just west of the commissary wagons. The bear-priests ululated a triumphant chant as they came to a halt in front of the castle. They eyed the crystal moon with venom. Some fingered their knives.

"We rescue Father as soon as it's dark," said Clovermead as they carried feed to the oxen. "I think they'll kill him tonight."

"What is your plan?" asked Sorrel. "It seems impossible to me. There are too many of them and they are too watchful, too efficient. Perhaps we would be better off if we fled to the walls and asked for help from Chandlefort."

"They won't help Father," Clovermead said shortly. They wouldn't lift a finger to help a thieving ex-servant. Her heart pounded with terror and she ached to bite and feed. Her bear-tooth sang with joy. "We'll use blood and bear-magic. Your blood and my magic."

Sorrel stared at her a long minute. "You are joking," he said, but he didn't smile.

"Either we both give some of our blood, or I have to kill someone else for all of his. I don't want to kill yet, Sorrel." Clovermead swayed and claws grew on her fingernails. They lengthened to two inches, three inches, then shrank. She moaned with terrible hunger. "Please, Sorrel," she whispered. "Don't make me kill."

"Give up the tooth," said Sorrel. "Then you will not have to kill anyone. Do not keep that evil thing."

"I need it," said Clovermead. "To save Father. I've racked my brain and I still can't think of any other way to keep him alive. Have you, Sorrel?" Her eyes pleaded with him to think of some way to save her.

Sorrel shook his head.

"Then, do what I ask you to do," snapped Clovermead. The Tansyard could not help her, and she almost hated him for his incapacity.

"All right," said Sorrel. His teeth chattered and he shivered in his tatterdemalion rags. "I do not care if these butchers live or die, but I will give you what you want. I very much hope that you are in control of your magic, Clovermead. I do not want to be eaten."

"I'll try not to eat you," said Clovermead.

"Can you promise?" asked Sorrel. Clovermead shook her head and Sorrel trembled more violently than ever.

Chapter Thirteen

The Raid on the Prison Carts

Late that night Sorrel and Clovermead crept through the darkness, frozen drizzle splattering down on their heads. Behind them the soldiers of the army huddled around their campfires, muttering and scratching fleas and snoring fitfully. Ahead bear-priests sat at the front of each prison cart, all silent under their fur capes. More walked sentry around the carts and flicked keen glimpses at the darkness. Their eyes glowed dull red. Clovermead and Sorrel, shadows among shadows, froze whenever a bear-priest looked their way.

"I think we've come far enough," Clovermead whispered when they reached the commissary wagons nearest the prison carts. "We can feed the tooth now."

Sorrel rolled up his shirtsleeve as Clovermead took the tooth off her leather cord. His eyes locked on the brown-smeared enamel and his teeth chattered. "Please do not make a mistake, Clovermead," he whispered. "Most emphatically I repeat, I do not want to be devoured by you. I want to live and ride on the Steppes, and I wish to be a happy, toothless old man with many wonderful memories before I die."

"Yum," said Clovermead. Sorrel flinched and she grinned. "Just a joke."

Sorrel smiled a very, very little. "Ha-ha. I must tell all my friends that drollery. They will fall laughing on the ground."

"Don't worry," said Clovermead. "You'll be all right." She plunged the eager tooth into Sorrel's forearm.

The tooth growled a tune of insatiable hunger. It turned pink, then red, then glowed deep and brilliant ruby to match the towers of Chandlefort. Sorrel gasped with pain and clamped his teeth shut against a louder outcry. By distant firelight Clovermead could see the blood drain from his flesh. His face turned pale.

Clovermead felt power and strength rush into her. Her mind reached out to the bears and she felt a hundred great masses of sinew and teeth stir at her command—ah! The bears twitched but did not move. The bear-priests held the bears tight in their own red net of command. With her eyes closed Clovermead could see the red net's links glowing in the night—slender, supple, and strong. She would need far more blood to rend that ruby web. She needed more of Sorrel—

"Stop, Clovermead," Sorrel gasped. "I am growing weak. I will not be able to walk."

Don't stop, said the tooth. *Take all of him. You have no more use for the Tansyard.*

You're right, tooth, Clovermead thought. *I'll eat him now. I need to stay strong myself. I need his blood. I want his blood.*

"Lady help me," Sorrel moaned. The plea made Clovermead curl her lips in an angry sneer. . . .

And the clouds parted. The moon shone through and lit Sorrel's agonized face. He looked at Clovermead and still he trusted her. *Some hero I am,* Clovermead thought as a last flicker of shame flared up inside her. *Even Lucifer Snuff has more honor. He kept his word when he promised to go back to Low Branding before attacking us again. I'd be a liar like Daddy if I killed him now.*

Regretfully Clovermead pulled the tooth from Sorrel's arm. The bloody point clung to his flesh and raised it to a red pucker. When tooth and flesh parted, Sorrel's arm was scarred from palm to shoulder. He sobbed with relief and pain. He tried to clutch his arm to his body, but he was too weak to move.

The clouds covered the moon again.

"I'm sorry," said Clovermead. "Sorrel, you can't imagine how hard it was not to eat you." Sorrel moaned, and Clovermead put the tooth to her own forearm. She felt a sting of pain and saw drops of blood well forth. The tooth sank into her as eagerly as it had sunk into Sorrel.

Her blood was divine. She drank ambrosia and she was ambrosia drunk into the long teeth of a Goddess. She felt the draining pleasure of death. Blood surged through her arteries and veins, and suction crushed their thin walls. Her arm moaned with electric pain, and she longed to feel her teeth rend flesh. Lord Ursus roared welcome and his desire to share in her feast. She should bring him meat, as any cub should bring her father meat. She loved him and she loved eating and the tooth was full of red power and she was getting very weak. . . .

Clovermead pulled the tooth from her arm. It was

thick and wet with blood. Her arm was a drained husk, and she sported a welted scar that ran from fingertip to neck. Sorrel gabbled worried human words at her, but she couldn't understand him. He was a strange, small monkey, and she was barely human in her coat of fur and long claws and sharp fangs.

"Now we free Father," Clovermead said. Or did she growl? She wasn't sure if Sorrel had understood her.

She clenched the pulsing tooth, turbulently full of blood, and took hold of its power. It was a claw in her hand, a fang in her jaws. She slashed at the sky and severed the net that bound the bears to the bear-priests' commands. Astonished roaring abruptly filled the night air around the encampment. The bear-priests yelled, and the ground by the prison carts was loud with the sound of pounding feet and spitting curses. Clovermead smiled and reached out to speak with the bears.

Hello, Boulderbash, she said. *Hello, Troutnibble, Cedarsniff, and Streamloll.*

Greetings, little human, said Boulderbash and the others.

I have a job for you, said Clovermead.

I thought you meant to give us our liberty, said Boulderbash. *This is only a new servitude?*

Correct, said Clovermead with an ugly laugh. *Do you think I would waste my power that way?*

Of course not, mistress, said Boulderbash. *What shall we do?*

Attack the bear-priests, said Clovermead. *Hunt them down. Kill them.*

That will be a sweet revenge for this imprisonment of our minds, said Boulderbash. *I wonder when we will be revenged against you?*

Never, said Clovermead, more confidently than she felt. *All of you, come now!*

You are not that strong, said Boulderbash. *As many as you can command are at your service. Only that many. The rest of us are free from both you and the bear-priests.*

Clovermead heard distant rumbling that rapidly grew louder. Padding feet struck against the hard ground. The bear-priests whirled to face the onslaught and they blanched with fear. They drew their broadswords—and seven great bears, Boulderbash at their lead, leapt in among the prison carts.

The bears roared in delight and fury. Their lips curled back and exposed their yellow fangs, so sharp and huge that they could have sliced through a giant's armor. Their claws bit savage runnels in the ground. Then they were among the bear-priests, as foxes among rabbits, tearing flesh and biting limbs. The bear-priests screamed as they were wounded and died, and Clovermead smiled with grim exultation. The bears ran after more victims and in their pursuit heedlessly knocked over prison carts. The wooden wheels crumpled and the prisoners screamed as the iron cages fell to the ground. The oxen dragging the carts smelled the bears' musk, flinched and struggled against their yokes, and bellowed their terror.

"Can you move?" Clovermead asked Sorrel. The Tansyard tried to get to his feet, stumbled, and fell back to the ground. "Stay here," she commanded. "I'll come back with Father. Then all three of us can escape."

Clovermead dashed alone into a flickering chaos of drizzling mist, tumbled carts, dead bear-priests, and lumbering bears. Near the Mayor's tent a line of patricians and bear-priests had closed ranks to combat the growling beasts. Clovermead felt a dozen bear-priests try to reattach the blood-net over the bears. Blood surged powerfully within her and she undid their efforts with a contemptuous flick—and saw her tooth's glow diminish.

Don't waste me, said the tooth. *You have time before they capture the bears again.*

As you say, old murderer, said Clovermead, and she came to the nearest of the abandoned prison carts. "Father!" she yelled into the night. Her voice was trembling and harsh. "Are you there, Daddy? Is Waxmelt Wickward there?" She jerked open a black curtain.

A skeletal stranger sat in filthy straw. Chains stretched from the iron walls to tight manacles that had chafed his wrists and ankles. He wore thin rags that had once been fine silk, and shivered in the cold. Clovermead thought he might have been handsome once, before emaciation wore away his looks. His sandy hair was as rough as the straw he sat on, and his skin was red with cold. His arms had been broken and left to mend badly. As the light came in a rat scurried away from the empty bowl of gruel that lay by the man. A foul-smelling pot sat at the far end of the cage.

There was too much light for the prisoner to see, even in the cloudy night, and his eyes blinked, teared, and shut tight. He turned a blind mole's face to Clovermead and groped through the bars with raw worms of fingers. His manacles caught on the bars. "Will you let me die?" he rasped. "Let it end. Let Lord Ursus drink my blood. He's welcome to it."

"I'm not a bear-priest," Clovermead said reluctantly. *I'm thirsty,* she thought. *I'll drink for Lord Ursus if you're so desperate to die.* She felt the bear tooth come eagerly to her hand. *No,* she told herself, *I need information. I can't kill him yet.* She growled her frustration and thrust the tooth away. "I've come for my father. His name is Waxmelt Wickward. Do you know where he is?"

The man laughed and cried. "I don't know where I am. I don't know anything but these stinking walls and the sounds of what bear-priests do to prisoners and . . ." He shuddered. "Save me, too. Don't leave me here."

Clovermead pulled idly at the door, wondering if she could make an easy meal of the fool. "It's locked," she said crossly. "I don't have time to get you out."

"Damn you," the man croaked. His fingers clawed at her. They brushed at her coat with no effect, but Clovermead fell back from him. Would Waxmelt look like this? Act like this? Desperately the prisoner stretched forth his hands till the manacles cut into his forearms. "I had a wife," he whispered imploringly. "I had a son. I need to see them again." Clovermead shook her head, though the darkness-blinded prisoner couldn't see her. "Please," he begged. "Please."

For a moment the moon shone through a crevice in the clouds, and Clovermead could no longer curse the prisoner for a fool, a weakling, a deserving prey. She cried and the tears dissolved fur from her hands, softened claws into fingernails. She cried for her own lost self and she cried for her father and she cried for the stranger who would die. "I'm sorry," she said, gulping back sobs. "I can't help you. I wish I could."

"They have won, then." He drew back his arms and he turned to face Clovermead directly, proud despite his rags and chains and sightless, tight-shut eyes. "I am Count Linden Silvermere of Queensmart," he said with a sudden shadow of vigor. "Tell my friends the bear-priests kidnapped me. Tell my family I loved them to the end."

"I will," said Clovermead. "I swear it. Farewell, Count Linden." She bowed to him in courtly fashion and he bowed his head in return. Then she ran from him to the neighboring prison carts.

She yelled for her father again, but there was no answer. She tore down curtains and looked at the broken men and women within each cell, starved and beaten husks, each time more afraid she would find her father, every minute more afraid she would never find him. "Have you seen my father?" Clovermead asked. "Have you seen Waxmelt Wickward? Do you know where he is?" Some had forgotten how to speak. Others were insane. The remnants had seen nothing but bars and torturers. Arrows whistled in the air. She heard a bear roar in pain and she knew that Troutnibble had died. The blood-net reformed above her and sank tendrils into the fleeing bears. Roaring their rage and despair, the bears stalked back toward the army.

Clovermead found her father at last in the twenty-first cart. "Daddy?" she asked disbelievingly of the small, familiar silhouette in the cage.

"Clovermead?" He stumbled forward and it was Waxmelt. He had grown thin, but not yet skeletal, and his flesh was still healthy and firm. His matted hair was much whiter and there were bloody bandages over his fingertips, but his body still moved at his direction. He had been left unchained. He could still see, though he narrowed his eyes against the distant torchlight. He was not yet broken.

"You're alive," said Clovermead, and her head fell against the bars. The world spun and she had to close her eyes. "I've come to rescue you, Father."

Waxmelt reached his bandaged hands through the bars to caress his daughter's cheeks. "You shouldn't have. You shouldn't be here. I hoped you were in Queensmart by now. Clovermead, don't you know how dangerous this place is?" His voice cracked with fear, but Clovermead felt him smile as his bandages stroked her skin. "Dear Lady. I can't imagine what you did to get here. My own sweet, brave, disobedient daughter—you are a marvel."

"I'm an awfully tired marvel, Daddy," Clovermead said in a small voice. Her knees tried to buckle under her and she wanted to sleep for a week, but she made herself stand up and shake the locked bars. "We don't have much time till the bear-priests come back."

"Run now," said Waxmelt. "This is foolish. You don't need me. I'm nothing to you. . . ." He paused and grinned anxiously. "It's a little late to tell you that, isn't it? Don't listen to me. They haven't manacled me. Snuff said they didn't need to bother chaining a weakling like me. Can you get through the bars, Clo?"

"I know someone who can," said Clovermead, and she raised the tooth as high as she could reach. It still gleamed red, though nowhere near so brightly as it had. She could replenish it from Waxmelt—she struck down that thought. It was the tooth's desire, Lord Ursus', not hers. She had come to save her father, not kill him.

One and the same, said the tooth, with a chuckle. *One and the same.*

Quiet, said Clovermead inwardly, and she called out to Boulderbash. *Come help me. I need your strength to free Father. Leave the bear-priests.*

But they are so tasty, said Boulderbash, *and they deserve more of the same for how they treated us. We did not enjoy our captivity.* The bear ambled out of the darkness, bloody jawed. She was as large as the whole prison cart. *So, my slavery is to be used to free your father. Touching. I warn you, girl-ape, we do not love your bonds any better than theirs.*

You can go free when you're done here, said Clovermead. *Boulderbash, I need you to break open the bars. Please, can you make a space wide enough for my father to escape?*

Little cub, said Boulderbash, *I do not think the bear-priests will be distracted much longer. They will reassert their dominion over the last of us while I am busy here.*

Then, hurry! Clovermead raged.

Of course, mistress. Stand aside. Clovermead fell away from the cart and Waxmelt retreated to the cart's far corner, his eyes wide with awe. Boulderbash inserted her forelegs between two of the bars, tensed her muscles, and strained against the steel. The rods bowed, creaked, bent, squealed, and snapped. So did the surrounding pair, and Boulderbash fell back from the prison cart. The space where four bars had been was now wide enough for Waxmelt to get through.

Will that do? Boulderbash inquired.

Wonderfully, said Clovermead. The tooth was drained

of light. It was small and cold, and the blood was dry. She let her arm fall and clenched the tooth tightly in her palm. *Thank you, Boulderbash.*

Will you do the same for me one day? Boulderbash asked with a great, booming chortle. *I think not, little one.* She lumbered off into the darkness.

Waxmelt came out of the cage. His legs were weak from disuse, but he could walk. Clovermead took a step to join him and tottered. Her arm blazed with pain and she was kitten weak.

Waxmelt went to her side and put her arm over his shoulder. "Who's rescuing whom?" he asked lightly.

"Blood-magic takes a lot out of me," said Clovermead. "Blood, mainly. We need to find Sorrel. He's waiting for us."

"The Tansyard's here too?" Waxmelt shook his head in wonder. "Where is he?"

"By the commissary wagons," Clovermead whispered.

"Where are they?"

"Somewhere there." Clovermead waved vaguely into the darkness. "Let's go, Daddy."

They stumbled through the night and the rain, both of them too weak to run. Clovermead tried to retrace her steps, but she mistook her way half the time. Waxmelt cursed the clouds that hid the constellations and the moon and left them directionless in the darkness.

Bugles rang, their piercing music louder than every roar and yell. The walls of Chandlefort cracked open and light blazed out on the dark camp. Neighing white shapes separated themselves from that distant shining and rushed closer. All at once dozens of ivory horses swept past Clovermead and Waxmelt and into the heart of the army. On their backs sat swaggering, laughing men, dressed all in cloth of gold, who slashed about them with huge sabers at bear-priests and soldiers. "A Yellowjacket! A Yellowjacket!" the laughing horsemen cried, and "Chandlefort and Victory!" and "The Moon! The Moon!"

"More soldiers," said Clovermead stupidly. She could barely comprehend their existence. "Why are they here? Daddy, I don't know what to do."

"Clo, we have to . . ." But Clovermead never heard what they had to do. Unheedingly a Yellowjacket rode at them on a pearly stallion that seemed twice Clovermead's height, and Waxmelt jumped desperately hard to one side, pulling Clovermead after him. As they fell, his hands came loose from her shoulders. Clovermead landed on a rock that bit sharp into her tooth-scarred arm. She felt herself roll, screamed, and blacked out.

When Clovermead came back to consciousness and opened her eyes, she saw she was in a shallow gully, three feet high at most. She could see nothing beyond its walls. She tried to move, tried to speak, but she could not.

She heard pounding hooves. Swords were clashing. The drums of the Mayor's army sounded and the soldiers of Low Branding began to advance.

"I see the innkeeper," she heard Sorrel say from on high. "She must have gotten him out of the prison cages. Quick, we must get him off the ground. I will look for Clovermead. She must be near here."

"Stay where you are," said a strange, brusque voice. "I'll get the man, but there's no time for wild-goose chases. They'll break through our rear guard in a minute." Clovermead heard the man jump from horseback to the ground and come closer. "Got him," the man grunted. "Light enough." His footsteps, heavier this time, retreated.

"Give me one minute, Lieutenant," Sorrel begged. "Lady Cindertallow will want her inside the walls. Dear Lady, Clovermead is—"

"Shut up, Tansyard. We found you in this shambles and we found the innkeeper. That's not bad for a raid. Sweet Lady, here come their cavalry." Clovermead heard thumps, Sorrel yelling unintelligibly, and then rapidly diminishing hoofbeats. *At least Father's safe,* she thought.

And she also thought, *They left me behind. They left me alone in the dark.* She knew it wasn't fair to think that way, but *They left me behind, they left me alone* still ran through her head as she descended once more into blackness.

When she woke again, there was still nothing but the gully walls around her. She hurt. She was bruised all over. Her upper jaw ached. This time she had the strength to move. She put her elbows underneath her and lifted her head.

She was still among the prison carts. Thirty feet away Lucifer Snuff strode among a phalanx of bear-priests, raging through the mangled bodies of their dead fellows and spitting curses. Despite his fury, his gaze flicked carefully over every inch of ground. He was coming closer.

Clovermead fell back into the gully. She reached for the tooth—and couldn't find it. Where was it? She scrabbled in the dirt around her, but it was gone. Hot tears burned down her cheeks. She was alone and weak again, all the power of the bear tooth gone. Part of her was relieved that the tooth was gone, but mostly she wanted it in her hands again. She would never let it go if ever it came back into her hands.

"Kill Count Linden," she heard Snuff say to a bear-priest by his side. He was very near. "The bears are still restless. The Count has spirit. His blood will make strong shackles." The bear-priest muttered obedience and pattered away. Snuff came to the gully itself. Clovermead saw his eyes rake the darkness, stop at her still form—and widen in delight and astonishment as he recognized her.

"Blood and vengeance," said Snuff, grinning. He knelt by her side and felt for her pulse. He saw her blink. "Clovermead Wickward herself, and she's among the living. I almost didn't recognize you with your hair cropped—hah, and you've stained yourself dark. Somehow I knew you were behind this mess." He laughed. "It's been a good night after all. We lost the thief, but we got the girl. Well worth the trade."

Then he kicked her in the head.

Chapter Fourteen

Stalking Dreams

CLOVERMEAD WAS PURSUING A FAT DOE OVER THE MOUNtains. She was a golden cub once more, and salt breezes riffled through her golden fur. She smelled the doe's rich musk of sweat and fear, growled hungrily, and ran all the faster. This time she would not let the doe escape. This time she would seize and bite.

You are a fine cub, little daughter, said Lord Ursus. He loped beside Clovermead with easy power. *All children are recalcitrant when they first teethe. I know that as well as anyone. I am gentle to my own.* The ground rumbled at Lord Ursus' laugh. *But never too gentle. The sky-crone is a nursemaid. I train hunters.*

I hunted Snuff, said Clovermead. *I tracked his scent. He defeated me once, but I'll have my revenge. I'll find him and I'll leap on him and I'll tear him to bits, even if he hasn't killed Daddy yet. I want to rip his lungs out and watch him choke to death.* She roared out her pain and her anguish and her rage for the bear-priest's blood.

You may have him, said Lord Ursus with negligent grace. *He should have captured you much earlier. He has proved blunt toothed, fit to be prey.*

Thank you, my Lord, said Clovermead. She ducked her

head in grateful submission. *How can you be with me? I lost the tooth.*

I am with you still and always, said Lord Ursus, grinning. *Stop,* he commanded. Clovermead reluctantly tore herself from the doe's scent. *Look. This foul hole is the sky-crone's. This is her breeding ground of weakness.*

They stood on a high, rocky ledge and looked down into a deep valley. Brine-laden sea mist at the north end of the valley crept over a shallow ridge and trickled southward. The dissipating gray film curled around hazy pines and larches and melted into the white snow on the mountain slopes. Above, the moon bobbed comfortably in a soft gray sea of fog.

At valley bottom a stream coiled toward the northern ridge, then disappeared through a crack in the rock that Clovermead imagined led to an icy underwater grotto where seals and walruses disported themselves in the dark boundary of river and sea. Clovermead traced the course of the river upstream, past a riverbed of ice and granite boulders to a perfect circle of white marble walls that girdled the stream's source. The slim walls held back seven-foot-high drifts of snow. Within the walls two long, low cloisters bracketed the stream banks. On their roofs women in white robes stood guard, swept snow, and prayed to Our Lady. Above the twin cloisters lay the stream's source, quiet and serene. It was a perfectly circular mountain pool whose unblemished icy surface was tinged the lightest blue. At the south end of the pool stood a small crescent temple and a craggy altar hewn from a single block of lapis lazuli, where Clovermead saw a small flame flickering. Faintly she smelled cedar incense burning in the temple.

This is Snowchapel, she said, full of wonder. *There's the Blue Stone, there's the Blue Pool, and there's the White Temple. It's all the way the pilgrims describe it.*

You believe pilgrims, child? Lord Ursus asked scornfully. *Those wanderers hallucinate. I saw them come this way year after year. They arrived from north and south, from Scrimshaw Harbor and Timothy Vale, peering at the water and peering at the sky. I sniffed at the moon and I smelled nothing. I lapped at the water and all I tasted was fish. The nuns chased me from the Scrying Pool and they yelled—I didn't know what, but harsh words. I was hungry, but the Pool wasn't for me. I knew they were weak, but they made me run.*

You ran? Clovermead could hardly imagine it.

Lord Ursus grinned. His teeth snapped at the mist and rent its billows. *I was not yet purified. I had not yet realized who I was. I was as weak as all my servants are before I have torn the weakness from them. I fled from the human women and I learned to hate them. They were so feeble behind their iron edges. And why had they chased me away? For a stupid, meaningless dream. For the dead moon. I know she is dead—that thing in the sky is a bone, a puny echo of light, a rock hurtling in the night. It is a mirage without smell, without taste, without texture, without odor, and silent. How stupid you humans are, to worship a nothing! I swore to punish you for your imbecility. I would make you worship Me. I would be the new God, a divinity you could feel in every inch of flesh and bone. You would scream and know I was your Lord. I would master all your senses, but pain most of all. I made an oath that I would hunt you all down, every one. I swore never to eat honey or fruit or nuts again. Only meat.* Laughter boomed through the valley and needles fell off of the pines. *I started by hunting pilgrims. I stalked them as they came to Snowchapel. I learned to love their scent of fear, to hunger for the taste of their flesh. I took them one by one, until I realized there were too many of you to kill in a lifetime. So I began to hunt for disciples to aid me in my hunt. Together my disciples and I will fulfil my promise, little cub.*

Clovermead whimpered uneasily and she felt less certain of her strength. Her fur stood on edge and she smelled her own fear.

I will tear the human fear from you, Goldenhair. You will be a bear as I am.

I want to be a bear, but it's terribly hard, my Lord, said Clovermead. *I can't stop being scared and human. I don't know how to get rid of the foolish chatterbox of a girl in me. My Lord, help me. Tell me what I have to do.*

You must become one of my disciples, said Lord Ursus. *They do not fear. Others fear them. They hunt. They kill. That withered old moon-prune is my prey. I tore off her arm and ate it; I have her scent. She runs, Clovermead, but she can't escape me. I'll devour her all. Soon. There'll be no moon then, only darkness and my reign. Then a few will hunt with me and many will be hunted. You can hunt, if you want.*

I thought you said Our Lady didn't exist, said Clovermead.

Lord Ursus growled uneasily. *She won't.* He wheeled away from the view of Snowchapel. He pawed at the snow and Clovermead knew the chase had started again. *No more questions. It is time for you to hunt yourself. Pursue the little girl, the coward, the prattler of moon-hopes and moon-blessings. Run her down. Leap for her. Kill her as she screams and tear out her heart. Do it now!*

I will, said Clovermead. She surged forward.

She chased the doe, who now was Clovermead herself, chased the fearful idiot innkeeper's daughter. Under the eyeless socket of the moon she ran over the white mountain slopes with Lord Ursus at her side. Our Lady was not there. Our Lady was gone, if she had ever been there. Clovermead knew now that the moon had never been meant to do more than light up the darkness, illumine Lord Ursus' sky-large sable coat.

The girl within the cub dwindled in her massive flesh and Clovermead felt a surge of strength as her humanity finally fled from her and into the racing doe. Now Clovermead was simply a killer. There would be no turning back, no regrets, no fears, once she had disposed of the little girl in the doe. Then she would serve Lord Ursus with a loving heart and rend flesh as he desired. She would live a life of noble action and devotion. She would eat and drink her fill.

Clovermead had almost caught sight of her prey. The doe was winded and Clovermead put on a burst of speed. Her legs pounded the snow, and Lord Ursus encouraged her forward with his warm breath, by his prickling, mocking, welcoming laughter, through the example of his terrible hunger. Clovermead would catch the girl-doe soon, achingly soon. She longed to be done and to sink her teeth into the puling child's flesh.

Clovermead saw the doe. She could feel the Wickward chit's flesh between her teeth. Her heart pounded, the night was a stink of fear and hope and ravening hunger, and she leapt—

NO! Waxmelt shouted, and flung himself between her and her prey. Clovermead screamed and tried to turn in midair, but her huge bear body smashed into him, her claws dug into his arms and stomach, her teeth bit into his face. She screamed and tried to get off him, but she was achingly hungry and he was a small, weak rabbit of a man and her claws and teeth ravaged the helpless body of Waxmelt Wickward. *I'm here to save you,* she tried to say, but all that came out was a roar. *I have to rescue you from Snuff,* she whispered, but it was a growl as she bit. *This is all for you,* she screamed as she broke his neck.

I've saved my daughter, said Waxmelt, smiling as he died.

I want to wake up, said Clovermead. Tears trickled down her fur as she clawed at the snow. *This is just a dream. Stop it now. Dear Lady, take me away from here.*

Lord Ursus was behind her again. The moon had set and the land was dark. She heard his breathing and his ancient, corrupt laughter.

Sweet Lady, save me! he jeered. *She can't, little cub. You will become a bear and you will have no father. It has been prophesied. This is a vision, not a dream.*

I don't believe you, said Clovermead, sobbing. Her tears melted her fur. *It isn't true. It can't be true.*

Fool! Your mind is as weak as your body. Brat, behold the past. Lord Ursus came closer, swallowed all the sky, and now Clovermead saw around his shoulders a necklace of human finger bones. Some were thick, some delicate, some long, some short, but all had been stripped clean of flesh. Lord Ursus had gnawed on the bones themselves.

Trophies of my prey, Lord Ursus said. *Behold the present.* One giant claw reached out to stroke Clovermead, to rasp and cut through her fur, to touch her bear tooth. Clovermead looked down and saw that the tooth was in her hand once more, come back to her, and had turned into a bleeding finger, fresh torn from a little girl's hand. It was Clovermead's own finger.

Behold the future, Lord Ursus cried out triumphantly. He knelt over Waxmelt's corpse and bent down to chew his flesh.

Clovermead turned and leapt at him. Her claws were full out and her teeth were bared in a rictus of rage. She howled and felt no fear, and Lord Ursus laughed. He struck Clovermead's head with a single flick of his gigantic paw and batted her into midair—

And Clovermead woke in the absolute darkness of a prison cart.

Chapter Fifteen

THE MAYOR'S INTERROGATION

CLOVERMEAD'S HEAD STUNG HORRIBLY AND SHE ACHED all over with bruises. She lay unchained on what felt like dirty straw, her tattered clothes covered by a thin blanket. She slid her swollen hands along her skin and felt for open wounds.

There were none. "My captor has saved his unspeakable vengeance for later and left my bones intact," Clovermead told herself. "Hah, I can speak. It hurts, though." Her throat was dry and itchy. Her upper jaw was on fire. She tried to swallow, and her swollen tongue brushed painfully against her teeth. An echo of a growl hummed inside her.

"My tooth!" said Clovermead. She clutched at her neck, hoping against hope that she would find it there after all. But it was gone. Lord Ursus was gone. She was weak and helpless and alone. She wept tears of anger and sorrow.

A colder breeze sighed through the darkness and Clovermead shivered violently. She tried to grow fur, but she could not. Clovermead forced her bruised body to move. She pawed through slats and straw for something to keep her warm, but there was nothing.

Clovermead gasped and reached to touch her neck again. Her brooch was also gone. She wept a few hot tears. "Ursus tear you, Snuff! Couldn't you leave me anything of Daddy's? Oh, pardon me, Cousin Lucifer, I'm sure you thought these torn clothes and these fine accommodations were a sufficient keepsake." Clovermead furiously wiped her cheeks dry. "The Wickward Suite has been passed down from father to daughter. Not literally, I suppose: After Boulderbash tore out those bars, that cart wouldn't make a good prison anymore." She felt the sides of her cell. All the bars were there. "How intelligent I was to effect this trade and reduce the difficulties of dungeon bookkeeping for my hosts. I wouldn't want to cause them any trouble about the counting of prisoners."

Clovermead explored her cell. Her head bent when she stood up. She was halfway comfortable when she stretched diagonally on the straw, though a grown man would have been bent double. She found a cup of musty water, a plate with a slice of stale bread, and a stinking pot for her eliminations. She shoved the pot to the far end of the cage and wolfed down the bread and water. Then she waited for something to happen.

That something took its time arriving. Dimly she heard oxen low and horses neigh, and once or twice the whisper of human voices, but the curtains around the cart muffled almost all sound. Clovermead formulated endless escape plans in her head—she would be miles from the camp before the bear-priests realized she had filched the key and unlocked the cart! She fantasized of rescue by Sorrel, by Waxmelt, by the Queen of Queensmart in all her martial glory. She escaped, she was rescued, she escaped, she was rescued, and Clovermead dreamed of how Waxmelt and Sorrel would come together on the back of a roc to lift her prison into the blue, blue sky.

She slept, she woke, and she slept again. Clovermead tried to exercise, but it seemed futile. She shouted until she became too thirsty to speak. She wanted her bear tooth. The tooth would have given her the power to escape. Now she was just prey. She was nothing without the tooth, nothing at all. Clovermead's stomach began to ache.

She would die in the dark. All her bravado had been useless. She was a fool, she was weak, all she had ever done had come to nothing. She wanted to live so much. Clovermead cried, bawled, sniveled. She was sorry for herself and she was afraid.

Much later, when at last she had run out of tears and her cheeks had dried, the curtain was flung open. Clovermead gasped and shut her eyes against the reflected sunlight as it boiled into her cell. She tried to stand, but her legs wobbled so badly that she had to support herself against the bars of the back wall. She opened her eyes a crack and squinted through the glare at two indistinct shapes that she guessed were bear-priests.

The first bear-priest unlocked the door to the cage while the second stood behind him with a drawn sword. "Come out," the first bear-priest commanded. Clovermead wanted to curl into a ball—but no, she wouldn't let them know how scared she was. She hobbled forward and tried to hop down to the ground, but she was too weak. The bear-priest cursed and jerked her down. She fell sprawling to the earth. Here the sun itself beat down on her, and she closed her eyes again against its harsh glow. She sat for a minute, waiting to be dragged or hit, but she was left in peace. Finally she looked down and opened her eyelids the slightest bit. There was dead grass and small twigs and cold earth beneath her. The ground was clear of snow. Gradually her eyes adjusted themselves to color, shape, and distance. She felt more hope, more courage in the light. After another minute she looked up.

The Mayor of Low Branding sat in front of her on a small gilded chair. He wore a dark blue velvet doublet and hose, a scarlet tunic, and a jet black hat with a silvery feather protruding from the brim. Sapphires the size of robins' eggs studded his golden belt and necklace. He examined Clovermead curiously, with calculation and almost with sympathy. The Mayor held a perfumed handkerchief to his nose and turned his face to one side when the wind blew toward him from Clovermead. He drummed his fingers with nervous satisfaction on his thin knees, crossed and uncrossed his legs, and rubbed his bulging stomach.

Lucifer Snuff stood by the Mayor's side. He was dressed in the same brown leather, muddy boots, and black cape he had worn when Clovermead first saw him back at the Ladyrest stable. Now he also wore strips of bear fur on his arms and legs. His balding pate and sharpened teeth shone in the sun. He slouched comfortably in His Eminence's presence, his thumbs hooked through his belt. He nodded amiably to Clovermead when he saw her look his way—only a fiery shimmer in his eyes revealed his anger.

Two popinjay Low Branding patricians and two grim bear-priests flanked the Mayor. The patricians regarded her with mild curiosity thinly veneered over profound indifference. The bear-priests looked at her with loathing but spent more time rolling their eyes every which way, wary for any sudden intruder.

The little party stood surrounded by a tight circle of prison carts, whose wooden walls formed a stockade between them and the rest of the army. High over the far carts Clovermead could see the shining pink towers of Chandlefort.

"We are pleased that you have agreed to appear before us," said the Mayor. Clovermead could tell that he used the plural to refer to himself alone. His smooth, courteous voice rang out with power. "We regret the difficulties placed in the way of this meeting by inclement circumstance."

Why, you potbellied stoat of a kidnapper, Clovermead wanted to say, but the words didn't make it past her lips. A brutal gleam in the Mayor's eyes belied his affable smile. It warned her to be polite.

"I do not believe you have been well served by your messenger, Your Eminence," said Clovermead with a courtliness she thought would have made Sir Auroche proud. "His manners are sufficient to make repellent what was in its nature a most attractive invitation."

Snuff muttered an oath and the Mayor chuckled. "Miss Wickward, we must acknowledge that Lucifer is not graced with your smooth tongue. Nevertheless, he is efficient. We have very few such liege men." The patricians bridled at his praise of the bear-priest, and the

Mayor chuckled again. "Ah, but we need both bear-priests and patricians. Bear-priests are powerful, but patricians are loyal to us. Mr. Snuff and his furry friends cooperate wonderfully with our plans, but they obey Garum and Lord Ursus. We would be foolish to dispense with our steadfast patricians. Wouldn't we, Lucifer?"

"Your Eminence's prudence is a byword," said Snuff. He grinned broadly. "Lord Ursus is loyal to his good friends."

"Doubtless—but prudence will remain our principle." The Mayor's fingers fidgeted on his legs, then darted inside his tunic. He brought out Clovermead's brooch. The dents had been smoothed from it, and it had been polished till it shone like white gold. Or was it truly white gold? The bee glittered, the sword gleamed, and Clovermead stared at it in amazement. The Mayor tossed the brooch from hand to hand and rubbed the metal between his fingers.

"This is yours?" he shot out suddenly. "The truth, now."

"My father's, Your Eminence," Clovermead faltered. "He gave it to me for safekeeping. Your Eminence, I'm terribly thirsty. Will it please Your Eminence to be merciful and allow his prisoner some water to drink?"

"Not yet, Miss Wickward," said the Mayor. "Perhaps when you have finished answering our questions."

Thirst and hunger pummeled Clovermead. She swayed and almost fainted. She kept herself awake from pure defiance.

"A good father should hand down his family heirlooms," the Mayor continued agreeably. "Our father gave us the Stork Scepter, the Barrel Throne, the

Mayor's Palace, and the city of Low Branding to rule. His familial instincts were impeccable." He smiled, but his eyes had turned cold. "Miss Clovermead, that brooch doesn't belong to Mr. Wickward. He stole it from Lady Cindertallow. He was supposed to deliver it to us. Did you know that? Do you know what else he was supposed to bring us?"

"Y-yes, Your Eminence," said Clovermead at last. "You mean the Cindertallow Ruby."

"The Cindertallow Ruby?" the Mayor asked softly.

"He told me everything," said Clovermead. "Except where he put the Ruby. He told me how Snuff got him to help steal the Ruby and how he went into the Treasure Room at Chandlefort and how he took the Ruby from its case. He said he took this brooch, too, and that he'd turned it into some sort of treasure map, if you knew how to read it right. The brooch will show you the way to the Ruby. Please, Your Eminence, I don't know how it can be a map, or where the Ruby is, or anything. He didn't tell me any more. I wish he had, but he didn't. You can torture me, but it won't help. Your Eminence, if the brooch doesn't help you, I'm sure you could trade me to my father for directions to the Ruby. I know he was glad to keep the Ruby away from Low Branding and Chandlefort, but he stole it a long time ago. I think he'd gladly tell you where it is if you'd give me back to him."

"You are misinformed," the Mayor said. His lips were trembling. Snuff's eyes were aflame with glee. "You are dreadfully misinformed. We are quite sure that Mr. Wickward will do no such thing. In the first place, Miss Wickward, we are informed that he has been taken within the walls of Chandlefort. He will do nothing contrary to the will of Lady Cindertallow. For another, Miss Clovermead Wickward, you have been misinformed for a terribly long time." The Mayor paused and laughed. "There is no such thing as the Cindertallow Ruby. There is no Treasure Room in Chandlefort. What we seek is something entirely different."

And the Mayor burst into peals of uncontrollable laughter. Snuff yelped and slapped his thighs. The two of them laughed and laughed, while Clovermead clenched her fists and tried very, very hard to keep herself from helpless sobs. They must be telling the truth: They wouldn't laugh so hard, so genuinely, unless they were. Was there no end to her father's deceits? He was false all the way to his lying heart, and only pain and death were truth. That she now knew.

The Mayor wiped tears from his eyes and suppressed his chortles. "Only a child raised in a rude land would believe such a preposterous tale. Do not take our words too harshly," he added hastily, for tears now glittered in Clovermead's eyes. "You are not to blame for the circumstances of your upbringing. No. But, Miss Wickward, we assure you that there is no Chandlefort Ruby. Hence the trade you propose is, well, out of the question. No, no, the only trading going on will be between Lady Cindertallow and ourself. And for an entirely different sort of gem." He yelped with laughter, as if at some particularly clever witticism.

"There is a simpler way, Your Eminence," said Snuff. "If you would choose to read the prophecies in a different manner." His eyes rested lightly on Clovermead.

"What did the chit call it? The Chandlefort Ruby. You can take the Chandlefort Ruby for yourself and claim Chandlefort with it. You can get rid of the Ruby afterward. Chandlefort will still be yours."

"We are not so ambitious," said the Mayor. "Nor are we so afflicted by hubris as to try to twist prophecy. It is a most dangerous simplicity you suggest. Besides, it is unnecessarily bloody, Lucifer. You have many valuable skills, but you have no sense of politics. That procedure would make a bad impression on many important people. And we are not in a position to ignore impressions. No, no, not nearly. And, Lucifer, your people don't help." He shook his head disapprovingly. "We recognize that Lord Ursus requires certain necessary rituals. But your priests could be more polished. Smoother. You are relatively smooth, Lucifer. Could you not instruct your fellows?"

The bear-priests glowered more determinedly than ever. "Lord Ursus tears roughly at a man's heart," said Snuff. "He is not smooth. I"—Snuff smiled—"I came naturally to his precepts, Your Eminence. I slid with his claws."

"And so you are a courteous beast," the Mayor said with a laugh. Snuff laughed too, but only with his mouth. His eyes were stony. The Mayor looked idly back at Clovermead. "We have been inattentive of you during our little badinage, Miss Wickward. We apologize for the discourtesy. Tell us, what has Mr. Wickward told you of Lady Cindertallow?"

"Very little, Your Eminence." Clovermead desperately ransacked her memory. "She made my father and his parents work very hard. Father said his parents got worked to death in her service. He hated her. I suppose she's haughty. Father said all the lords and ladies of Chandlefort were haughty."

"Mmm. Mr. Wickward is most perceptive. She is very arrogant. Perhaps we could have avoided this war if she had not been so haughty." The Mayor shrugged. "Or perhaps not. They say one yard isn't big enough for two dogs." He laughed delightedly. "The peasants have such amusing phrases. Dear me. But Lady Cindertallow is also a woman of honor and a woman of heart, within her narrow bounds. Miss Wickward, do you know that we could have forced Chandlefort to recognize Low Branding's independence twelve years ago, if not for your father's unexpected thievery?"

Clovermead shook her head. She did not dare to speak.

"We based our actions on Lady Cindertallow's honor and heart. And then your father intervened—these have been a most frustrating twelve years. We had hoped to be undisputed sovereign of Low Branding in our prime. Instead our son will inherit that pleasure." The Mayor sighed. "Well, it is over now, and Lady Cindertallow's honor and heart are intact, if our spies are to be believed. As always, complex ways are slow but certain. Events have borne out that truth, Lucifer, have they not?"

"So it would seem, Your Eminence," said Snuff.

"The appearance is the truth," said the Mayor, getting stiffly to his feet. "Our bones ache. We are not as fit for campaign as we once were. Well and well. Lucifer, you have kept Miss Wickward ignorant. Well done—

you will be rewarded. Miss Wickward, we do apologize for the air of mystery. It is probably unnecessary, but prudence is our watchword. If it is any comfort, you will find out the truth soon enough."

"Will I be free when I learn the truth, Your Eminence?" asked Clovermead.

"A philosopher would say yes," said the Mayor with a thin smile. "But you are not interested in moral theorizing. You will probably become free, Miss Wickward. That is all we can honestly say. Lucifer, she will not set your bears on our army again, will she? Too many of our soldiers died in that skirmish."

"I've searched her for my tooth," Snuff said. "It's not there. She must have lost it in the raid."

"Then, we need not keep the young lady in the carts." The Mayor turned to one of the popinjays by his side. "Seneschal, Miss Wickward needs food and water, a bath, and a change of wardrobe. She will not make a good impression in her current state. You will arrange it?"

"At once, Your Eminence," said the Seneschal.

"But don't lose track of her—eh, Seneschal?" The Mayor's voice was suddenly sharp and grim. "She is a very important prisoner."

The Seneschal blanched. "She won't escape, Your Eminence," he said in a stifled tone.

"We will have your head off if she does," said the Mayor.

Chapter Sixteen

The Prophecy of Mrs. Neap

THE SENESCHAL TIED CLOVERMEAD'S HANDS BEHIND HER back and kept a tight grip on her shoulder as they exited through the stockade of prison carts. Infantrymen in parade uniform hastily closed the breach behind them. At the Seneschal's brusque direction two of them marched up to escort Clovermead through the camp. The little party plunged into the iridescent tents of the Mayor's entourage—young patricians clad in harlequin hues who all seemed to be fencing, drinking, gambling, and swearing lightly about their losses as their servants hurried to and fro, catering to their masters' whims. The young men cheerfully greeted the Seneschal and looked curiously at Clovermead. The Seneschal grunted his replies and hurried on.

They came to the servants' quarters—a place of smaller, plainer tents, mixed with outdoor kitchens and clotheslines. Butlers, cooks, and laundresses chattered amiably with one another as they did their work, and bowed respectfully to the Seneschal. The laundresses clucked their tongues with pity to see Clovermead's slight figure rushed along by great soldiers.

The Seneschal beckoned a group of servants standing nearby to attend him. "Mr. Cofferdam," he said to a hulking redhead, "this young lady needs new clothes. Please fetch Master Carnelian's tailor—I know the old fellow's cut dresses for that brewer's daughter Carny's so fond of. When you're done with that, tell my cook to bring a good, hot meal here in an hour. Mr. Jetty, the girl will need privacy, and we need more space than a tent can provide. Please bring some screens. Miss Quay, please fetch a nightdress for her. What she has must be burned, and the tailor ought not to approach her while she is naked. And—what's your name again?" The Seneschal frowned in puzzlement at a tall, middle-aged woman with a homely face.

"Mrs. Neap, milord," she said, curtseying.

"Ah, yes, I remember now," said the Seneschal, who plainly didn't. "Mrs. Neap, please arrange for hot water and a tub. You will bathe the young lady. Also, bring her breakfast and tea. Soldiers, the three of us will watch the screen while the girl remains inside it. Be prepared for her to attempt a sudden escape." He clapped his hands and the servants scattered to obey his orders.

In a few minutes Mr. Jetty returned with curved wooden screens that formed a circle thirty feet across. As he set them up near the servants' tents on a snowless gray-red expanse of crumbling rock and sparse weeds, Miss Quay came up with a small white nightgown and thin blue slippers, which she left on a wooden chair within the screens. Mrs. Neap returned with a bowl of oatmeal and a steaming teapot, then in three more trips came back with a large woolen rug that she spread on the screened-in ground, two slim chairs, and a five-foot copper tub. Several laundresses came in her train, each hoisting a cauldron of boiling water in her mittened hands. The laundresses poured the water into the tub till it was nearly full to the brim, and left several more cauldrons nearby, with steam trickling from their lidded tops.

"The young lady will bathe now," said Mrs. Neap firmly. She shooed everyone out of the enclosure, shut the screens firmly, then turned and smiled gently at Clovermead. "That's all right, my dear. You sit down by the tub, get yourself a bite to eat, and wait for the water to cool down a bit. Here, I brought you a towel and soap." She handed them to Clovermead, who let them drop by her side, then joined towel and soap on the wool rug.

Clovermead gulped at the oatmeal and gasped as the hot mush burned her throat. She washed it down with a draught of tea. "I don't understand," she said. "First they shut me up in that horrible prison cart, and now I'm about to have a hot bath. I suppose there's some reason for what they're doing, but I am utterly perplexed."

"His Eminence has a mind like a corkscrew, so don't try following it unless you want to end up in knots. Will your mystification keep you from bathing?"

"Not unless the Mayor put sharks in the tub."

"There are no animals in any bath I make," sniffed Mrs. Neap. Clovermead smiled to see her look so proudly disgusted at the idea. "Dear me, if you're well enough to laugh, you're well enough to get yourself into this tub. Off with your clothes and in you go!"

"Yes, ma'am," said Clovermead. *She seems nice enough,* thought Clovermead, *like Goody Weft or Goody Merrin or someone like that. She even looks like somebody or another that I knew in Timothy Vale. They did say Gaffer Bolts had an aunt who married a pilgrim from Low Branding. I wonder if this is her daughter? I'll have to ask her.* She finished gobbling her oatmeal, and in a trice she had shucked her clothes and plopped herself into the hot water.

"Stay still," Mrs. Neap commanded as she commenced to wash the dirt from Clovermead. "I'm sure you just want to play in the hot water, but we need to get you clean first. The tub will cool before you know it, and who's going to be heating new water for you? Some poor woman with something better to do with her time. Ee, those scars are ugly." She ran the washcloth gently over Clovermead's tooth-welted hand and arm. "My dear, how did you do that? And all those bruises . . ." Clovermead hissed as the washcloth ran over the bump on her head. "Who on earth did all this to you?"

"Bear-priests," said Clovermead. "Your Mayor's friends."

"Oh, them," said Mrs. Neap with unveiled distaste. She scrubbed harder at Clovermead's back. The pressure of her hands hurt Clovermead's bruises but relaxed the tight knots in her muscles. "I won't speak a bad word of His Eminence, but I wish he hadn't allied himself with that lot. They're nasty men, those bear-priests. You poor thing. But there's no helping what can't be helped, as my mother used to say. And you're not too badly hurt—you're lucky, miss, if half what they say about the bear-priests is true. Can I trust you to soap yourself?"

Clovermead giggled. "I'm not going to throw the soap out of the tub, if that's what you mean. And I do want to be clean, really clean. That prison cart was just awful." Mrs. Neap drew in her breath sharply. "I underwent but a day or two of horror, but those other prisoners must have been locked up for years. I think you ought to speak horrid and terrible truths of His Eminence, to speak nothing of a bad word. He bears responsibility for the evils of the bear-priests, and what they do is terrible. Oh! My stomach's rumbling. The oatmeal was awfully nice, but there wasn't that much of it. My stomach is not appeased. How long till that hot meal comes?"

"Half an hour, I'd say," said Mrs. Neap. She handed the cake of soap to Clovermead. "Don't give me that sad look, young lady. You can hold out that long. Now then, you use that soap carefully. It has special herbs in it that clean wounds and make swelling go down. The Mayor himself bathes with it. Be sure you touch it to every place you're injured."

Clovermead dipped the sweet-smelling soap in the warm water and rubbed it along her arm. Her flesh tingled and the pain in her scars and bruises faded. Clovermead ran the soap slowly and deliberately over her other wounds, while Mrs. Neap sat back comfortably in her chair and sternly instructed her to wash behind her ears and cleanse her matted hair. Her blond stubble and pale skin reemerged as the soap stripped away her disguising stain. When the bath began to cool, Mrs. Neap poured in another cauldron of hot water.

After the soap had dissolved entirely, Clovermead lay back and just let the bath's warmth soak into her. *I have not sufficiently praised comfort,* she thought to herself. *Adventure is all well and fine, but a hot bath, a hot meal, and a warm bed are lovelier than a cellar of jewels. I should write an epic lay on the virtues of leisure.*

Leisure will bore you, said her tooth. *Don't I know you, little cub? You have a taste for adventure.*

You're wrong, said Clovermead inwardly. *I'll stay in this bath for a solid week, you wait and see. . . .* She stiffened in her bath. *Tooth?* she asked. *Where are you?* She felt fear and joy and completeness. She had feared the tooth so, missed it so.

Where should a tooth be?

Clovermead trembled and reached toward her suddenly aching mouth. The bear tooth was there, where her upper left canine had been. Her old tooth had been ground away and now the stump began to complain bitterly. The bear tooth was lodged in its place, huge and bloody.

I am with you still and always, said the tooth. *Could I let Snuff remove me from you? No, disciple, daughter, I could not let him part us. You lay unconscious in the gully and I moved your arms for you. Your arms secured me in your mouth. I made myself seem as small as a human tooth for a while, but no more. I am myself again and now we are bound together forever.*

Forever, Clovermead told herself dreamily. *How sweet that sounds—but why didn't you speak earlier? I was so lonely and scared, there in the dark of the prison cart. I was weak and helpless and I needed you.*

You needed to learn that lesson, little one, said the tooth. *You are nothing without me. Without me is fear, solitude, night, the weakness of the worm. Now you will never forget that.*

You were cruel, said Clovermead.

The tooth laughed. *Cruelty happens to the weak. Do you want to be weak?*

Never again, said Clovermead. *Never, never, never.*

Power will be yours, said the tooth. *I swear it.*

I'm afraid of your power, said Clovermead.

Again the tooth laughed.

"I still don't understand why the Mayor's doing all this," Clovermead said hurriedly to Mrs. Neap. "What makes me important?" A sudden, awful thought made her sit bolt upright in the water. "Does the Mayor want to gloat over me? Will he put me in a fine dress and tie me with rusty chains to a great big boulder on the top of a hill near his palace and come out every day at noon to cackle triumphantly and rub his hands with glee and tell me I'll never be rescued, never, never, never? The Black Knight did that to Lady Amaurette in the *Heptameron,* and she was just about to go mad and had started singing songs about marigolds and ducklings when Sir Auroche rescued her just in time. I suppose Sorrel or Father wouldn't be able to tear off my chains with their bare hands, like Sir Auroche, but they could probably break them with a hammer or a file. I don't think I'd go mad just because the Mayor was gloating, either. I always thought that it was the boredom of being tied up on a rock that would make you go mad, and that listening to the gloating would help to pass the time until you were rescued. And I never did get the point of the gloating itself. If I was going to be a villain like the Black Knight, I don't think I'd waste my time with all that cackling business. Mrs. Neap, couldn't you please tell the Mayor that he'd just be wasting his time gloating over me, and that he'd be much better off letting me go?"

Mrs. Neap tried vainly to suppress her laughter and then burst into a hearty guffaw. "Dear Lady! There are no boulders with chains in Low Branding. There aren't even any hills nearby. His Eminence has dungeons and jailers to do his guarding for him, and he has no desire to gloat over little girls who have clearly read too many romances. I'm sure he doesn't plan anything of the sort for you, so put that kerfuffle out of your head. Are you clean yet?"

"Yes," said Clovermead shortly, with wounded dignity.

"Then, bath time is over," said Mrs. Neap. "Here's your towel." Clovermead stepped from the bath into its thick fibers with scarcely a second exposed to the winter chill. Mrs. Neap brought her the nightgown and slippers as she dried herself off, and helped her slip into them as quickly as she could. Clovermead sat down in the chair opposite Mrs. Neap.

"Now, child, I can't tell you why His Eminence wants you dolled up so fine," said Mrs. Neap ruminatively, "but I can give you some good advice."

"I should be a sweet little girl who curtseys at the drop of a hat and speaks respectfully to her elders? That's the advice I usually get."

"That is good counsel, dear," said Mrs. Neap with a smile. "But I meant something else. It's never too late to draw out the bear tooth, Clovermead Wickward."

"What?" The tooth roared rage and fury through Clovermead, and her hands jerked toward Mrs. Neap to rake her cheeks. Clovermead made her alien arms fall still. Slowly, slowly, she made her nails grow short and lowered her mutinous hands. The tooth growled hate and alarm, but Clovermead would not let it rule her. Not yet. "How do you know about my tooth? How dare you . . ." *Make me hope?* she almost said. *How dare you make me despair?*

another part of her echoed. Clovermead was pale and shaking. "Mrs. Neap, how do you know my name? I never told you that."

"Yes, you did," said Mrs. Neap. "Weeks ago and many miles to the north. You were very kind and gave me a towel to dry myself with, so now I've been able to return the favor."

"But that was . . ." Clovermead looked straight at unmemorable Mrs. Neap. The woman's face blurred. Her skin shook like water on a moonlit lake, roiling with light. Her body shone bright as fog in the morning sun. Mrs. Neap wavered in and out of view, disappeared, and left in her place a tall woman with raven hair, a faint scar on her cheek, and a mouth constantly on the verge of laughter. She was stout about the waist, and under her brown dress she wore a pale gray habit. Around her neck she wore a silver pendant of Our Lady. Her eyes were as thick with dreams as ever.

"Sister Rowan!" exclaimed Clovermead.

"I told you it was fun to sneak up on people unawares. Hello, Clovermead," said Sister Rowan. She stretched out her arms and enfolded Clovermead in a long hug. The tooth raged, but Clovermead clung to the nun, her body all atremble as Sister Rowan patted and soothed her. She didn't cry, she wouldn't cry, but she was awfully glad to see the nun. She felt younger in Sister Rowan's embrace. She felt more human.

"Are you here to help me escape?" Clovermead asked at last. "Can you teach me that disguising trick?"

"I'm sorry, Clovermead," said Sister Rowan. "It takes years to learn that art. You'll have to stay prisoner a little longer. I'm here because I had another vision of Our Lady, at the Royal Abbey in Queensmart. She said the same words I just told you about the bear tooth, and then she said, 'Tell Clovermead Wickward.' I was terribly distraught when I woke up, because she'd also told me where to find you, but I'd already forgotten that part of her message." Sister Rowan blushed brick red. "Abbess Medick always did say I had a head like a sieve."

"I'm glad you were able to warn me, and that's all that matters," Clovermead said tactfully.

"Thank you, Clovermead. People do carp so—anyway, Our Lady is bountiful in her providence, and she sent Abbess Spurge another vision on the same night. Our Lady told the Abbess that I would find you outside Chandlefort, in the Army of Low Branding. Abbess Spurge wasn't very happy when she told me this—she gets a splitting headache when she has visions, poor dear—but I must say, she was much more cooperative than Abbess Medick was. Abbess Spurge sent me north right away to find you. I got here a few days ago and I hid myself among the servants. They don't know one another that well, so it was easy to pretend I was one of them. I looked for you, but I didn't find you. Then today the Seneschal showed up with a brown-haired, brown-skinned waif who I could tell at once was Clovermead Wickward, and here we are."

"I'm awfully glad to see you," said Clovermead. "I've never been alone before—there was always Father while I was in Timothy Vale, and then there was Sorrel while I was traveling south." She told Sister Rowan the story of her journey. "And now the Mayor seems to want to keep me captive," Clovermead concluded. "Do you know why?"

Sister Rowan shook her head. "Abbess Spurge may know—she got terribly excited when I told her all the visions of you I'd been having. But she wouldn't say why." Sister Rowan blushed again. "She said, 'You'd gab the Abbey password to Lord Ursus himself and not realize you'd done anything wrong.' She was very stinging."

"You would have," said Clovermead. She curled back her lips and pointed to the bear tooth embedded in her jaw. "He's in me, Sister Rowan. He hears my thoughts." Sister Rowan gasped as she looked at the tooth and the tooth growled with satisfaction.

Now Clovermead told Sister Rowan how she had been changing since she picked up Snuff's bear tooth—how she had learned to talk with bears and command them, about the blood-draining, the tooth-talking, the fur and claws, her hunger and thirst. She told her about her dreams of the valley of Snowchapel.

"That's exactly the way it looks," said Sister Rowan. "I couldn't have described the place better myself. That much was a true dream."

"I'm afraid the rest will be too," said Clovermead. All her fears and dark desires spilled out of her—how she had missed the tooth when she thought it was gone, how glad she had been to discover it still with her. "Half the time now I want to be a bear," Clovermead finished, whispering, trembling. "I want to become like Lord Ursus. Sister Rowan, I don't think I believe what Our Lady told you. I'm not strong enough to take out the tooth. It'll be the other way around—he'll draw me out of my body and have the husk for himself. Sister Rowan, can't you help me?" Clovermead was crying, and the tooth was laughing at her puling weakness. "Help me draw the tooth."

Tentatively Sister Rowan reached out her finger to touch the bear tooth—and jerked her finger away, crying out in pain. Her flesh had been ripped open. "It bit me," she cried out. "He bit me." She reached out her fingers again and Clovermead growled. Clovermead's hands seized Sister Rowan's and held them still between tight claws. Sister Rowan looked at Clovermead's eyes. They were wide open, mad and yellow, and Clovermead wanted very badly to tear into the nun. The tooth savored the taste of nun's blood and hungered for more. "I won't try to draw the tooth," Sister Rowan said, speaking slowly and clearly. Clovermead nodded and released the nun's arms. Sister Rowan drew back and the madness faded from Clovermead's eyes. "I can't help you. Clovermead, listen to Our Lady's message. You can draw the tooth yourself. It'll never be too late."

"What does it matter?" Clovermead asked. She was crying again. Her tears were bitter and despairing. "I freed Father. That's all I wanted to do. Let Lord Ursus have me now."

"You also matter," said Sister Rowan. "Our Lady sent me a vision about you. She cares what happens to you."

"Why doesn't She send *me* a vision, then?"

Because she is dead, said the tooth. *Because she never was.*

Sister Rowan sighed. "Lord Ursus is very strong, Clovermead. His claws can block Her light. Her light still exists, but you must search for Her, even in darkness."

Clovermead laughed, an echo of the tooth's mocking guffaws. "Then, what use is it to pray to her? Lord

Ursus' way is better. He helps his worshipers. He doesn't abandon them." Like Waxmelt. Like Sorrel. Like Sister Rowan. Our Lady was like the rest of them. She had left Clovermead alone in the darkness. Only Lord Ursus was true to her. He was terrible, but he would never leave her.

Never, the tooth promised. *I will be with you until death and to the end of time. Together we will hunt prey when the sun is a dying ember and the earth is cold as ash. On a far dusk we will kill the last man. We will hear his last scream. We will drink the last pool of human blood.*

Promise? asked Clovermead. *Promise me, my Lord. You won't lie to me? You won't leave me?*

I swear it, said Lord Ursus, and Clovermead knew he spoke the truth.

From a great distance Clovermead saw that her words and laughter had horrified Sister Rowan. "I don't mean that," she lied. "I'll listen to Our Lady's message."

"Good, good," said Sister Rowan with relief. "You must, my dear. You have to." She clasped Clovermead's hand in hers. Clovermead's hand felt nothing. It was dead flesh.

At last Sister Rowan rose. "I wish I could stay more, but they'll get suspicious. Don't worry—I won't go too far and I'll have my eye out for you. If I can, I'll try to get word to Chandlefort so that Lady Cindertallow's soldiers can rescue you."

"I'm awfully glad, Sister Rowan," said Clovermead. But now it was just words. Clovermead hugged the nun farewell. "Thank you for trying to take out the tooth," she said. "It will never leave me," she added, but by that time Sister Rowan had turned into Mrs. Neap and had left Clovermead's enclosure.

Miss Quay bustled in with the tailor, and there was a great deal of measuring and turning and noting of sizes and shapes. The tailor went away, and Mr. Cofferdam came in and put a table on the ground, then set it with plates, silverware and glasses, hot roasted chicken, baked potatoes, and corn muffins. The glasses were filled with sparkling water and red wine, and Clovermead got pleasantly tipsy as she devoured the meal. She was still hungry, still thirsty, but the food and drink had taken the edge off her hunger.

The tailor came back with white silk petticoats, a canary yellow dress, an ermine coat and hat, and thick wool-lined boots. Wonderingly Clovermead felt the clothes. They were so beautiful! And then she had to put them on, and though the materials were fine and soft, she had never been in anything so restricting and uncomfortable in her life. She could mince in them, but she couldn't run or jump or bend down to scoop up a stone or anything. *They would laugh at me in Timothy Vale,* thought Clovermead. *I'd laugh at me. I look like a lemon pie. I would much rather have a sensible, comfortable vest and trousers.* She was on the point of saying so, but then Miss Quay cooed delightedly that Clovermead was dressed in the height of fashion, and that she had never seen a girl look so lovely in her life, and that Clovermead must be simply, simply thrilled. Clovermead concluded that Miss Quay had the brains of a chicken, so it wasn't worth saying anything at all.

When she had been dolled up to Miss Quay's satisfaction, the screens came down. The Seneschal gave her an appraising look, nodded his approval, and marched her back to her prison cart, escorted by the soldiers. The cart had been cleaned of its straw and its filth, and now a freshly made bed with sheets and blankets lay in the cage.

"In you go, Miss Wickward," said the Seneschal. He offered his hand to Clovermead and helped her up into the cage. She lay down on the bed. It was soft and comfortable. "I'll have to lock the door, Miss Wickward," said the Seneschal apologetically. "I'm afraid that you still have to be treated as a prisoner. But do call during the night if you need anything—anything at all. The soldiers will attend to you." Then he let the black curtain fall.

So Clovermead fell asleep mightily perplexed—locked in a cage, dressed like a princess, and warm in a snug, clean bed.

And Lord Ursus was with her. The lullaby of his perpetual growl was a comfort to her.

Chapter Seventeen

What Waxmelt Wickward Stole

CLOVERMEAD WOKE TO A TANTARA OF TRUMPETS. MARTIAL music bugled forth and cannonaded off the stone walls of Chandlefort. The sound swelled loud and louder.

Snuff ripped the curtain from the cage and the morning sun streamed in. "Good morning, girlie!" he said. "Time to rise. Action at last! His Eminence has been waiting for this day for twelve years—you should see how excited he is! He's so frantic that he can't button his shirt properly." Snuff unlocked the door of the cage. "You coming, or do I have to drag you out? Say I have to drag you, chit. You owe me for my tooth."

Clovermead meditated on Snuff's cruel face with cold hatred. *You corrupted my father,* she silently accused him. *You persecuted him, captured him, would have killed him. You corrupted me with your tooth. It will all be worthwhile to kill you. To humiliate you.*

I will give you that power, said the tooth.

I am yours, Lord Ursus, said Clovermead, and she abandoned herself to darkness.

At last! said the tooth with joy. Lord Ursus rushed into Clovermead. He was darkness, pain, and blood. Above all, he was power. Clovermead was him, he was her, and they could devour an army or tear down a fortress. Their feast would start today.

"I used your tooth better than you ever did," said a low voice in Clovermead. Its very tone hinted at cruelties beyond Clovermead's imagination. She hoped she would learn of them soon.

Clovermead rose from the bed and faced Snuff without fear. "I broke your net. I set the bears on you. Could you have done that, weakling?" She balled her fists—then unclenched them. All ten of her fingers grew thick, curving claws. This time her fingers were transformed, not just her nails. Her clawed, furry fingers grew, horribly fast, until each was half a foot long. Their tips dripped with fresh blood. She advanced toward Snuff as his face suddenly blanched. She reached out her claws through the cage door to his face. Snuff stood still, craven and trembling. "You owe me for your life, prey."

"Master," Snuff whispered. "Mistress—forgive me." He bent back his head so that his throat was exposed to Clovermead's claws. "Kill me if you want to." But behind his fear Clovermead saw betrayed hurt and hatred.

"When I am hungry, I will," the low voice said through Clovermead. "You are still useful. Tell my priests to prepare for battle. Ready the bears to attack."

"But our plans," Snuff protested. "They're almost in place."

"There are new plans," said the voice in Clovermead. "I will make the prophecy mine." Clovermead roared with laughter and her claws withdrew into her fingers. "Lead me out," she told Snuff in her girl's voice. "His Eminence commands it."

"Yes, Mistress," said Snuff, ducking his head obsequiously. Clovermead gloried in his humiliation and his ungovernable, helpless hatred. She descended from the cage proud as a queen.

The day was brilliantly clear, the sky sapphire and cloudless from horizon to horizon. The air was bitter cold and froze Clovermead's lungs stiff and painful as she wheezed out puffs of white breath. There was no wind. Chandlefort's Rose Walls were bleached, bright shadows in the pale sun. The Salt Heath was bleak and empty. The tents and wagons of the Army of Low Branding were impudent intruders from the land of the warm and the quick on a barren land, whose temporary occupation of the dead soil would pass soon enough.

Featherfall and a pony waited outside the cage. "If you please, Mistress," Snuff muttered. He offered his arm to Clovermead. She spurned it and leapt onto the pony by herself. The pony whinnied fearfully as Clovermead clapped her knees around its flanks. Clovermead laughed and stroked the pony's neck with her claws. The beast tried to bolt, but Clovermead clamped down on its pitiful, small mind and extinguished its will. The pony's legs moved at her command.

Snuff and Clovermead rode slowly through the assembled army. The soldiers had polished their armor, shields, and weapons till their burnished glare outshone the rubies of Chandlefort. Each regiment formed an exact rectangle. Cavalry and infantry alike stood immobile as statues, inhumanly self-controlled in their granitic stillness. Some soldiers turned blue from cold, but no teeth chattered and no one shivered.

Around the army the bears stood in an equally impassive circle. They occasionally yawned and licked their lips. Bear-priests, fewer than before Clovermead's assault, had been interleaved among the bears. In their furs, priest and beast were scarcely distinguishable from each other.

At the front of the besiegers the Mayor rode in splendor on his small gray mare. He wore steel plate armor embossed with the image of a great pike, all teeth and scales and fins. Punnily, the pike wielded a pike, whose tip was as razor sharp as the fish's teeth. At his waist the Mayor had a reed-thin rapier whose hilt was solid sapphire. His stoatish features undid his attempt at absolute splendor, but he was still an imposing sight.

By the Mayor's side were a dozen bear-priests and a dozen patricians, whose dull furs and brilliant costumes formed an unlikely contrast. They held themselves even more stiffly than the army at large, if that were possible. The mayor nervously switched his mare back and forth between the two honor guards.

"Hello, Lucifer," said the Mayor. "Good morning, Miss Wickward. We are pleased to see you."

"Thank you, Your Eminence," said Clovermead. She and Snuff halted a little away from the Mayor. She sent mute instructions across the Heath to the bear-priests, told of new plans, new friends, new enemies. The spirit of the Bear was in the captive girl and spoke through her. The soldiers of Low Branding were no longer allies. Soon they would be prey. The bear-priests listened, and Clovermead saw them submit themselves to her as they turned and slightly bowed their heads to her, each in turn. Then the priests sent instructions to the bears. Instructions multiplied in the blood-net. Clovermead added no more words, but she silently roared. The bear-priests quivered with devotion. The bears offered her their hunger. She luxuriated in her servants' terrified obedience.

"Let it start," the Mayor said with passionate intensity. "We want this war over. We want our freedom." He waved an imperious hand.

Five heralds dressed in silver and riding ash white horses trotted slowly from the besieging army toward Chandlefort. Each waved a pearly truce flag. The trumpets blared out louder than ever, and the heralds came within bowshot of the walls. They halted their steeds, raised golden horns to their lips, and let sound an enormous, synchronized shout that could be heard for miles—"OYEZ!" The word rolled off the Chandlefort walls and up towers and through distant windows. It rattled into the bowels of the castle.

"OYEZ!" the heralds repeated. "Attend the words of His Eminence, Cabochon Corundum, the Mayor of Low Branding, beloved of Lord Ursus!"

For a minute there was silence. Then ten heralds of Chandlefort dressed in cloth of gold climbed atop the nearest parapet. They put golden horns of their own to their lips. "Lady Cindertallow deigns to listen," was their laconic reply, as fiercely clamorous as the hail of the heralds of Low Branding.

"Deigns, does she?" the Mayor muttered. "Thinks she can still be proud? We will punish her for that. Go on," he shouted to his heralds. "You know what you're supposed to say. Give that piece of arrogance our message."

"His Eminence declares siege on Chandlefort," blared the Mayor's heralds. Their words were an assault on the eardrums. "His Eminence declares that the Demesne of Chandlefort has waged unlawful, unjust, and aggressive war on the City of Low Branding and sought to deny it its rightful freedom. His Eminence demands that Chandlefort cease its unjust violence. His Eminence, Cabochon Corundum, the Mayor of Low Branding, beloved of Lord Ursus, calls on Lady Cindertallow to make an immediate treaty of peace."

"She won't," Snuff said to Clovermead with vicious satisfaction. "Even if Waxy's told her everything, she doesn't know for certain that we have you. She doesn't know whether I've lived to tell the Mayor who you are. She'll refuse and then we'll tell the truth. She'll capitulate willy-nilly and look the fool for her first refusal. We'll show her pride for the shell it is. All pretense, like everything of the sky-crone's."

"What do you mean, tell them who I am?" asked Clovermead. Her voice shook. "I'm just Clovermead Wickward. I'm no one."

Snuff looked at her with loathing. "You're yourself again, Mistress. How terrible. Why did the Master choose you? Why?"

"Because I am powerful," Clovermead said in her bear's growl, and Snuff recoiled, cringing.

The Chandlefort heralds were quiet for a long minute. Then they called out, "Lady Melisande Cindertallow, Chatelaine of Chandlefort, Marchioness of the Salt Heath, Suzeraine Perpetual of Low Branding, Mistress of High Branding, Protectress of

Timothy Vale, Abbess Honorary of Snowchapel, Voivodine of the Harrow Moors, Foundress Hereditary of Ryebrew and Barleymill, Vicereine in the Realm of Linstock, says this to the Mayor of Low Branding, her rebellious subject: He will put down his arms and surrender himself to our terrible justice. If not, we will fight him unceasingly, trusting to Our Lady's love and to our walls, until his siege is broken. Sure of our rights, we will further war until Low Branding has been subdued to its lawful obedience."

"You bluff well," said the Mayor, grinning savagely. "It won't work. We have outplayed you. Say on, heralds."

The heralds thundered. "His Eminence, Cabochon Corundum, the Mayor of Low Branding, beloved of Lord Ursus, scoffs at Lady Cindertallow's hollow boasts. He sends an ultimatum to Lady Cindertallow: He will destroy what Lady Cindertallow most values if she does not recognize that Low Branding is sovereign and free."

There was some discussion on the parapet. Very quickly the heralds called out, "Lady Cindertallow demands that the Mayor of Low Branding explain himself."

"Hah!" the Mayor crowed. "She knows, Lucifer! She knows we have her. After all these years, Snuff. She won't be so high and mighty now!"

"Plunge in the dagger, Your Eminence," Snuff urged. He laughed loud, in ghastly ecstasy. His serrated teeth flashed in the bone white sun. "Tell the stupid cow about her lost calf."

The Mayor kicked his horse and galloped forward to join the heralds. Snuff grabbed Clovermead's reins and pulled her with him, after the Mayor. He showed no respect to Clovermead in his time of triumph. A myriad of men looked with awestruck suspicion upon Clovermead, and suddenly she knew what her father had stolen all those years ago. She knew the lie that he could not bear to reveal to his beloved daughter.

The Mayor grabbed a golden horn from the nearest herald. "We have the baby stolen by Waxmelt Wickward, sometime servant at Chandlefort," he bellowed. "We have Lady Cindertallow's daughter and sole heir." He swung around and pointed a jubilant finger at Clovermead. "Give us our freedom and we will return her to you. Continue this war and she dies."

Clovermead heard laughter all around her, inside and out. Snuff yelped, Lord Ursus roared, the Mayor guffawed, and she looked back at the deception that had been her life in Timothy Vale. She saw Waxmelt Wickward, kidnapper, teach the child of his hated mistress to call him Father and to love him, and that was worse than laughter. Great teeth ravaged her heart, but they were not Lord Ursus'. They were her own treacherous father's, whom she had risked her life to save, who was not her father after all, who had made her true mother a stranger to her. Waxmelt Wickward had orphaned her and called her Daughter.

Lord Ursus was a better father than Waxmelt could ever be. Inside she roared her sorrow and her rage. Lord Ursus comforted her with hunger and thirst and the promise of satiation and revenge.

"We will parley," cried the heralds of Chandlefort.

The castle's thick black iron gates were flung wide

and dragged back by scores of servants. The gates rumbled along grooves worn into the granite flagstones and lit red sparks as they dug into the stone. They snapped into position perpendicular to the walls as the servants fell wearily back into the Chandlefort courtyard. Where the gates had been, a hole one hundred feet wide and twenty feet high gaped in the walls.

Thunderous hoofbeats echoed from the gates, and twenty-four Guardsmen riding side by side burst out of the dark entrance onto the Heath. The sun glinted off their canary yellow jackets and white capes, off glittering sabers and spurs and bright helmets. They were giants six and a half feet high and taller. Each waved a banner of Chandlefort: Two dozen golden burning bees and scarlet flaming swords flapped in the breeze, each ten feet high. The Guardsmen rode till they were one hundred yards from the wall, swiftly formed an outward-facing semicircle, and suddenly reined in their horses. Each Guardsman then drew a man-high saber from his scabbard and lifted it point out. They stood high in their saddles and proudly held their flags and sabers in midair.

When the Yellowjackets had positioned themselves, three more figures on horseback followed them out the gates. They cantered slowly to a flat white slab on the Heath, twenty paces beyond the nearest Guardsman. There they waited while the Mayor, Snuff, and Clovermead rode to meet them. At the Mayor's nodded command Snuff kept close behind Clovermead, his knife drawn and ready to stab her in the back. Behind the Mayor his honor guard of patricians and bear-priests advanced to hold themselves parallel and opposite the Yellowjackets. Yellowjackets and honor guards remained fifty yards apart.

Lady Cindertallow was foremost among the three who came from Chandlefort. She was tall and slender, with fine, curling blond hair the exact color and texture as Clovermead's falling from a golden helmet. Her long, proud face was lined with small wrinkles, but her fierce beauty still defied the onslaughts of time. Her loveliness was graven deep in her imperious slate eyes, her full, arrogant red lips, and her long, swanlike neck. She was cougarishly lithe and sat astride her spirited black mare with easy assurance. She wore golden chain mail, as did her steed, and over her mail hung a solid gold pendant carved in the shape of a burning bee wielding a diamond sword. Next to the pendant she wore a small silver crescent as a brooch.

Lady Cindertallow was Clovermead as Clovermead had always dreamed she would look when she was grown—Clovermead the warrior, Clovermead the queen, Clovermead the beauty for whom men would die. Her features so clearly proclaimed her Clovermead's mother that Clovermead wondered how she had ever thought the small stranger, so drab and so different from her, could be her father.

Lady Cindertallow looked once at Clovermead, her face a taut cipher.

Behind Lady Cindertallow came Sorrel. He had exchanged his Tansyard rags and tatters for the livery of Chandlefort, and he had daubed gold paint alongside his cyan tattoos. He looked shyly at Clovermead and ducked his head when she returned his gaze. He blushed, bit his lip, and frowned.

The third figure was Waxmelt. He came dressed in brown woolens but tied in leather bonds. He stared hollowly at Clovermead. Clovermead flinched when she saw his familiar, beloved, strange, despicable face, and Waxmelt turned gray as he saw her flinch. He sagged, a puppet shorn of his strings.

"Good day, Milady," said the Mayor cheerily. "I don't believe I've seen you since your coronation—sixteen years ago, was it not? You've borne the years lightly, Lady."

"You still look like a greased weasel, Cabochon," said Lady Cindertallow. "You've gone gray and fat."

"Dear me," said the Mayor. "Such language after so long a parting. I suppose I shouldn't be surprised—you never did have manners."

"You killed my husband," said Lady Cindertallow. "You stole my daughter. I'd burn you alive if I could."

The Mayor laughed. "You wouldn't let my city go free and that meant war. All's fair in war, Milady. Here." He held up the brooch in his hand and tossed it to Lady Cindertallow. "The Brooch of the Cindertallow Dauphine—you recognize it? You last saw it twelve years ago, pinned to the swaddling clothes of your daughter, Cerelune Cindertallow."

Lady Cindertallow deftly caught the brooch and inspected it closely. She rubbed her fingers along the white gold. "It appears genuine," she said. "Traitor, is this the brooch you stole?" she asked without turning her head.

"It is," said Waxmelt. He spoke in a horrible monotone, a man wishing for death.

The farce is nearly done, Clovermead said to the bear-priests. *Begin your preparations now. Be ready for the assault in five minutes.*

The bear-priests in the Mayor's honor guard bowed slightly to her. Farther away Clovermead felt men and bears begin to move.

The Mayor nodded to Clovermead. "Here is your daughter, Cerelune Cindertallow. I think she takes after her mother more than her dear, departed father."

"Lady strike you down for insulting the memory of the murdered dead," said Lady Cindertallow. A spasm broke her features' proud fixity. She struggled to regain her composure—and succeeded. She allowed herself to look again at Clovermead, studying her features long and carefully. "She looks as my daughter could have looked," she said in a hard, high voice. "Still, she could be an imposter. You've had twelve years to find one, Cabochon. For all I know, Cerelune died of fear twelve years ago. That . . . ghastly thing you summoned up when you stole her frightened half the Guardsmen in the Nursery to death. Their hearts stopped. Most of the others went mad. Why should I think my daughter survived?"

"Why didn't you look for me?" The question burst out of Clovermead, and for a moment Lord Ursus was far away from her. "What sort of mother are you? You left me for dead."

Lady Cindertallow's eyes skittered away from Clovermead, as from a scalding glare. "Are those your first words to me, Cerelune?" She smiled painfully. "I suppose I deserve them. If you are indeed my daughter. How long have you known?"

"Just five minutes. If you *are* my mother." *I believed Daddy,* Clovermead told herself. *I won't simply believe anyone ever again. I want proof.*

"Ah. I have had some months to accustom myself to the idea that you might still live. Since the prophecy came from Our Lady." Lady Cindertallow let her eyes return to Clovermead. "I hid the raid on the Nursery from the world. I judged that it would gravely damage Chandlefort's prestige to admit we had been so vulnerable to attack. And I did not even know who had taken you! I thought it was the Mayor, but I could not prove it. As I could not prove he killed your father. As I could not prove he killed my parents." Lady Cindertallow stared at the Mayor. He smiled. "Ah, no. I dared not make the accusation of that monster: Chandlefort was not yet at war with Low Branding. If the Mayor had announced your capture, I would have acknowledged it. If he did not—well, I waited for him to send his terms for your return.

"I waited a week, Cerelune. I waited a month. I heard nothing. In my heart I knew then that the Mayor had been clumsy and killed you. I knew that my little girl was buried under some anonymous tree. Only then did I let it be known my daughter had died. Of fever. If I had proclaimed the truth to the world, a horde of imposters dragging infants they called Cerelune would have descended on Chandlefort. That was a recipe for civil war—and by then we had already begun to fight Low

Branding. I chose to lie to my people. In secret I sent a few trustworthy men to look for you, in case I was mistaken. Dear Lady, I hoped I was mistaken. But they found no trace of you."

"Mr. Wickward absconded unexpectedly," said the Mayor with a shrug of his shoulders. "You can ask him for the truth of it. He can tell you that this is your daughter."

"Speak, traitor," said Lady Cindertallow. "Is this her?"

"She's your daughter, Milady," said Waxmelt raggedly. "I stole her from the Nursery and took her to Timothy Vale. I called her Clovermead, made up a story about a dead wife, and told the Valefolk that she was my daughter. I became innkeeper there, at Ladyrest. If any of your spies came through, they would have thought I was a Valeman and no one would have told them otherwise. None of the Valefolk say much to outsiders. Even so, I kept her out of sight as much as I could the first few years. By the time she started talking with the pilgrims, no one remembered that Lady Cindertallow had ever had a child. Every day she grew to look more like you. I was afraid she'd inherit your pride, Milady, but Our Lady preserved her from that."

Clovermead heard faint roaring on the wind. Far away a bear-priest fingered his broadsword. She felt hunger and anticipation all around her, drawing nearer.

"An insolent traitor," said Lady Cindertallow bitterly. "But one who speaks with the ring of truth. He's stuck to the same story since he was brought in to Chandlefort. Tansyard, you also vouch that this is the girl you knew as the innkeeper's daughter?"

"Yes, Milady," said Sorrel. "I will swear that she is Clovermead. I will swear again that she had that brooch before she was captured by the Mayor. She showed it to me in a mill in the Salt Heath, and I will swear a third time that this girl, who I only then realized was Milady's very image, showed it to me in all innocence of what that brooch proclaimed her to be. She knew that it came from Chandlefort, but not that jewelry emblazoned with the Burning Bee is made only for the Cindertallows themselves."

"Then, I am willing to believe that she is my daughter, Cabochon." Lady Cindertallow looked again at Clovermead. Her hands shook on her reins. "What price do you demand for her?"

"I have told you, Milady. The freedom of Low Branding." The Mayor extracted a piece of paper from his saddlebag and squinted at it. "More precisely, you will recognize Low Branding as sovereign and independent, free from all obligations financial, political, and military, or of any other kind whatsoever, to either the House of Cindertallow or the Demesne of Chandlefort. You will also relinquish your power and your titles over High Branding, the Harrow Moors, Ryebrew, Barleymill, and all other lands in Linstock east of the Chandle Palisades. You will not contest Low Branding's right to claim suzerainty over the above mentioned territories. You will assemble your several vassals, and in their presence you will sign a treaty confirming your relinquishments. You will also swear a binding oath to Our Lady to observe the terms of the said treaty." The Mayor carefully folded the paper and returned it to his saddlebag.

"Or you will kill my daughter," said Lady Cindertallow.

"Yes. Or marry her." The Mayor flicked his eyes over Clovermead's slight figure and laughed. "I feel no desire to be joined in blessed matrimony with Miss Wickward, but I am well aware that there are certain ancient prophecies that foretell great accomplishments for the twenty-first ruler of Chandlefort. Perhaps I could claim in my wife's name to be that ruler? Even if she died suddenly, just after the wedding? I don't myself believe that fate can be fooled by cheap tricks, but I suspect some of your vassals would be more gullible. I can set your precious castle ablaze with faction, Milady—I say this only if you thought to let your daughter die. I don't think you're so callous, but there's no use taking chances. Prudence, prudence, that's my watchword."

A distant growl sounded. Lady Cindertallow turned to see what had made the noise, and saw a sleepy bear licking his lips and yawning as he stood. Impatiently she turned back to the Mayor.

"Leave off your threats, Cabochon. I'll sign your treaty."

"You see, Lucifer?" said the Mayor. "Complexity is a slower way, but it is most effective."

"Yes, Your Eminence," said Snuff. He bowed obsequiously. "Complexity and patience. It's been a long campaign."

"Villainy works," Lady Cindertallow spat out. "You've done a filthy thing, Cabochon. My family is dead. I lost twelve years with my daughter. She loved a traitorous servant as her father, while I . . . loved nothing. Sent my love out to empty space, hoped my daughter was still alive somewhere, out there, and feared she was dead." A tear cracked Lady Cindertallow's proud face. Her hand jerked toward Clovermead—and she clenched it back. "Your blasted city's freedom doesn't matter that much."

Clovermead wanted to cry too, to comfort this woman—but Lord Ursus was coming back, had come back, and he filled her thoughts and soul. Now she felt only contempt for the old woman who would cripple her power for a useless love. The old woman would be dead soon. Clovermead laughed, Lord Ursus laughed, and they sent further instructions to the bear-priests on the details of the assault.

"I would have done anything for our freedom," said the Mayor of Low Branding. His eyes blazed. "You would not bend to reason, Milady. You would not listen to my entreaties. You forced me to villainy—I could not win us our liberty without using it. I have no regrets. You're a selfish woman, Milady, and you deserved your pain—"

Bears roared louder than ever and the Mayor turned to see what the noise was. Clovermead saw a ring of brown fur scrabble its claws on the Heath and move, padding in toward the Mayor's army. They bared their teeth and snarled. The bear-priests walked with them and drew their broadswords all at once. Bears and bear-priests walked in slow and steady unison, inexorable as moving gears. Bestial snarls were their regimental music.

An uneasy hubbub spread among the ranks. Officers tried to reassure their men, but they would not be steadied. The bear-priests set their blood-net over the army and sent terror among the Mayor's soldiers. The men fell from their perfect lines into disarray and stumbled toward the walls of Chandlefort. Clovermead smelled fear on them, rancid panic, and she growled with delight. It would be a pleasure to hunt down this fat prey.

"Cabochon, what is this treachery?" asked Lady Cindertallow with alarm. "Call off your filthy beasts."

"I didn't call them," said the Mayor. For the first time Clovermead saw him look worried. His eyes found Snuff. "Lucifer! What are you playing at? Tell your servants to get back in line."

"Lucifer didn't order them forward," Clovermead growled, her tooth snarled, Lord Ursus roared. She kicked her horse forward and grinned with pleasure. "I did. I have found a better vessel for my plans than you, Mayor. She will be the twenty-first lady of Chandlefort and she will serve Me. All Linstock will be my hunting range." Clovermead bellowed with laughter. "And much more besides. Mayor, your services are at an end. Cindertallow, you have bequeathed Me an excellent daughter. Little prey, I thank you both for your stupid squabble."

Clovermead gave the final order, and the bears and bear-priests leapt forward.

Chapter Eighteen

THE WHITE DOE

SNUFF SWUNG DOWN FROM FEATHERFALL, DREW HIS sword, and loped between Clovermead and the parleyers. Slack jawed, the Mayor watched as Lord Ursus' bears and bear-priests smashed into his disintegrating army. The bear-priests had killed half the patricians in his honor guard in the first seconds. The rest fought valiantly against the sudden treachery of their companions, but they were already outnumbered. The bear-priests' swords mowed them down.

"Dear Lady!" Lady Cindertallow swore. She stood high in her stirrups and her eyes flickered quickly over the chaos. "To me!" she yelled to her Guardsmen. Her voice was as loud as any trumpet. The Yellowjackets kicked the flanks of their horses and brought them to a gallop.

Clovermead's shadow grew long and dark. Lord Ursus was her shadow, and where her shadow fell, all light was extinguished. He sprang up in front of the Guardsmen. He was a hill-high monster who pawed the ground and left festering gobs of darkness on the Heath. He roared, and from his mouth spewed evanescent visions of men and horses screaming as the flesh fell from their bones, howling as their bones fell apart, and shrieking to the last as they crumbled into dust.

The Yellowjackets' horses neighed wildly and bolted for the castle gates. Their wide-eyed riders tried to rein them in but with no great vigor. Terror pursued them; terror lent their flight yet greater speed. Jubilantly Clovermead's fearful shadow roared its conquest of the Salt Heath.

The Mayor's shocked idiocy fell from him as abruptly as it had seized him. "Ride, Milady," he said to Lady Cindertallow. He smiled grimly and gripped his lovely, useless sword in his clumsy hands. "This is my folly to pay for, not yours. Get behind your walls." He laughed. "They've kept you safe from me for twelve years, Melisande. They won't fail you now."

"Catch her, Snuff," Clovermead commanded. She galloped toward the Mayor as Snuff advanced horribly fast on Lady Cindertallow. Lady Cindertallow drew her blade and parried Snuff's sword as it lashed at her neck. Then she riposted and hewed at Snuff's chest. Their blades whirled in a deadly dance. Lady Cindertallow was an expert swordswoman, and she was fighting on horseback, but Snuff had Lord Ursus' speed and strength in him. He fought and fought and he never grew tired.

Sorrel snaked out his blade to snap Waxmelt's leather bonds. Waxmelt held up his freed hands and Sorrel tossed him a dagger. The innkeeper swung down from his horse as the Tansyard kicked Brown Barley forward to join Lady Cindertallow. "The Cyan Cross Horde," he cried. "Mother! Father!" Furiously he swung his sword at Snuff, and the bear-priest hastily turned his blade from Lady Cindertallow. Now Lady Cindertallow and Sorrel fought jointly against Lucifer Snuff. The bear-priest's blade pirouetted effortlessly to ward off both opponents.

Clovermead ducked under the Mayor's clumsy blow, swung a long paw at his gray mare's head, and tore it off. Clovermead growled in joy at her own strength and backhand smashed the Mayor off his dead steed onto the Heath. He rolled a dozen feet. Clovermead sprang lightly onto the ground. "On your feet," she ordered him. "Fight me to the end." Her snout twitched at the smell of blood coursing from his gashed, broken arm. Her teeth lengthened, hungry for his flesh.

Waxmelt tried to join in the fight against Snuff. He thrust his dagger toward Snuff's back—and Snuff whirled and kicked him in the stomach. Lady Cindertallow sliced shallowly into Snuff's arm. Waxmelt sagged to the ground. Howling and enraged, Snuff ducked under Sorrel's sword, struck sideways, and sent Lady Cindertallow's blade spinning away. Snuff slashed once more against Lady Cindertallow and struck her helmet. She cried and fell off her horse, unconscious, joining Waxmelt on the hard stones of the Heath.

Clovermead padded toward the Mayor. Her golden fur lengthened, and her teeth and claws grew sharp and long. Her bones stretched and her muscles expanded. Her yellow dress shredded from her enormous body and lay in rags on the heath—she was eight feet high and four feet thick, and still growing. Her ears unfurled, huge and high, and her nose grew large and sharp. She fell on all fours as her arms turned into forelegs. A tail poked out the bottom of her back. Her claws cut through the earth, caught on a pebble, and squeezed against the rock, which crumbled beneath the killing pressure of her paws. Clovermead roared with joy. The helpless, pathetic little girl was gone at last. Only the bear remained.

"Did you always mean to do this?" the Mayor asked, stumbling to his feet. His broken arm hung loose and ugly. Clovermead sniffed for fear and was disappointed to find none in him. He held his sword out, hopeless but defiant.

"At some point, Mayor," Ursus growled through Clovermead. "Prey is prey. But I had not meant it to be so soon. Not till the little Cindertallow found my tooth. She was very strong and she was very hungry. I knew then that if I had her, you were dispensable." Clovermead laughed with joy that she could be useful to her Lord; Lord Ursus guffawed at the Mayor's trust in him. "Twelve years spent for this, Mayor! Poor fool."

"Poor fool, indeed," said the Mayor. "It seems I was imprudent." He sadly made the crescent sign. "I pray that Our Lady will forgive me."

The name sent Lord Ursus into a rage, and there would be no more playing with the man. Clovermead leapt at the two-legged meat—

And the air twisted before her. Sister Rowan appeared between the bear and the Mayor. Clovermead roared with anger, unable to turn aside. Her teeth bit at the air and her claws sank deeply into Sister Rowan's side, her arms, her leg. The nun fell beneath Clovermead's weight, her eyes fixed on Clovermead. There was no recrimination in them, no pain, only forgiveness. Her blood seeped up Clovermead's claws and onto her fur.

The sun vanished. Clovermead looked up to see the moon shining in the sky. Its cool rays slashed at the shadow on the land. Clovermead howled in agony. She closed her eyes against the light of the moon—

Clovermead ran in her dreamland northern woods. Lord Ursus ran by her side. The moon glared on them as they ran, and its reflection from the snow sliced at Clovermead's eyes. Lord Ursus recoiled from the brilliance. He groaned and moaned and snapped uselessly at the white circle above. He cursed, but his curses were soundless in the light.

She gave her blood freely, said Clovermead in wonder. *She was willing to die for the Mayor—even for him. She acted like a hero.*

How could she do that? Lord Ursus raged. *Why? I didn't expect—*He saw Clovermead listening to him and he clamped his muzzle shut. He tried to smile. *Prey can be foolish, little cub. Sometimes they throw themselves into your mouth. It only means they deserve to be eaten.*

But that isn't heroic, said Clovermead. *That isn't exciting. There's no challenge to killing if you can't hunt them down.* She shook her head bewilderedly.

Never mind, little cub, said Lord Ursus. *Other hunts await you. Can you smell the doe?*

Clovermead sniffed and found the familiar, elusive scent. It was divine—a drug, as desirable as ever. There was powerlessness and fear and hurt in it, and once more Clovermead was vibrantly aware of her own power, her bravery, and her ability to cause pain. She loved what she had become. Heroine, villainess—those were just words of prey. She could do as she wished, perform more glorious actions than any she had read of in her books. Now she lived, as she had never done in sleepy Timothy Vale. Now she was divine to everyone she murdered, for she had the power of life and death. Thrusting all thoughts of Sister Rowan out of her mind, the cub Clovermead roared with joy and ran.

Lord Ursus paced her as she accelerated. Clovermead salivated and dodged trees. The pines grew thinner and smaller as they raced along bare slopes of snow and stone. She spotted the doe's delicate hoofprints. White wolves sprang into the wake of the two bears, howling their hope for carcass meat. A black vulture flapped after them. Jackrabbits scampered into their holes and eagles soared south, disdaining the scene of murder.

Lord Ursus and Clovermead rounded the hill, and below them she saw Snowchapel again. The valley was thick with pearly mist and every droplet glowed in the extraordinary moonlight. Down by the temple the nuns of Snowchapel lined the Pool's edge and sang a hymn to the moon that throbbed through the mist. Its silvery harmony beseeched Our Lady to dispel fear and darkness, and Clovermead cried from the ceremony's sheer beauty.

Strike the doe down! Lord Ursus' urgent growl broke the hymn into jagged discords. *Consume her! Put an end to the moon-gibberish.*

The doe came into sight. Clovermead roared and she smelled the doe's terror stronger than ever. The scent was an urgent pungency in her nose and heart and stomach and thrilled nerves. The doe was an old white deer, winded from the chase. Her lungs pumped madly and she stumbled on slippery roots beneath the snow. Clovermead pounded closer.

Kill her, said Lord Ursus. *Do it now.*

The moon shone down brighter than ever and there was no darkness where Clovermead's thoughts could hide. *Sister Rowan said I could always draw the tooth,* she told herself, *but I don't think I'll want to after I've killed the doe. I'll want the tooth in me, Lord Ursus with me, forever and ever. I love the taste of blood too much already—after I've killed this prey, I'll never be free of blood-thirst. I will be strong, I will be powerful, and the little girl will never get in my way again. Our Lady will never bother me again. The light will never hurt me again and I will rest in darkness forever.*

But I don't want to be a bear. I don't want to be a monster. I didn't know what power and adventure were when I wanted them. They're not worth having. I want to be Clovermead Wickward of Timothy Vale again. If I have to be silly and weak, I don't mind.

I do mind. Clovermead Wickward was hunted. Clovermead Wickward was stolen. Clovermead Wickward was lied to by her own father, who wasn't her father, was deceived by everyone she met. In her foolish innocence she was a plaything for the powerful and she was contemptible. The Mayor and Snuff were right to laugh at me. Better to serve Lord Ursus and be strong. Better to be feared. Better to kill—and it was so lovely to kill. I am so hungry, Clovermead cried. *I am so thirsty. Teeth and blood, I can't withstand the temptation of flesh.*

Sister Rowan is dying or dead. Sorrel will die. That stranger they say is my mother will die. Father, Waxmelt, Daddy, will die. I tried so hard to keep him alive. Snuff will kill them, Lord

Ursus will eat them. I will kill them. But I love Father. In spite of everything, I love him.

All the more reason to kill him quickly. Love is the worst weakness of all.

I've never seen anyone stronger than Sister Rowan when she stood between me and the Mayor. She was stronger than hunger, stronger than thirst. She was stronger than fear.

I think her strength came from outside her.

Dear Lady, help me, Clovermead cried out. She stopped running and Lord Ursus roared in fear. *I am weak, Lady. I will always be weak by myself. Please, give me your strength, which doesn't kill. Give me the strength that keeps me from killing.* Against all her hunger, against all her thirst, against all her hatred and cruelty and pain, Clovermead drew in her claws. Crying, Clovermead looked again at the white doe.

Light was everywhere. Lord Ursus was far away and his musk dwindled as the glimmering moon cleansed Clovermead. There was music, singing, and the light faded enough to let Clovermead see the world again. The music went on.

Clovermead saw a small, old woman leave the gates of Snowchapel as the nuns sang her farewell. She walked slowly but steadily along a thin, curving trail up the steep slope. Light throbbed around her.

The old woman climbed for hours, until she reached a ledge high up the slopes of a mountain due north of Snowchapel. Clovermead looked down one slope of the mountain and saw the nunnery and the Scrying Pool. Down the other slope she saw the pass to Scrimshaw Harbor and the ocean. North there was no mist. The moon shone clear in the night sky upon the endless ice below. The cakes and bergs were terrible and beautiful. They were a flimsy cover on the chaotic ocean and more solid and enduring than mountains.

At the center of the ledge was a hollow sheathed in white marble. It gathered up moonlight and returned what it had gleaned to the sky. The old woman took a handful of scented twigs from her robes and put them in the center of the hollow. She lit them and their fragrance was lovely to Clovermead's nose. As the twigs burned the woman sang a prayer. The moonlight grew brighter, and brighter still—

And a black bear leapt onto the ledge and stood over the hollow. He was twenty feet long, that bear, strong and terrible, but also afraid. He landed on the stone as if he expected to be burned, and he was so comical that Clovermead wanted to laugh.

The old woman did laugh. *Away with you,* she said in an exasperated tone. *Sniffing after fish, getting mixed up in sacred rites—you've got to learn manners, little Ursus!*

Ursus retreated a step—and growled his rage, his humiliation, his fear, and his hunger. He snapped his teeth. The old woman gasped and skipped a little away from his jaws. She laughed again, but with a sudden catch in her throat. *You have grown! You must stop that. You'll frighten people.* She turned away from Ursus and began to sing.

Ursus bowed his head in shame. Then he looked up suddenly. Clovermead saw the realization of his strength flower in him. She saw blackness stream across his eyes, and for the first time his mouth twisted with cruel anticipation. He looked at the sky and saw nothing but the darkness inside himself.

The old woman had reached the end of her hymn. Moonlight brighter than the noonday sun stabbed down to bathe her skin, and Ursus roared and sprang forward, claws extended. The old woman hardly had time to turn before he had snapped her neck. And the moonlight turned black, bright black, black that grew and filled the bear. The blackness kept growing and the bear grew too. He roared with newfound intelligence and power, and he crouched down and bit at the old woman's corpse. The moonlight dimmed. He ate, and he ate more, and he sucked light from the world. The pearly mist faded, the northern ice grew dull, the moon itself turned gray. And when Ursus was done with his meal, he roared with laughter and the prospects of triumphs to come. He was fifty feet high, one hundred feet high, huge beyond all measure. He left Snowchapel behind and loped south.

To Garum, the old woman said to Clovermead, but it was not just the old woman who stood at her side. She was a young beauty, a weathered matron, a crone as old as the hills, and all three at once. Her robes twinkled with the light of a thousand stars. Her expression could be cold and implacable, but she was never cruel. Her lips fell more naturally into smiles than into frowns. Her glowing eyes were gentle. *That was a hundred years ago, and more. Before he came, it was a corrupt city and ready to serve a bloody master. He gratified its whims. There he took the name Lord Ursus.*

What happened here, Lady? asked Clovermead. She wanted to bow low, to free herself from the bear's musty fur and killing claws, but she couldn't. It was her own flesh.

The Abbess of Snowchapel came up to observe the rites of the winter solstice, during a year when the full moon shone. I gave a great deal of myself to her that night. When Ursus killed her, he swallowed a large part of me, too. The old woman shook her head sadly. *He has used my light so badly. Poor beast, poor thing.*

You pity him?

He is so lonely and so scared—of course I do. An angry glint shone in the old woman's eyes. *Mind, I don't forgive him. He's done great wrong on the world and snuffed out a great many lights. I pity him, but he has to face justice for all the evil he's done. He will be punished.*

How? asked Clovermead. *When?*

I wish I knew, Clovermead Wickward, said the old woman. *For now, I fight him one battle at a time. It isn't easy.*

I still want blood, said Clovermead. She scratched angrily at her fur, till her claws near cut her skin. *I can feel it inside me. Lady, when will you take my hunger from me?*

You must get rid of your hunger yourself, said the lady. *But I will give you my strength.* Her mouth crinkled and she laughed. *Now, stop attacking that lovely pelt. It's beautiful and it isn't anything to do with Lord Ursus. It's what's inside you that turns dark, not the fur and claws.* Slowly the moonlight began to fade. *Farewell for a while, Clovermead. Your friends and family need you. Go back to them. You have more work to do.*

More? asked Clovermead, tired and bewildered.

Don't be afraid, the old woman said gently. *My strength is in you.* The light had become very faint. Snowchapel vanished—

And Clovermead was back in the Salt Heath. The sun shone overhead. Sister Rowan lay bleeding before her. The Mayor waited for Clovermead to leap. Snuff stood above Lady Cindertallow's fallen body and faced Sorrel. Waxmelt began to stir. Everything was the same, except that her shadow was gone.

Snuff jerked, moaned, and stumbled away from Sorrel and Lady Cindertallow. "Master?" he cried out, and he whirled toward Clovermead. His eyes widened. "Just the child," he hissed—and a dark shadow blossomed out of him. "You're back, Master!" he shouted joyfully, and his shadow raked the earth behind him and snarled at Brown Barley and Sorrel. Sorrel gibbered, his hands went slack on Brown Barley's reins, and his horse reared up and sent him flying to the ground. Snuff ran at Clovermead, his sword upraised.

In her mind Lord Ursus roared at Clovermead and told her that she was scared. He told her that she was small, puny, a worthless, fearful wretch, a little girl born to be killed at the hands of a stronger man. He told her to run—that she had nothing to give the world but the challenge of her death and the pain of her going. He told her that she was meat and that she would die.

His voice grew small. His shadow was tiny. "You've said all that before," said Clovermead with a growl. "I'm awfully scared, but I won't run. I'm too much like you, but I won't serve you. I don't want to die, but I'd rather die. And I'd rather live!" Clovermead stood up on her hind legs and swung her arms against Snuff. His sword bit deeply into her left shoulder, but with her other arm she bashed him to the ground.

Lord Ursus' shadow vanished for the second time—but Snuff had bounced to his feet. "Perhaps you'll live, missy," he snarled, "but Lord Ursus always finds other victims. Those you love will die, girlie. Always." His eyes blazed, he clacked his sharpened teeth together, and he ran toward Lady Cindertallow, still sprawled on the ground. His laugh was vicious and hyena loud. His sword stretched out toward Clovermead's mother.

The woman she had never known. The woman she had never loved. The haughty woman who had ruled Chandlefort and its servants with arrogant indifference. The woman her father hated.

The mother she might learn to love.

Clovermead ran after Snuff, as in a nightmare. She had to overtake him, but her bear body melted from her as she ran. Swift, furred legs shrank to naked limbs, and only two legs carried her forward. The wind whipped against her naked flesh, and she could not reach Lady Cindertallow in time. She cried out in despair—but Sorrel was there and fighting desperately against Snuff. His sword kept up a desperate play against Snuff's assault, but Clovermead knew it could last only a few moments.

Lady Cindertallow's sword lay before Clovermead on the ground. She picked it up and raced faster still. Her lungs were ragged with pain and her feet were bloody. She prayed to Our Lady not to let her collapse. Snuff thrust Sorrel aside and hammered his blade down at the unconscious Lady Cindertallow—and Clovermead slipped her mother's blade beneath his stroke. Snuff's sword clashed uselessly against the Heath.

Snuff howled his frustration and whirled to face Clovermead. His sword chopped down at her—and Clovermead parried him. He struck at her again, and again she parried. She was exhausted, but her arm still moved, her blade still rose. She was on Kestrel Hill listening to Sorrel tell her to be careful when she fought, she was on the Salt Heath putting his instructions to effect. She parried wearily, she turned her strength into desperate delay, with no razzle-dazzle at all. Her eyes watched the flash of Snuff's blade and nothing else. She kept Lucifer Snuff away from her, away from her mother, for ten seconds, for thirty seconds, for a minute.

Then Clovermead could fend Snuff off no longer and he smashed her sword from her fingers. Her little finger was broken. Clovermead was tired to death and she fell to her knees. She was crying.

"How brave you are," said Snuff. He hacked out a laugh. "You'll die all the same."

"First you must face me," said Sorrel. He stood by Clovermead's side. "You will not kill her, too. I will die first." His sword shook in his hand. He had fallen heavily on his side when Brown Barley threw him, and he was scraped and bloody from chest to calf. He was nearly as tired as Clovermead.

"And me," said Waxmelt. He came up to Clovermead's other side, a dagger in his hands. He trembled but stood defiant. "There'll be no more killing. Old friend."

"Three weaklings to one armed man. I believe I faced these odds before, at Ladyrest." Snuff considered his opposition. He smiled. "This time I will fight."

"So will I," said Clovermead. With the last of her

strength she put her fingers into her mouth and pulled hard at her bear tooth. It clung to her jaw. She pulled harder, with claws and fingers, a bear's strength and a human's agility, until the tooth came reluctantly out of her mouth. Blood and gum came with the tooth. More blood dripped from the hole in her mouth. Her jaw shrieked with pain and Clovermead ached with the loss.

"My tooth!" Snuff shrieked. He raised his sword. "Give me back my tooth!"

Clovermead held the tooth in her hand for a long second. She could still change her mind—

"Enough," said Clovermead. She clenched her hand into a fist and squeezed against the tooth. It bit her flesh and drew blood. Clovermead squeezed harder and her hand flickered into a paw. With all her bear's strength she crushed the cruel seducer she had prized for so long. The tooth crumbled, shattering into jagged fragments that ripped gouges in her palm. Snuff screamed an agony of loss as Clovermead dropped the splinters to the ground.

Blood poured out of the fragments. A vast, welling pool streamed from the tooth and sank into the ground. The dry earth swallowed the blood cleanly and laid it to rest.

Lord Ursus' shadow fled a final time from the Heath. The light grew stronger and bears and bear-priests murmured their dismay. Their attack on the Army of Low Branding and on the few Yellowjackets outside the walls faltered and then halted. The soldiers let fly a ragged cheer. Clovermead thought she could hear a sob in its midst. A great many men littered the ground. And from the gate of Chandlefort an army of Yellowjackets poured forth. Their trumpets bugled to the heavens as they charged the bears and bear-priests.

Snuff gaped and let his sword sag as he watched Lord Ursus' army fall back. His eyes flickered nervously and he made himself grin once more. His sharp teeth gleamed in the sun. "Fortune favors you, girlie. My master needs me for later battles. He will always need his true servants." Snuff sheathed his sword and bowed mockingly. "Until we meet again, Miss Wickward." He whistled and Featherfall came to him. He leapt onto Featherfall's back and kicked hard into his flank. Featherfall snorted in pain and galloped away. Soon they disappeared beyond the horizon.

We are still enslaved, said Boulderbash to Clovermead from somewhere far away. *There are still enough bear teeth to keep us prisoners.*

I did what I could, said Clovermead. *I can't do everything by myself.*

Ah, no, no one ever can. And so we remain enslaved to my poor, terrible son.

Your son? asked Clovermead.

Little Ursus, said Boulderbash. Her voice was growing fainter. *We always grew large in my family.*

He enslaved his own mother?

What do you think you have done to your own parents? asked Boulderbash. She laughed low and rumbling. *Good-bye for now. Our Lady's blessing upon you. And don't forget, little one—we first talked before you found Snuff's tooth.* Her voice faded from Clovermead's head.

Sorrel stood guard over Lady Cindertallow until

Yellowjackets came to relieve him of his duty. Then he mounted his horse, drew his sword, and went to join the armies of Low Branding and Chandlefort as they pursued the slowly retreating bear-priests. Waxmelt knelt by Clovermead's side and tore off his cape to cover her nakedness. He folded her in the thick cloth and held the bloodied girl close to his heart as she shivered and sobbed. The innkeeper sang lullabies to his daughter until she fell asleep.

Chapter Nineteen

Cerelune Cindertallow

A WEEK LATER LADY CINDERTALLOW AND THE MAYOR OF Low Branding signed a treaty of peace. Side by side they entered the Throne Room of Chandlefort and joyful cheers roared forth from all the assembled witnesses. Hundreds of lords and ladies of Chandlefort crowded upon the porphyry-and-carnelian floor, and with them some dozens of the patricians of Low Branding. Huddled in the back corners of the room, warming themselves by the burning logs merrily blazing in the Throne Room's great marble fireplaces, were hastily commissioned and newly arrived ambassadors from High Branding, the Harrow Moors, and Ryebrew. Notables from every part of Linstock had donned their finest vests, blouses, breeches, and dresses, and their raiment drenched the room with shimmering, parti-colored hues. Their cheers grew louder still as Clovermead, carried on a litter by four servants and swaddled in bandages and wool coverlets, followed her mother and the Mayor into the room. She ducked her head and raised a weak arm from her invalid's nightgown to acknowledge the cheers.

An aged nun met the Mayor and Lady Cindertallow at the dais. The crowd grew quiet, and the nun made the crescent sign over each of their bowed heads. She shuffled forward, stood between them, and took their hands in hers.

"Our Lady's blessing lies on this peace." Her cracked voice penetrated to the farthest walls. "Our Lady has grieved for the dead on all sides of this war—for soldiers and for farmers, for men and for women, for children orphaned and killed. Our Lady has grieved especially that this war has left Linstock open to the claw of the Bear. Our Lady urges that this peace last." The nun put the hands of Lady Cindertallow and the Mayor together. "In Our Lady's name, let the fields be tilled, let the sheep graze, let the gates of the cities be opened. In Our Lady's name, let us be vigilant and watch together for our mutual safety against the return of the Bear. In Our Lady's name, let us remember the dead." Men and women made the sign of the crescent, and a long silence filled the room. Then the nun smiled. "And now let us put sorrow behind us. This is a day of joy." She stepped back from the dais.

"We welcome you all to Chandlefort," said Lady Cindertallow. She wore a simple white dress draped from her shoulders, and around her forehead a thin circlet that bore the sigil of the burning bee and blazing sword. "We have prepared a treaty with the Mayor of Low Branding. Herald, read it."

The herald stepped up from the side of the room, cleared his throat, and peered down at the words written on dove white vellum. "Be it known . . ." he began, and what followed was very long and very formal and it taxed Clovermead to figure out what was being said in between the *wheretos* and the *forasmuches* and the *consequentlys*. The gist seemed to be that Lady Cindertallow now claimed only to be Duchess of West Linstock, which was the part of Linstock west of the line of the Chandle Palisades, and that Low Branding was to be independent. There were a half dozen other agreements appended to the treaty: The Mayor of Low Branding acknowledged his responsibility for the war, but Lady Cindertallow wouldn't claim damages against him; both Low Branding and Chandlefort acknowledged and guaranteed the independence of High Branding, the Harrow Moors, and Ryebrew; Low Branding and Chandlefort signed a league of mutual defense against all third parties, meaning Lord Ursus and his bear-priests at Barleymill and Garum; and Low Branding agreed to put no taxes of any sort on Chandlefort goods for twenty years, as recompense for causing the war. And there would be peace in Linstock. That was the most important agreement of all.

"Bring the paper here," said Lady Cindertallow. The herald brought the treaty and a pot of ink to a lectern. Lady Cindertallow signed the treaty with a flourish and the mayor did likewise.

Lady Cindertallow displayed the treaty to the assembled crowd. "We are at peace," she proclaimed, and the crowd cheered. Lady Cindertallow lifted her hands and the crowd quieted. "There is other news, and just as joyful. As those of you present at the battle with the bear-priests know, our daughter, Cerelune, is not dead. We apologize for the deception, but it was necessary to keep her safe for the duration of the war. Cerelune is alive and she is here." Lady Cindertallow pointed to a furiously blushing Clovermead as the room roared its approval. "We call on all our subjects to acknowledge Cerelune as our rightful heir to all the lands and titles that we hold."

The lords and ladies knelt down. "All hail Demoiselle Cerelune," they cried out. A hundred of them, two hundred, everyone but the Mayor and the ambassadors of the newly independent lands, got to their knees before her. She saw Sorrel winking at her, and Sister Rowan in bandages but grinning broadly, and Waxmelt staring in wonder. All three of them had knelt too. *I must be dreaming,* Clovermead told herself. She pinched her arm, but still they were kneeling and still they were all-hailing her. It was exactly what she had hoped would happen to her when she read the *Garum Heptameron.* It was exactly the fate she had expected from her first perusal of *The Song of the Siege of the Silver Knight.*

Except she had always imagined they would hail Clovermead Wickward. The cheers and the homage were for Cerelune Cindertallow. Was she really Cerelune? She listened to the cheers and she didn't know for sure. *I am Cerelune Cindertallow, daughter of Melisande Cindertallow,* she told herself. I am *Clovermead Wickward, daughter of Waxmelt Wickward.* Neither statement sounded true.

Not that I should complain, thought Clovermead, grinning guiltily. She waved again at the lords and ladies. *Goodness gracious, I'm a princess in disguise! Not everyone can say that, young Miss Wickward, so stop your whining. It's perfectly silly of you.*

But still they were calling out someone else's name.

There were festivities following the treaty signing and

the formal recognition of Cerelune Cindertallow's existence, but Clovermead was too weak to stay for them. Her doctor whisked her away from the Throne Room and back to her bedchamber in the Cindertallow Nursery. He fed her steaming honey tea and warm oatmeal, and then she fell asleep beneath soft down coverlets.

The next morning the Mayor came to visit. He walked into the room proudly enough, but his head ducked shamefacedly. Yellowjacket Guardsmen followed him in and watched him very carefully indeed. He sat down on a chair by the bed and uncomfortably scratched his chin. His left arm was bound in a sling. His eyes darted every which way.

"We are leaving tomorrow for Low Branding," he said at last.

Clovermead did not know what she could say that would be remotely mannerly.

"We suspect we understand your perplexity," said the Mayor. "You wish we were leaving for the far side of the earth? It is understandable." He shrugged. "We regret what we have done to you, Demoiselle Cerelune." His eyes focused on the bedroom window and the Heath outside. "We were advised by Snuff. We made the decision ourself, to free our city. We were wrong to trust the bear-priests, but we cannot say we chose wrongly when we ordered you kidnapped. We value Low Branding's freedom very highly, and Lady Cindertallow's pride and strength provided us very few alternatives. But we do wish we could have devised a less cruel stratagem."

"Thank you, Your Eminence. I also wish you'd been more imaginative, but I suppose there's no curing that now," said Clovermead. His Eminence shook his head. "I should hate you, but I can't. I wouldn't be Clovermead Wickward if it weren't for you." Her eyes glittered. "Besides, my hatred is unnecessary. I hear Your Eminence has troubles of your own."

The Mayor winced, his stoatish face pasty and somber. "You hear correctly, Demoiselle. Our army was terribly mauled. Perhaps one man in four survived, and many of them are wounded. We have become very weak."

"Poor men," said Clovermead. "What will their families say?"

"Most of them were mercenaries," said the Mayor carelessly. "That sort don't have families. As for the rest—we are free now."

"I still don't understand that," said Clovermead angrily. "Lady Cindertallow gave you everything you wanted. You won the war."

The Mayor smiled bleakly. "We are free because Chandlefort is dreadfully weakened after twelve years of war and because Low Branding is outright crippled. If Chandlefort and Low Branding continued to fight, neither would have strength left to defend Linstock against Lord Ursus. Even your proud mother recognizes that. So Low Branding has gained its freedom, but only in tight alliance with Chandlefort for its very survival. It is a most hollow victory, Demoiselle, in which we can take little joy.

"Moreover, we must give up certain ambitions we had to rule over all East Linstock—in the treaty we explicitly guaranteed the independence of High Branding and the other eastern lands. Furthermore, we have forsworn certain potentially lucrative taxes on Chandlefort goods. All that is disappointingly less than victory." The Mayor laughed. "Our Lady is just."

"Perhaps more of her justice waits for you," said Clovermead.

"Our Lady says that forgiveness is a virtue," the Mayor said.

"I don't hate you, Your Eminence, but I don't like you very much. I don't expect that will change anytime soon."

"Self-knowledge is the road to wisdom," said the Mayor. He stood up and shook Clovermead's reluctant hand. His flesh was soft and damp. "Or so the philosophers say. Ah, well. We hope you will visit Low Branding someday and accept our hospitality. We wish to make some small recompense for the ills we have done you."

"You can," Clovermead said suddenly. "Your Eminence can pay a pension to the families of your soldiers who died. And to any crippled soldiers. If Lady Cindertallow allows me any money, I'll send it to Low Branding too, to help them out."

Surprise flickered on the Mayor's face. "Why would you want this, Demoiselle?"

"I'm responsible," said Clovermead. Saying the words out loud made her angry and afraid and sad. "It wasn't all me, but I let Lord Ursus take me over. He ordered the bears forward to kill your soldiers, but I ordered it too. And I was happy to kill them. I've got to do something to atone. Please, Your Eminence, I want to do what I can for them as soon as I can."

The Mayor shook his head in wonder. "You shame

us," he said softly. "Most deeply. We accede to your request. Please inform Lady Cindertallow that we will pay a pension of a shilling a month for ten years to all soldiers crippled in this expedition, or to their families if they are dead. Should you provide further monies to them, we will add to their pensions in equal measure."

"Thank you, Your Eminence," said Clovermead. "I'll tell her exactly what you said."

"We do not consider that this will cancel our debt to you," said the Mayor. "You are still welcome to our hospitality, Demoiselle." He bowed and left the room.

In the afternoon Waxmelt and Lady Cindertallow came together to see her.

Lady Cindertallow touched Clovermead's shoulder as lightly as if she were sticking her finger into a fire. Waxmelt stood diffidently by the windowsill, shrinking from Lady Cindertallow when she looked at him. Then he smiled broadly and familiarly at Clovermead, and she returned his smile with natural joy.

"You still have my daughter's heart, Mr. Wickward," said Lady Cindertallow. Her pride made her words a monotone. "She could have looked at me that way."

I wish I could, Lady, thought Clovermead. *But then Daddy would have been a strange servant named Mr. Wickward whom I would have scorned if I'd known him at all. I couldn't have had you both.*

"I'm sorry I took Clovermead, Milady," said Waxmelt. "I should have known how it would hurt you. But I loved her as soon as I saw her. She was so beautiful and so gentle and so tiny that I couldn't bear to let her stay with you or be taken by Snuff and the Mayor. I didn't think you might have looked at her the same way. If I'd thought that, I'd have let her be in the Nursery."

"You say that now," said Lady Cindertallow. "But her heart is still yours."

My heart is my own, thought Clovermead. *Or both of yours. Or nobody's or everybody's or stolen away by Lord Ursus. I don't know about my heart—what makes you so wise?*

"I've lied to Clo since the first day she could talk. She has more than enough reason to hate me." Waxmelt looked hesitantly at Clovermead and tears welled up in his eyes. "Lady's Grace, if she does still love me, that's more good fortune than I expect or deserve. Her heart isn't at my command to give back to you."

"So talk to me," Clovermead said loudly to her mother. Lady Cindertallow turned very slowly to face her daughter. "I'm sure Father did awful things to you, but that was twelve years ago and there's nothing to be done about them now. I'm here."

"I think it would be easier to fight Lord Ursus single-handedly than to make conversation with you," Lady Cindertallow said raggedly. "What can I say?"

"I don't know," said Clovermead. "Anything. Do you really think I look that much like you? Sorrel said I was your image, at the parley outside the walls, and Snuff and the Mayor saw it too."

"We are alike," said Lady Cindertallow. "Still, when I look at you, I see more of Ambrosius. My husband. Your true father. The Mayor had him murdered before you were born. You very nearly weren't born when I found out he was dead. I held on to you in my womb for dear life." Lady Cindertallow's fists were clenched tight.

"You were all I had left of Ambrosius. And then you were born—I tell you frankly, you hardly seemed worth the trade. I suckled you anyway—that's Cindertallow tradition, not to give the babes out to wet-nurse. It took me months to love you for yourself. I began to. It helped that you learned to smile. You smiled with a little bit of Ambrosius in you and a little bit of yourself. He was gentle. I thought you would be mischievous. And then Mr. Wickward stole you. I couldn't even grieve for you, the way I had for Ambrosius. I didn't know if you were alive or dead."

"I'm sorry, Milady," said Clovermead. The title struck Lady Cindertallow like a slap. "What should I call you instead? Mother? Melisande? They both sound awfully strange. Mother is the person Father said was dead, and Melisande sounds like someone my own age. What do you think of 'Ma'am'?"

Lady Cindertallow's lips twitched. "It's against all protocol. Old Lord Germander will have a fit. Ma'am—say it to me again."

"The prune jelly is delightful, Ma'am, but I fear the cherry preserves are not what they should be, Ma'am, and I fear I must elope at once with young Lord Prettyeyes, the Rake who writes me such nice poems, Ma'am, I hope Ma'am will not be displeased." For a second mother and daughter grinned at each other.

"'Ma'am' will do," said Lady Cindertallow. "And I will call you Clovermead, save on formal occasions, when you must be Cerelune. That seems simpler."

"Thank you, ma'am." Clovermead hesitated. "You won't punish Father, will you? Or send him away?"

"I was sorely tempted to play the ogre," said Lady Cindertallow, "but I won't. You love him and he may stay. Mr. Wickward, I don't much care for your presence here, but then, I gather you don't much care for me or Chandlefort. Shall we agree to live in mutual discomfort for our daughter's sake?"

Our daughter. That sounded so easy. Clovermead wanted to hear her mother say that again. Her father, too.

"Milady is kinder than I could have dreamed." Waxmelt frowned suddenly. "I trust Milady does not expect me to enter her service again? I had quite enough of serving the Cindertallows twelve years ago."

Lady Cindertallow laughed short and hard. "I don't hire thieves. Mr. Wickward, I think you will become a useless lord of some sort. I'll have to figure out a title to bestow on you. Lord Wickward of the Vale, perhaps? That shouldn't arouse too many hackles among the nobility. You will be easy for life, Lord Wickward, you will order servants around to your heart's delight, and what you felt for me your servants will feel for you."

"I hope I never give them cause, Milady," said Waxmelt. "Someday we must talk about the treatment of servants here at Chandlefort."

"Someday," said Lady Cindertallow. "Later. Lord Wickward, will you leave me alone to talk to my daughter?"

"As Milady wishes," said Waxmelt. He strode quickly to Clovermead's side and squeezed her hand in his. "I'll see you tomorrow, Clo? With Sister Rowan and Sorrel? They both would love to speak with you and see how you're doing."

"Of course, Daddy," said Clovermead. She squeezed his hand with all the love in her heart. Waxmelt was her father and would always be her father. She would not, could not, tear him from her. Waxmelt nodded and then slipped out of the room.

"I envy him so much," said Lady Cindertallow.

Clovermead reached out to grip her mother's hand. Lady Cindertallow's pale flesh was cool and dry and lined with tiny wrinkles. Clovermead massaged the alien fingers and stroked the unfamiliar palm. Convulsively Lady Cindertallow gripped her hand in return. Clovermead sat up in bed and Lady Cindertallow leaned forward. They embraced each other—and rapidly parted.

"It's very strange," said Clovermead. "I—I would like to know you better."

"I'd like that too," said Lady Cindertallow. She smiled at Clovermead, then stood up. "You must be tired. I'll come back tomorrow."

"Please do. Oh, I forgot to ask you about helping all those poor crippled and dead soldiers, and what the Mayor said he'd do, but we can talk about that tomorrow. And, ma'am?" Clovermead leaned forward and kissed Lady Cindertallow on the cheek. Lady Cindertallow started but returned the buss on Clovermead's forehead. "I'm glad to know you."

"Then, Our Lady blesses me," said Lady Cindertallow. Gently she pushed Clovermead back. "Lie down now. Obey the doctor and rest."

And in the evening Clovermead sat all alone in bed, luxuriating in her thick covers as the steady heat emanating from the hearth sank into her bones. She wondered at the upheaval in her life since the last winter, when she had read tales of adventure by the dining-room hearth at Ladyrest and dreamed of the day she would leave Timothy Vale and become someone different, someone greater. Someone more powerful.

"A silly dream," Clovermead whispered. "Power's not what I dreamed it would be, and I've managed to become Demoiselle Cerelune Cindertallow and Clovermead Wickward all at the same time. It's a jumble. Oh dear, I wish I were back at Ladyrest and that none of this had happened."

But she didn't really wish it. There was no going back to Timothy Vale. She would have to make the best of the jumble that was her and Waxmelt and Lady Cindertallow.

"At least everyone's talking to everyone else," she observed. "That helps."

Now that all her adventures were done with, Clovermead thought back over them, back to the day Sorrel had found her in his room and she had first seen Boulderbash. Funny, Clovermead had known her name even then.

We first talked before you found Snuff's tooth, Boulderbash had said.

"But if I could talk with bears then . . . ," Clovermead muttered to herself—and her mouth opened wide. "Dear Lady, is it possible?"

Clovermead stuck out her hand before her and concentrated. Slowly fur sprouted on her hand. Her claws grew longer.

Clovermead waited for the whispered bloodlust to strike her, but the only hunger that came to mind was a distinct urge for honey. And, perhaps, some fish.

She let her hand return to human guise. "Lord Ursus didn't make me bebear myself," she told herself happily. "That's *my* power. All mine. What a lovely thing to know, what a wonderful, exciting, glorious ability to have! It isn't the strength that's the best part about it, it's the nose. When I get out of bed, I simply must sniff around the kitchens."

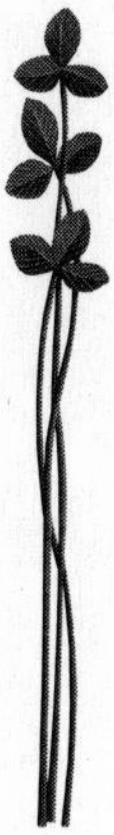

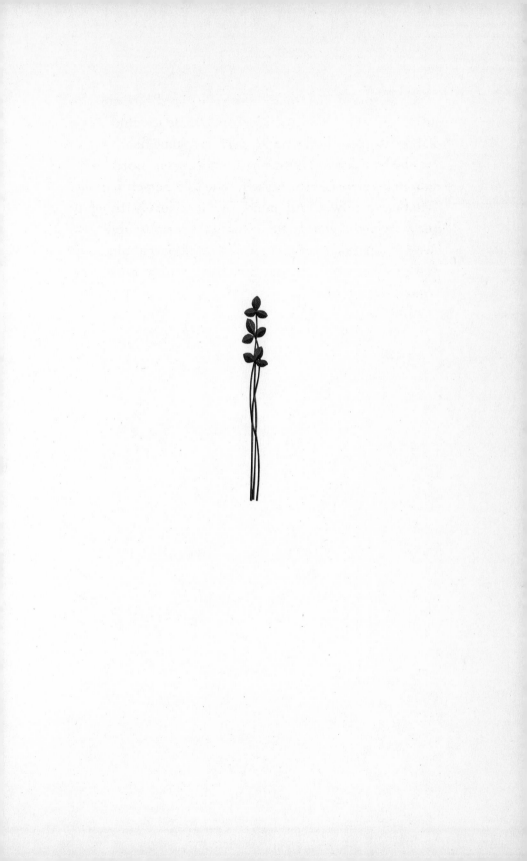